LEGEND OF NEVERWHERE

AND THE LOST TOTEMS

AN ARCHY LAWRENCE PORTAL FANTASY

DAVID A. TROTTER

DEDICATION

To my children, who inspire this adventure I call life.

CONTENTS

"THIS IS THE DAY YOU FAIL," I said as I picked myself up from the ground, a trickle of blood dripping from lip. I raised my gauntleted hand to wipe the blood away before popping a healing flask from my bandolier. I drank quickly, the crimson liquid burning sweetly as it flowed down my throat.

Beep.
Beep!
Beep!!

My health was not full, but it would do for this. I raised my sword, the slivery leaf-blade crackling with light. Music started to play once more, a haunting, angry tone reverberating from all around me. Three weeks ago, this would have utterly freaked me out. Right now, I needed to focus. I didn't have time for fear or failure.

The boss's health bar stretched all the way across my *Heads Up Display* though a good third of it was gone. It was also blinking with a ghastly maroon afterglow.

Pervading Pustulous Plant.

Hey, don't look at me. I don't name the spells. I don't really use them either.

But I'm getting ahead of myself, aren't I?

Let's go back a few weeks ago to before all of this craziness. Because who I am today, well, no one would have ever believed I was the same kid from back then. And it all started when Dad got a call to move us from our house in New York to a small town in Arkansas.

Why, you may ask?
Well, let's start there.

PART ONE
JOURNEY INTO NEVERWHERE

Chapter One:
I Move To Arkansas

"ARCHIBALD CHADWICK LAWRENCE JR., look at me when I am talking to you," said Mom, her normally melodic voice reaching near glass-breaking levels of shrillness. This sound, along with the art history book pointed up at me, wholly captured my attention.

I looked down at her, sheepishly. Despite already being a good five inches taller than her—thankfully taking after Dad in that regard—my mom was a domineering personality. Five foot six, bouncy blonde hair, with sharp hazel eyes, she was not one to take lightly. She had been a prolific singer and acclaimed voice actor when she met my dad, and she often used her bravado to take control of situations. Which was often necessary with my wandering mind.

What had she been saying? I couldn't quite recall. It had

something to do with the note my teacher had sent home with me. Not that it was anything about my grades; those were always fine. No. This one had to be from Ms. Thayne. Again.

If one could say that a sixteen-year-old boy could have an arch-nemesis, mine would be Ms. Thayne, my Phys-Ed teacher. More like a military instructor. And, if I was being fair, it wasn't her fault. Not really. But who wants to do push-ups and throw balls, anyway?

"Honey, that is the third time this semester you have skipped class." Mom's voice washed over me again, drawing me back into the moment. Something she had to do often, as I always seemed to find my mind wandering at the most inopportune moments.

"What's the point? I hate Phys-Ed," I muttered under my breath, not looking my mother in her eyes, but down at the watch Dad had given me for my eighth birthday. Dad, like Mom, was a bastion of correctness and priority, and taught me to always look people in the eyes, but it was so hard to do it. But unlike Mom, Dad was tall, dark-haired, and had bright blue eyes that seemed at times almost too clear, as if he could see through any lie or misguided attempt at deceit. Which came in handy in his line of work.

I hated disappointing my mom because she really was a good mom. She tried everything to teach me how to be a model member of society. But when she was upset? Oh man. Don't let her size fool you. I liked to imagine my mom could face down the minotaur from Greek mythology, or out-scream a banshee from an Irish folk-tale if she wanted to. My mom could out-argue any of my father's business partners, and do it with a smile that made them feel like they had won, anyway.

Me, on the other hand? I was tall, like my dad. Freckled, like my mom. Somehow I got unmanageable black hair that liked to poke up awkwardly at my crown, my mother's more slender build instead of my father's muscular frame. I got stuck with my dad's obsession with collecting, building, and tinkering with things, though.

"What is the point, honey?" asked Mom, doing her best to calm her voice. "Your father and I have taught you better than that."

"Ugh," I groaned, finally looking up from my Rubik's Cube, which I still was turning with nervous fingers.

Mom's face looked strained. It had been a hard month. Dad's work—he was an ancient art appraiser for an illustrious art acquisition firm—had been struggling lately. A lot of the problems overseas were causing the transition of various pieces to slow. Or something like that. I hadn't paid all that much attention to it until I was told I was no longer getting my weekly allowance. Which sucked. How else was I supposed to get the new DLC when it dropped? The only friends I had were online, and if I didn't get it, I'd be left behind.

"Honey, listen." Mom's voice was calm now, back to her normal tone. She could have been the singer she had always talked about being before she and Dad had me. She ran a hand down the necklace she always wore, the one with a thumb-sized ruby set into the white-gold chain. She always did this when she was on edge. "Your father is very stressed, and getting D's and skipping classes is not helping him. I understand you do not like your Physical Education class, but do try and attend. That is the very least you could do."

"Mom, I am a straight-A student. How is throwing a ball going to help me in life?" I countered, not wanting to dive into this subject again. I was sixteen. I had two offers for scholarships at both Cornell and Dartmouth. My 35 on the ACT, 1520 on the SAT, and my father's attendance at Dartmouth, where he was a two-time national fencing champion, pretty much assured me a place at university. Why was she so hung up on Phys-Ed?

"There is more to life than just school and playing video games," Mom said as she placed the book gently on the Akra coffee table in our parlor, one of her favorite pieces in the house we currently lived in.

That is the other thing. We moved. A lot.

You might not have guessed this by now, but I don't make friends easily and I have a little bit of social anxiety. It is true that, save my nemesis, most adults in my life find me agreeable, especially my teachers. I had won two prestigious STEM awards and helped my last school earn its first-ever SHPE. Oh, and I am pretty sure I also have ADHD, but Dad doesn't think it is real. So there is that. If it weren't for our three Cairn Terriers, Hephaestus 'Heph', Hermes, and Artemis, and an old Siamese cat named Bastet, (I know, Super original) I wouldn't have any friends at all.

"I am sixteen, Mom," I answered, trying my best not to roll my eyes. Mom spotted it anyway, her brows narrowing.

"Sixteen and never had a job. At your age, I was already working twenty hours a week."

"Not this again."

"Sixteen, and you do not go out with friends. You do not go to games. You do not do anything but sit in your room and play on that stupid game station or build Lego."

"If you did not want me to have it, why did you buy it?"

Oops.

Oh no. No, no, no, no.

"Excuse me, sir?" Mom's brows fully shifted positions from a narrowing 'V' to nearly flying off the top of her head.

"Mom, I didn't mean—"

"I did not mean. Honestly, Archy, you would think you had been raised by simpletons, the way you speak to me. I hope you do not speak to your teachers in such a manner. As for the game station, I do believe your father will have words with you when he gets home. Now, off to your room. And I had better not hear that gaming system turn on!"

"Yes, Mom," I groaned.

"Now, off with you."

I headed up the stairs to my room on the far side of the house. Mom's yelling had excited the dogs, who yipped and barked at me along every long step, past the guest rooms—which were often occupied by relatives who wanted to see Upstate New York and bum off my family—and my father's study, which was the only place in the house that I wasn't allowed to enter, though the door was always open and I could clearly see everything inside the large room. It was packed with statues and figurines from dozens of ancient civilizations, every wall either covered with bookshelves or old charts and maps. The desk in the back of the room, lit by two gorgeous stained glass windows depicting the Battle of Agincourt in one and the Burning of Jean d'Arc in the other, was an immense hunk of gaudy wood and marble, covered in neatly stacked papers and folders and dusted to perfection. There were the three little figurines carved from gemstones of dull green, whose origins I had never quite figured out. They reminded me of some of the artifacts from Thailand, but the markings were just wrong, as were the proportions. Then there was the stone itself. I had never seen a green quite like that, so pure and bright it was almost disturbing. But I did not linger on the mysteries of my father's study on my trip to my room.

I flopped onto my bed and was then immediately ambushed by Heph, Hermes, and Artemis, who seemed more interested in fighting one another than actually attacking me. Bastet sat on her perch built into the wall, a jumbled maze I had built myself that burrowed through my room and three of the guest rooms, connected by multi-colored tubes and walks so that Bastet could have ultimate freedom of the house and escape her three adopted siblings that were bound to the ground.

All in all, my father's house was practically perfect for everyone. Everyone but me.

As I stared up at my ceiling, which was adorned with posters of some old N64 Games, a few music posters from bands I loved, and a hand-painted map of Roshar—Dad had done that for me and it was one of my favorite birthday memories—I let my mind drift. I had always enjoyed the idea of going off on some great quest like Link. Or wandering across the Shattered Planes of Roshar or fighting alongside the Bloody Nine. Who was I kidding? I would've been worthless at any of that stuff. The sad part was that despite my grades, I didn't even feel that smart. I just liked to put things together, and tests and quizzes were like puzzles. But as for knowing things that seemed important? I had nothing floating around my constantly shifting mind. My whole life it felt like my brain was a TV, and every few seconds, someone beyond me was flipping the channels. I would hyper-fixate on something for two nanoseconds and then move on. It stressed my dad out and made my mom worry. With two parents who could've been prom king and queen,

I wasn't unattractive, just awkward and klutzy. I didn't like sports. I had run track and swam, and that was fine and all, but team things...that was never really for me. Too many people worry about. Too many punishments for things I didn't do.

Ding!

"The light. The light is fading. Help us!"

Shadows swirled around me. I felt as if I were falling.

I heard laughter, dark and malicious. I could not see from whence it came.

Panic tugged at my heart.

I saw black fire, and then...and then I saw a man. Or not a man. A being of beaten bronze, with eyes of darkest red, and in his hands, he held a bident of lightning.

I don't know how long I lay there, tossing about at this uncomfortable nightmare, before a knock came at my door. Bastet, who had found her way onto my lap, nearly jumped out of her skin, sending the three dogs yapping and yammering like aliens were invading. This sent me leaping to my feet, hands sweaty and heart hammering.

I had always had problems with nightmares. Mom said it was an overactive imagination. Dad seemed unbothered about them, often talking to me about them and having me write them down. But no matter what, after every one of them, he would always touch the face of the watch he had given me and say, "It is better to break than to bow, for we Lawrences do not bow to anyone."

I never really thought much of the saying and just

assumed it was an old dictum that was passed down, having long lost its meaning. I would just politely nod and do what was asked, trying my hardest to forget about it as quickly as possible.

Mom poked her head in the door and said, "Come on down, Archy, your dad is home."

Quickly, I tried to wipe away the sleep from my eyes and focus, because there was still some kind of faint afterglow. A fuzzy blue light that was flickering away that made my head kind of ache.

"Is everything okay?" Mom asked, and I could tell she was troubled.

"Yeah, it's fine," I answered, not even catching the fact that she did not correct my language.

What I came down to, nothing could have prepared me for.

"Hey buddy." Dad's tired, but loving voice met me at the kitchen table. It was so smooth and strong, it really made me jealous at times. "There is something we need to talk about."

This wasn't good. The 'There is something we need to talk about' conversation always ended in one of two ways. And with how Dad's business was going, I was pretty sure which direction this one was going.

On the table sat several loose papers, maps, and other notes that appeared to have been spilt from two manilla folders. On top of them rested a locking briefcase made out of metal, almost like something you'd see in a spy movie. I had seen dozens of these. Dad would carry formerly-priceless pieces of art in them so he could take them to his study.

This briefcase was open and inside were three polished totems unlike anything I had ever seen before. I could not tell if they were Tibetan or Gaelic. They had no one regional marker, but were an amalgamation of all of them. One was green and onyx, one was red and gold, and one was blue and pearlescent.

"Son," Dad, noticing my attention, quickly shut the case, looking a little flustered at himself. He gathered his poise and started talking with an even, level tone. "I've been given a huge opportunity. There was a big discovery, lots of First Nations People's art found in a cave in Arkansas."

"What?" I stammered, cutting off my dad in the middle of his explanation. I did not like where this was going.

"Did you know that there are over two thousand known caves scattered throughout the Ozark Plateau in Northern Arkansas?" Dad said, attempting to move the conversation forward.

"What your father is trying to say, Archy, is that he got an offer to go and appraise several of the pieces and work with one of the local museums," Mom said, wrapping her hands around Dad's arm for support. Dad was struggling. I could see it.

But I was, too. Perhaps it was selfish, but I was struggling with this news and I knew where it was going. I did not want to hear it. It took everything I had within me not to run off to my room and slam the door.

Yes, we moved. We moved a lot. But never out of the state. Not to Arkansas. What was there to do in that place? I only knew about two things from there: Walmart and chickens. Okay, three things. There was a really cool casino there that Al Capone used to visit and watch horse racing. But that was it.

"The movers are coming tomorrow to gather the important stuff," Dad said, his voice sounding far off in my ears.

"We will be leaving a lot of the big stuff here, Archy," Dad said with forced optimism. "We will not be there long. Perhaps nine or ten months. We will be coming back."

"I... I..." I couldn't think of anything to say. Mom had made food, the smell of which turned my stomach. I felt tears stinging at the back of my eyes. I did not want to move. Honestly, I didn't know if I could.

"Archy, better to break than to bow, son," said Dad, his voice finding its familiar strength. "We will get through this together. It will be like one of those adventures from your games."

'Better to break than to bow'. He was citing his grandfather's words. I had never met him, Dad's mother, either. Dad said they both passed when he was a young man in a terrible accident. He did not like talking about it. He had met Mom not long after. Her family had practically begged her to marry him, though she was just as smitten with him as they were.

I digress. Better to break that to bow meant that we Lawrence's would meet everything head on, choosing to break rather than bow down and give up. It meant we were up against a challenge and Dad was choosing to rise up and meet it. He was asking for my help in that same struggle. I could tell. I just didn't know if I had the courage to do so.

Okay. I can do this. I could do this. I repeated in my head, building up the will to speak. "It's okay, Dad. I understand."

That night I did not sleep. What was the point? I wasn't going to school the next day. I was moving. To Arkansas. I spent the whole night looking up stuff on my phone.

Did you know that there is a town in Arkansas whose

mascot is a hillbilly? An actual hillbilly? Why? What were they thinking? Also, did you know for every person there were ten bajillion bugs? Yeah. I didn't either until I started doom-scrolling all night long.

When the sun finally came up, my eyes were red and my head ached from staring at a screen all night. But the day was here, there was nothing to be done about it. A U-Haul sat in the driveway. We had never taken a U-Haul before, but Dad said he would drive it while Mom and I took me, the three dogs, and Bastet in the car.

"Why can't we just fly?" I groaned as I threw my bag into the backseat of the car next to a lockbox Dad had placed back there before he got into the U-Haul.

"You are going to scratch the leather, and do not slam the door that way, you are going to rattle my ears, Archy." Mom's voice faltered a bit as she tried to remain poised, but she was hurting.

This made me feel all the worse. Every night Mom and Dad had stayed up late, thinking I was in bed, talking about what was to become of them. Dad had tried to reassure her that everything was going to be fine, that a lot of people were hurting in this economy, and that we were doing better than most still. But Mom never seemed to buy into it. She had even said something about selling her necklace, which Dad vehemently opposed, stating that was one of the first things he had ever bought her. She then brought up selling more of his collections, but that argument went nowhere fast.

Anyways. The drive to Arkansas was long and boring that first day. I just watched out the window like a movie, grey skies and rainy. It was late October by now and the thought of going to a new school mid-semester was heavy on my mind.

Did Arkansas have a good STEM program?

When I looked it up online, they sure seemed proud of it.

What about activities?

From all I could find, these people did nothing but fish and duck hunt. What was I supposed to do? I hated bugs, and all I could find were articles on hiking trails and swimming holes.

A shudder ran down my spine at the thought of swimming in still, murky waters. Who knew what could be living in those things? I had read about flesh-eating bacteria and I was almost certain that was the case for every bit of stagnant water in Arkansas.

We stopped at a little town outside of Columbus, Ohio. I don't know why we didn't stay in one of the nicer suites like we always did on family trips. Not then. Besides that, Dad had been acting strange all day. Every time we stopped to get gas or take a break, which he seemed to do way more than needed, he would always get out and walk around, checking everything. After he was done with that, he'd come up to our car, and look into the back at his lockbox.

The Holiday Inn was fine, I guess. There was nothing 'wrong' with it; I was just more accustomed to nicer places. I was a little surprised when no one stepped out to take our bags or park our cars, leaving us to do all of this alone. Dad went in to pay, telling Mom and me to stay in the car until he got back, urging us not to leave the car.

The town didn't look foreboding or dangerous. There were a myriad of streetlamps and illuminated signs for half a dozen or so chain restaurants and a big parking lot for a strip mall. However, when Dad came out of those sliding doors, you would have thought he had seen a ghost.

"Melissa, get your things, and let's get up to the room," Dad said as he popped open the trunk of the car, pulling out an overnight bag and his briefcase with haste, which he thrust into my arms without meeting my eyes. He then wrenched open the back door and grabbed that lockbox and my backpack. "I'll carry these. When we get to the room, I'll order pizza. How's that sound, Archy?"

Well, now I knew something was up. Dad never ordered pizza. But the thought of cheap, hot pizza far outweighed the oddity of my dad's behavior in my pubescent brain. I was ravenous. "Sounds great!" I said with feigned enthusiasm, but Dad gave me a smile for it all the same.

Our room had two queen beds, dingy carpets, and smelled like cheap cleaner. The sheets were white and nothing looked too dirty on a second pass. That being said, I was still hesitant to sit on my bed, thoughts of who else slept here, amongst other things, racing through my mind.

My Dad, true to his word, pulled out his cell and ordered two pizzas, one pepperoni and one ham and pineapple, Mom's favorite. Though I was almost certain she wouldn't like the taste of "Zappie's Pies" as much as the wood-fired pizzas our private chef made in our brick oven on our back patio. I wondered where Rogier would go now and felt a pang of sadness knowing we would no longer pass jokes back and forth as he chopped imported vegetables or shared made-up stories as he seasoned meats.

After about half an hour had passed—me spending that time watching a Sci-Fi movie on the one TV in the room—a knock came at the door. My father nearly jumped out of his skin. Mom rested a hand on his shoulder as she called out, "Be right there," then turned to my father and said, "Archy, it's just the pizza boy."

Mom, as always, was right. It was just the pizza boy. Lean and tall, covered with acne, with curly hair, I felt a pang of empathy for the delivery boy. He, like me, had not been dealt the nicest cards. But unlike me, he could not look Mom in the eyes - a trait my father instilled in me through many awkward moments - and turned away bashfully as she handed him a few twenties and told him to keep the change.

When the door shut, Dad nearly hit his head on the ceiling as he leaped to his feet. "That was a hundred dollars, Melissa!"

"Did I underpay?" she asked, reaching her hand back to the door, confusion on her face.

Now, Mom was not dumb. But, we had been accustomed to finer things. Dad had been the one to order too, so I don't think Mom knew that a large pizza was only like twenty-five dollars. So I was not surprised at all to see the resolution stiffen her chin as she tilted her nose up at my father and said, "We are not peasants. We can afford to pay a boy for his services. You made money enough on my table for that."

"Not with the Akra again..." groaned my dad as he took the two boxes from Mom.

"Thanks for the food, Dad," I interjected positively, rushing up to the table and sitting down with not-so-feigned eagerness. I hated when my parents were upset with each other. It made me feel weird. Honestly, I was maybe twelve before I realized they even argued. They were a perfect couple in my eyes, never yelling or belittling the other. But this week had tested them both, pushing them to the bounds of their mental borders. "And I am sure that kid is beyond thankful for the pay. Can't imagine he gets good tips here."

"Archy is right," Dad said, demeanor softening. "I am sorry, Melissa."

A small smile spread across Mom's lips as she blinked rapidly to clear her eyes. Quickly, she too found her seat, and soon the poor pizzas met their demise. We ate as if we hadn't in two weeks, each of us tossing manners to the side for this one singular meal. Even Mom did not stop and wipe her mouth with the slightest smudge of red sauce touched her cheek. No. For one glorious evening, we just were us and eating, and not worrying about anything. At least, I thought we weren't.

"Listen, Archy," Dad whispered in his soothing voice, the one he used to use when nightmares would thrust me from my sleep, crying and yelling. "I know it is a lot to ask of you and your mother, but we have to do this. I need your help, son. I need you to be strong. A lot is going to happen over the next few months. I have a new job that will take me away quite a bit and we're moving to a new town. Can you do that, Archy? Can you be strong for me?"

I hated when my dad would talk to me like this, like I was a child. I hated it even more that it comforted me, putting my mind at ease and my imagination to rest. "Yeah, Dad, I can do that."

"That's my boy," Dad said in a louder, more pronounced tone, tapping the watch he had given me. "Let us be off, then. Remember, we Lawerences do not bow to tasks. Better to break than to bow, like Grandfather always said."

My Dad was great at two things: he could always bring someone up, and he just had this air of motivation and inspiration about him. On the other, he could also ruin a good moment with a corny joke or a terrible quote.

We drove on until we reached a town called Springfield, Missouri. Dad wanted to stop so we could sleep there and not get to our new house after dark. He was weird about it, and he and Mom argued about it a little louder than some of their other disagreements. Which, I will have you know, were few and far between. Like I said, my mom and dad loved each other a lot. Sometimes an embarrassing amount. But ever since Dad lost his job, well, everything just seemed tense and strange.

Eventually, Mom lost out and we got another hotel in another small town. Dark was just falling and Dad spared no time at all to get us and his lockbox up into the hotel room. We had takeout again, which I knew was going to hurt later, but I didn't care now. I was starving. Hot noodles and salty beef. What more could a teen ask for?

I flopped onto a thread-worn chair in my room - that is right, this hotel had a separator, so I didn't have to sleep in the same room as my mom and dad - eating my food and watching one of my favorite animes. Sometimes, I did wish I lived in some world like that. The hero gets all the powers and swords and girls. But I had ADHD and could probably tell you the exact number of times on one hand a girl had shown me any interest at all. Despite my anxieties and worries, I slowly drifted off into a restless slumber.

Standing in the sky, bathed in brilliant amber light, was what I could only describe as a pyramid. Except it was more blocky and squarish, like the ones from South America or Mesopotamia. That is beside the point. On the top of the pyramid, in the altar room, stood a figure of light, whose eyes were red flames and skin was molten metal, and in their hand, they held a bident of lightning. That inhuman being began extending its hand, taking hold of one of the little figurines my dad had in his case, only this one was much bigger. As the demon thing touched it, the figurine began to leak an inky fluid, a fluid that ran down the pyramid and turned the world to darkness.

Filled with fear and dread, I did what my dad had told me to do over and over again when I was a little kid and having a nightmare. He had always said, "Archy, dreams aren't real. It is all in your brain, and your brain doesn't like pain. So, if you ever want to wake up from a dream, just pinch yourself. You'll wake right up."

The pyramid vanished, like a movie you thought you had watched years ago, but now you weren't even certain it ever even existed. Despite the grandeur, like waking up from a very vivid dream, every detail was rapidly becoming a blur of the anime I watched and the sodium-dense meals I had scarfed down the last two days.

Chapter Two:
I Meet Georgia Stoddard

Arkansas.

It was hot, humid, green, and empty. I had never driven that far without seeing anything at all other than trees and rundown gas stations in my life. But we made it to our new home, or at least the place we would call home for the next few months while Dad explored these new dig sites. Which he was acting kind of weird about.

Dad always liked going to dig sites and exploring. This time, however, he seemed distracted and worried, as if something were wrong. Mom, to her credit, did everything she could to help me get settled in.

The first day we arrived was all just moving in and settling. Our three dogs seemed to be the only ones taking to the new house and extended back yard. That part was kind of cool. I had spent so long in the big city that having an actual yard was wild to me. Bastet just found a perch on the second floor of the house near Dad's new office and ignored us, per usual.

The second day was all about getting registered for my new high school, Cottonwood. Something I was not too keen on, if I was being honest. I looked it up, and it was sorely lacking in all of the things I was looking forward to. If you were to ask any student, football was Arkansas' number one export, with baseball and basketball tying for second. Great. Just great.

"Welcome to Cottonwood High, I am Ms. Johnston," announced the school's superintendent. "If you don't mind, I'd like to show you around and introduce you to some of the faculty and staff."

I had gone to new schools several times. Normally, I just went to the classes Mom signed me up for. I had never really been given a tour. This seemed weird, and everyone kept looking at me and waving. I wanted to disappear through the floor.

"Good Lord, boy, you play ball?" shouted a rotund, balding man wearing a polo and athletic pants.

"This," said Ms. Johnston with a sigh, "Is Coach Makleroy, our head coach for the basketball team."

"You gotta be six two!" said Coach Makleroy, extending a meaty hand toward me.

"Six foot four," said Mom, blocking off his hand and taking with her own. "Tall like his dad, academic like his mother." She spoke firmly, for which I was both thankful and mortified by.

"Archibald is new to northwest Arkansas, and we are just doing our tour, Coach," said Ms. Johnston with a firm edge to her words that was both sweet and also cutting. I had heard that people in the South spoke differently, less direct and more, well, like this. But watching it happen live was a little wild to me. "If they're interested in our extracurricular activities, I'll have them look you up afterwards."

"Well, I also teach history, so if you want, I'd love to have y'all in my class," said Coach as he walked away with a wink.

This encounter was, despite all things, only par for the course for me. I was tall. People always assumed I played basketball. However, I had all the hand-eye coordination of a one-eyed snake, a fact that Dad tried to drill out of me. He was a collegiate fencer in his day, touting not one. but two titles from Dartmouth, his alma mater and where he and Mom met.

Yep, Mom had been a stage performer and vocalist while my dad fenced and studied ancient archeology and art. And they had a son who couldn't look girls in the eyes or catch a ball to save his life. They never gave me any grief over it once they realized I wasn't physically gifted. But I could swear, in the moments when they thought I wasn't looking, that I could see their disappointments and frustrations.

"This is Mr. Highfield," said Ms. Johnston. Somehow, we had walked down the hallway and into a classroom. I had utterly blanked. "He teaches Anatomy and Physiology. Mr. Highfield, this is Archy Lawrence, our newest student."

Mr. Highfield was tall and white-haired, though his face belied his age, causing him to look much younger than he must have been. He had a goatee and a smile that could thaw winter's chill. He wore a short-sleeved checkered button-down, which seemed odd to me, and jeans. Most of the teachers at my other schools wore dusty jackets and khakis.

"Oh my," he said, his accent thick as molasses. "Mr. Lawrence, is it? A pleasure, a pleasure. Why don't you take a seat? Looks like I have one open by Ms. Stoddard over there!"

Mr. Highfield pointed across the classroom, which was eighteen stations, two students to a table. To my dismay, a girl sat at the station, her nose deep in a book. She had auburn hair done up in two poms on either side of her head, a flannel shirt with the sleeves rolled up over a superhero t-shirt, and a pair of denim shorts and Converse on.

"Georgia, hello?" Mr. Highfield added, further making the tenuous situation more awkward. A couple of the students sniggered at this.

"Uh, sorry!" Georgia said, lifting her head up from her book, her freckled face starting to turn the faintest sheen of red at the attention. "What is it?"

"Mr. Lawrence here is new," Mr. Highfield said, pushing me forward with a gentle, but firm, hand. It was strange being the same height as a teacher; normally I would tower over my instructor. His hand was thick and firm and I could feel the calluses through my button-down.

What the heck did he do outside of the classroom? I wondered momentarily as I was pushed toward the open seat at Georgia's station, which was clustered with books, notebooks, and papers, along with a polyurethane replica of a ribcage, little sticky notes denoting separate bones.

"Yeah, come on then," Georgia said, clearing her throat. If I had thought Mr. Highfield had a strong accent, it did not hold a candle to Georgia's. I could not help but stop and blink at it hearing her speak, a motion that did not help the awkward tension between the two of us.

Not wanting to cause a further scene, I dropped my bag to the floor and plopped myself in the raised seat next to Georgia, eyes locked forward, heat rising up the back of my neck.

"I don't bite, I promise," Georgia whispered under her breath as Mr. Highfield resumed his lecture on the Sternocleidomastoid, pointing to parts of the skeleton and talking about the muscles there.

"Uh-huh," I muttered, unable to think of a response, eyes locked in front of me.

"You're high-strung as all get-out, ain't-cha?" she said with a laugh, her voice just above a whisper.

Apparently, whatever had caused Georgia the momentary embarrassment at her introduction did not debilitate her as it would have me. She elbowed me softly, adding, "Come on, Mr. Highfield's great, you're gonna love him. He's everyone's favorite. Besides, who doesn't like learnin' about bones and stuff?"

"Aren't we talking about the muscular system?" I asked, barely hearing her words due to my heart hammering in my ears.

"Sure," she said with a shrug. "Anyways, where are you from?"

"New York," I answered, trying my best to keep my voice low and even.

Mr. Highfield loudly cleared his throat, "Ms. Stoddard, let's not distract the new kid. He is very behind, m'kay? Let's focus, you two."

I felt heat blister the back of my neck. Great. First day and I was already getting in trouble.

"Don't sweat it, he's the best. We'll chat after class!" Georgia said.

True to her word, Georgia was quiet the rest of class, taking diligent notes all while doodling. She had drawn three or four mock-ups of what Mr. Highfield was projecting, pointing little arrows at the muscles and describing them.

"You know you can just look that up, right?" I said, worried that these people didn't even know how the internet worked out here. In hindsight, that was a pretty elitist thing to say, and I wanted to take it back almost instantly.

"Y'all folks think us pig farmers ain't never heard of the interwebs before down here in the sticks?" Georgia said in an overly sardonic and Southern accent, deeper than her already thick one.

"I didn't..." I groaned as everyone else was packing up their books.

"Geeze, don't be so uptight," Georgia said as popped up out of her seat and taking up a green backpack covered in enamel pins, one of them being the triforce, which immediately drew my eyes. Quickly, she slid the contents of the table into her backpack. "We have phones here. We ain't dumb."

"I'm sorry," I answered sheepishly.

"Lighten up, too," she said with a wink of her emerald eyes. "You'll be fine. See y'all tomorrow?"

"I guess," I answered.

"Bye now," Georgia said brightly as she slung her bag over one shoulder. "I gotta get goin'."

I walked into our new house, the smell of fresh, warm bread wafting through the air. Mom had found time to make bread? There were also the familiar tones of classical singing playing over the radio, Mom's preferred genre.

"How was school?" Mom asked as she set a salad bowl on the table. One day and she had already bought groceries, got a table setting placed, and matched all the curtains in the house.

"Fine," I answered, mind still wandering through all of the different things that had gone down today. "My Chemestry teach is nice, she is from Michigan. Our art teacher, Mr. King is cool too."

"What about that Mr. Highfield? He seemed a little," Mom stopped, trying her best to choose her words correctly. If my mom was anything, it was proper. "Unorthodox."

I literally laughed out loud, to which Mom joined in.

"I think everyone is unorthodox here," I finally answered.

The door to the house opened, followed by three yipping dogs scrambling forward. "What is everyone laughing about here?" Dad said in a feigned stern voice, but I could see the cracks of excitement in his expression, his blue eyes practically shining with delight.

"Honey?" Mom asked as she floated to him, kissing him on the lips. I rolled my eyes, but couldn't help but feel a bit of warmth in my chest. Despite the move, the hardships, the awkwardness, we were together. "Did you find something?"

"Let us eat, Melissa, and then we will talk," Dad said as he placed his silvery locking briefcase on the counter before taking his shoes off.

"Okay then," Mom said, her smile bright. "I did the best I could with what I had."

Mom's idea of not much or 'the best she could' resulted in a four-course meal with lamb shanks, sauce, and a truffle-cake. Everything was delicious, down to the last morsel. Part of me wished I knew how to cook like her, but I did not have the patience for it. When I had been younger, Dad had placed me in Boy Scouts, and I had to make campfire meals, which more often than not resulted in burnt amalgamations that not even the dogs would deign to scarf down. This led to many late night drives to burger joints Mom would never have approved of.

"Alright, Archy Sr. Time to tell," Mom said as she placed her fork across the top of her plate. "What has you in such a bright mood?"

"Why do we not start with our boy?" asked Dad, turning the attention onto me in a way that I knew infuriated Mom in the best way. "How was your day, son?"

"It was fine," I answered, my stomach feeling full to bursting and my mind wandering off into imagination's paths.

"And what of the girl? Was her name Georgia?" Mom asked.

My mind snapped back into place as my eyes shot to Mom's. She was smiling over a cup of tea, eyebrows lifted in triumph. Oh no. She had noticed before she had left with Ms. Johnston. Dad, who had caught Mom's expression leaned forward, "Girl?"

"Ugh," I groaned. "I am just at her table. We have Anatomy and Calculus together."

"Two classes? Archy, I did not know about the second!"

If I could have carved a hole into the floor and hopped in head first, I would have. Georgia and I hadn't talked much, but she was nice to me, which was uncommon for girls. I was tall and could have be somewhat considered conventionally attractive, if it weren't for my stick figure build and my stupid hair that never lay right. But Georgia had just been nice, talkative, and inclusive. She hadn't postured like other girls I had dealt with, nor had she laughed behind my back.

"Well, son, tell us about her," Dad prodded, clearly now drawn in to this conversation, placing his own announcements off to the side.

"She likes Zelda and lives with her grandparents," I grumbled. "I don't know much else."

"Archy, it is do not. Just because we have moved does not mean you can start slipping with your contractions," Mom scolded, but I could tell she was still more excited than upset.

"Mom," I groaned aloud. "Is it really that big of an issue?"

"If you are going to interview well, you need to be able to speak properly," said Mom, speaking with clear diction. "I am raising a future leader, not a mumbling baboon."

"Melissa," Dad said, raising an eyebrow. "He is just a little flustered, that is all."

Dad's words did not help the situation; if anything, they made it worse. The next few minutes devolved into the importance of proper etiquette and speaking clearly. Don't get me wrong, I was not upset by this. It took the spotlight off of me and away from girls. Well, girl. I smiled, picturing her there, smiling warmly.

"Anyway," Dad said, clearing his throat. "We had a huge breakthrough today. When I took this job on, I had no idea just what was being unearthed here. Honey, we have found artifacts from the Gillish Dynasty."

Mom's eyes widened, a shocking move between excitement and concern. "Arch." She was using her nickname for him, something was serious. "Are you sure?"

"Yes, positive." Dad's voice was brimming with elation.

"I have been search for years. I thought—" His words cut off in a choked up bout of excitement.

"It is alright," Mom said, but then her eyes darted between Dad and I, the concern returning. "What will this mean?"

"Nothing yet, Melissa," Dad said as he scooted his chair away from the table. He hurried across the room and grabbed his silvery case. Quickly, he thumbed the combination, opening the box to reveal those three figurines, along with a pearlescent seashell necklace.

"What is that doing in Arkansas?" I asked, my curiosity piqued.

"Archy, there is a big world out there," Dad said excitedly, nodding to Mom, as if assuring her everything was alright. "And I cannot go into all the details, yet. But I can say this, we're going to go to the caves soon, and I will explain everything there. It might seem like a lot, but Archy. I cannot wait to show you more."

"Is that...?" Melissa asked, looking at the necklace.

"Yes," Dad said, staying the rest of Mom's question. "Just give me a few days so that I can verify a few things. But Melissa, this could be it."

I did not understand the excitement. What were they going on about? We never had hurt for money, but was this something that was about to change our lives forever? Dad had always had grandiose ideas of finding some lost or hidden treasure. But what person who pursued a degree and occupation in ancient art and artifacts didn't? However, this attitude was different. I could almost feel the energy flowing from Dad. There was something more here.

"Are you two going to just talk around me, pretending

like I am not here?" I asked, feeling a little frustrated, but also intensely curious.

"Archy," Dad said, scratching at his chin, one of his excited ticks. "Just a day or too more. The caves are still a little unstable. They are putting up scaffolding right now. But I promise, as soon as that is done, I am taking you both there. I will explain everything."

"Everything?" Mom asked.

"Yes, Melissa, everything."

Chapter Three:
I Find a Cave

THE NEXT THREE days of class were unbearable. I tried my best to not be distracted, but all I could think about was how Dad and Mom had reacted to that little necklace and those strange figurines. And to make matters worse, Dad was almost never home now, staying out until after I had gone to bed and leaving before daylight, which I wasn't about to wake up for.

"You alright? You look plum tuckered out," Georgia said. "My Pawpaw always says early to bed early to rise, but I don't like that at all. I need my sleep."

"Why do you live with your grandparents?" I asked without thinking, trying to keep the conversation going, but away from me. Sure. I had been curious about it, but I figured it was a taboo subject.

Georgia got real still and quiet for a long minute, and I was about to apologize profusely, when she looked back at me and said, "Car wreck. I was twelve. Ain't much I can do about it, so I don't want any fawning. I don't like talkin' about it, because folks treat me differently when they find out."

"I'm sorry," I said, feeling absolutely terrible for bringing it up.

"Not your fault," Georgia said with a shrug, but I could see the hurt in her eyes, the way she seemed to look through me. "It happened a long time ago."

"I can't imagine," I muttered, not sure what else I could even say.

"Then don't," Georgia answered flatly. "I gotta get going, Pawpaw needs some help on the farm."

"What about class?" I asked, confused as to her statement.

"Not all of us come from money." Georgia's words weren't meant to cut, at least I don't think they were. They seemed matter-of-fact. But it did not take the sting from them.

Before I could do or say anything, Georgia popped up from her seat, snatched her backpack and left the room. Mr. Highfield's eyes shot over in my direction, a hardness to them he rarely displayed. Disapproving.

I wanted to say I hadn't meant to hurt her, to bring up something that would have caused her to storm out. Once again, my mouth couldn't form words. So, I did the only thing I could do. I slumped down and began to rigorously study my notes.

The rest of the day went on like that, me stewing in my own pot of frustrations and self-deprecation. I always seemed to make matters worse when I talked. Why couldn't I have just kept my mouth shut? Or talked about comics or books? Georgia loved books. Why on earth did I bring up her parents?

It was with these bitter thoughts bouncing around my head that I walked into our new house. I did not recognize the heaviness in the air at first. I was so absorbed in my own head. It did not take long, however, for me to catch on.

The radio was silent. Mom was always listening to music. Next was the lack of food being cooked. And then came the heaviness. Across the house, there was silence. Even the dogs were demure in their own little way, no yipping and barking. Bastet was nowhere to be seen, when she normally spent her time perched in the windowsill. When I finally spotted Mom, my heart nearly stopped beating.

She was sitting across the room, eyes open wide, seeing nothing.

"Mom!" I cried out, dropping my bag and rushing toward her, shoes still on, tracking mud and dirt across her clean floor.

She blinked, her eyes bloodshot and cheeks tear stained.

"Mom, what's wrong?" I asked, falling on my knees before her and grabbing her in a hug.

She latched onto to me. Her breathing was erratic, sobs still heaving in her chest. I do not know how long she had been her, nor what had happened, but I was determined to help in whatever way I could.

"There was a collapse." Mom's voice was distant, a thousand miles of unbelief spanned in an instant. My mind had been wholly focused on her that I had not even stopped to think about what would cause her to be in this state.

Too many thoughts came on at once. All leading to the same place.

"Dad!" I said, panic ripping a hole into my chest. The shock of my own voice, of the thought of Dad being hurt or... no. I tried to tug away, but Mom latched onto me, the fierceness of her grip causing pain. Or was that pain coming from my head, my heart?

"Archy, there was a collapse at the caves," Mom tried again, her voice shaky. "Your father... he... they. I just got the call."

No. No. No.

I had just. We were supposed to talk. There was something. He wanted to tell me something. My thoughts broke like glass, my will shattering into a million pieces, taking with it any semblance of strength or control I had mustered.

I felt hot tears stream down the side of my face. This was not happening. This was not real. I was having another bad dream. There was going to be lightning or terrible monsters or sky demons. Something else. Something fake. Something Dad would wake me from and tell me was all in my head.

I couldn't breathe. I needed air. I needed...out.

Mom's hands fell from me as I stood. The room seemed to spin, my stomach lurching. I wanted to lie down. I wanted to scream. I wanted my Dad.

"Archy." Mom's voice was coming up from somewhere very far away. "Archy, we don't know yet. Just there was a cave in. They're bringing a team. We will know more later."

My mind was reeling. I could not see straight. But it latched onto something obscure. Mom had just used contractions. She wouldn't do that. She didn't do that.

Panic gripped my heart, and I ran. I ran across the house. I ran to Dad's study. Mom was calling for me, but only weakly. Her voice died off before I had reached the top step. Before I burst into Dad's study.

Papers littered his desk. Papers, and notebooks, and journals. And...there. There was what I was looking for. His contractor's binder. It was where he kept all of the documentation on every project he worked. It was under another metal locking box, this one was open and empty. It must have been a spare for carrying any more artifacts. I knocked it to the ground as I tore through the contractor's binder. Page after page, he had checked off or marked completed. That was until I got to the pages tabbed as 'Open'. I read rapidly until I found a page titled: *Arkansas, Dig Site.* Underneath it in Dad's scrollwork handwriting was written a single word with a question mark next to it. *Totems?*

There were other notes. Pictures he had taken. Strange pictures I did not take the time to study. They were hand painted though, that much I could tell. Five different symbols. And an orb beneath them, like a sun breaching the horizon, a ray reaching to each of the symbols. I turned another page. More of his handwriting. It was growing less and less neat, more and more hurried. Things were underlined, others circled. Pictures were stapled here and there, random bits of pottery captured in my father's meticulous manner, everything numbered, everything placed.

At last I found what I was looking for. Coordinates.

Unlike every other trip, Dad had not told me where this dig site was. He had not taken me too it. He said he was going to. But he hadn't yet. I needed a way to find it, and now I had it. I took no thought, other than I needed to move. I needed to act.

I rushed down the stairs, phone in one hand, the cave's

coordinates in the other. Mom was in her chair and the dogs were barking now. She wasn't moving. I rushed to her side.

"Mom," I said, trying to steady my voice. "I'm going to see if I can help."

She did not answer. She just stared forward. I had never seen her like this, ever. And it only strengthened my resolve. I needed to do this. For her. No matter what. I could not leave her in this state of hurt and confusion.

"I'll be right back," I said, unsure as to what I was going to do.

The dogs were going crazy. Yipping and barking. I needed to think. Mom wasn't moving and my brain was trapped in overdrive. I just needed to get outside. Get some fresh air. I could make a plan. I just needed to breathe.

No sooner had a stepped outside, then did I spot the cause of our trio of dogs' alarm. Tumbling down the driveway in an old pickup truck was Georgia. What was she doing here? The dust hadn't even settled when she hopped out.

"Hey," she started in, before I could get a word out. I could tell by looking at her she was embarrassed, and there was just something about her that kept me for interrupting her. "I just stop to come by on the way to the feed store and apologize for what I said in class. It wasn't fair, and I'm sorry."

I blinked.

"Cat got your tongue?" She said playfully. But then she must have seen it in my face, the way I was staring wildly or the redness in my puffy eyes. All levity fell from her demeanor. "Archy? What's wrong?"

"There was a cave in," I answered hollowly. "Dad..."

I watched as her eyes caught on to the unspoken words. "Oh, no." They sounded as if she had been hit in the gut.

I don't really know what happened next. Georgia was on her phone, talking frantically with someone. I was sitting next to her, the sound of the truck's engine and the wind coming through the open windows buffeting my thoughts and my ears. I was in haze. Georgia had asked me where. I didn't answer. I only gave her the papers with my Dad's contract. We had stopped for a few minutes somewhere, a little house with a large garden and smells of animals. I couldn't focus. I might have been crying again. My phone hadn't rung. No new messages. Nothing from Mom. Nothing from Dad.

We were driving again, far into the hills, away from busy streets onto unpaved roads. We bumped and bounced. My mind was spinning. I wanted to throw up. I wanted anything, any sign. Then I saw them. Blue lights flashing, and Georgia was arguing with someone and pointing at me.

An officer walked up to my window, tapping it lightly.

"Hey son," said a calming voice, though I could hear the resolution behind it. "I can't let you go further. It's too dangerous."

"It's his dad," Georgia said across the bench seat of the single cab. "Y'all gotta let him up. It ain't right not to."

Another blow. Another disappointment. I was numb.

They argued back and forth, but ultimately Georgia lost. And she should have. We had no right to be here. What was I thinking? Running to a collapsing cave? What was I going to be able to do?

"Hey," Georgia said after we parked, about two hundred yards or so away. "You alright?"

I didn't answer.

Silence followed.

"Well, we got two options, the way I see it," said Georgia eventually, breaking the chasm between us. "We either wait here for the next while until one of them officers come down and tell us the news. Or, we go up ourselves. We'd have to hike in, but I know these hills. My Pawpaw used to take me up hiking through here. Never knew they meant much to anyone. But I know my way around."

"Why?" I asked, still staring at my feet.

"Why what?" said Georgia. She sounded perplexed. I still couldn't look at her.

"Why are you helping me?" I asked, allowing the hurt open my mouth.

"Because," Georgia said, and then stopped. "Because no one helped me. No one took me to my mom and dad. I just... I saw it on the news. Small town. Local news. I recognized the car. Next thing I knew, I was living with Pawpaw and Meemaw."

More silence followed.

I wish I could say I felt sorry for her loss, that I could commiserate with her. But my own wounds were too fresh, too open. I couldn't think straight. Had I been able to, I never would have done what I did next. I opened the door of the truck and got out.

I wasn't outdoorsy. Dad had put me in Boy Scouts in an attempt to help me 'get in touch with nature'. I don't think it stuck. I wasn't good at much of anything that didn't connect to a screen or have to do with math or puzzles. But this was kind of like a puzzle, wasn't it? And I wasn't going to abandon my Dad. I wasn't going to leave Mom sitting in that chair wondering. I would do something for the first time in my life, I would be more than just a kid who was scared to act.

"Alrighty then," said Georgia, sliding her green backpack over her flannel shirt. "I got a few things from the house. We won't be gone long, I hope. But I got a light and some snacks. We can head up the hill over yonder and get going. How's that sound?"

"Yeah," I muttered.

We walked in silence, Georgia leading the way. She did seem to know her way around here, I had to admit. Because, despite the pain and confusion that was wracking my brain, I was slowly starting to come to grips with this, well, stranger helping me. Sure, she had been friendly in class. And I would be lying if I said I did not enjoy her company, her spunk and her energy. But she didn't owe me anything. Yet here she was, helping me. A spark ignited, the tiniest ember of something other than icy dread and dizzying fear. Hope.

After about twenty minutes, we came to the mouth of a cave. It was not what I was expecting, I do not know why. In my mind, I expected a massive maw, a gaping cavern. This was more like a shelf of rock, an awning of stone. At the back of the awning, a small hole wound its way further into the mountainside.

"We stay close, and if it get's too tight, we go back," Georgia said with an air of authority.

"But, this isn't where my dad is?" I said, confused.

"They kinda link up," Georgia answered as she pulled out one of the two lights from her pack.

"How do you know?" I asked.

She pointed her light in answer, illuminating some ancient hand paintings of an enormous two-headed bird circling a mountaintop. "There are paintings like this all around these caves. You said your dad was into art and stuff, I figured this would be an easy place to start."

"Okay," I said following her, hearing the words she said, but not fully comprehending them. All I knew is I needed to find my dad, and if Georgia thought she could find him this way, why shouldn't I follow?

We wound deeper and deeper into the cave, the walls of the cavern growing tighter and tighter as we descended. It grew cooler too, and I was growing increasingly more and more thankful I was wearing a hoodie. Georgia even rolled the sleeves of her flannel down, though I wondered how much that truly helped, what with her wearing shorts. I did not wonder long before something happened that would alter my life forever.

"Hey, you see that?" asked Georgia, shining her light through a narrow crevasse. Something caught the light, drawing my attention.

Dad's silver locking briefcase!

"Oh no!" The words came out like a gut punch, taking the wind from my lungs. Tears began to form, misting my view. I ran forward, disregarding anything and everything.

The case was open and empty, the figurines gone. I searched around the floor frantically, searching for any signs of them or, more importantly, my dad. I found nothing save for a narrow shaft in the floor that went straight down.

"Archy," Georgia said, apprehension tinging her voice. "Maybe we should go back now, tell someone what we found."

"Dad!" I screamed into the void, leaning over the hole.

"Archy, get back, the ground looks—"

Whoosh!

Lights, sounds, colors. They all melded together as I plummeted down, down, down into the void. I cried out in fear before all went black.

Chapter Four:
I Fall into Neverwhere

I HIT THE GROUND HARD. The impact took the wind from my lungs and sent spots of pulsating white and zigging blue flashing across my vision. My first reaction was to cry out, but I found I could do no such thing. It felt as if a clamp was wrenched down on my chest. My second reaction was running my hands all over my body, making sure nothing was protruding that shouldn't be. As I was haphazardly combing myself for bodily injury, I heard a whimper.

Georgia!

I rubbed at my eyes and looked about me, unsure if my vision was still messed up because the colors that flooded my vision did not seem real. But I did not have time for that now, Georgia was somewhere, and she sounded hurt.

Now, as I had just said, there were strange colors at the

bottom of this cavern, and they were way too bright. Not just their hue, it was way too bright down here to be a cave. Moss and fungi grew, brilliantly blue like electricity from a comic book. The mushrooms did not look like anything I had ever seen before and the moss shone with iridescent light. A stream ran through the cavern, and where the water met the stone, scale-like gleaming formations manifested.

How hard had I hit my head?

"Georgia," I managed to wheeze out the word, though my voice sounded as though a truck was parked on my chest.

When I finally spotted her, something odd was hovering over her. Now I knew something was up. Three little hearts hung just above her head, two of which were a dull red, the third one half dull half vibrant and blinking. Two small bars were beneath the hearts, though they were very short, one blue and the other green. Off to the side, what I could only describe as an icon appeared:

Georgia Stottard

Human

Level 2

Special Skill - Insightful Glance

What in the world was going on? I looked down at my hands, and as if by some of magic, I saw my own name, marked in the same scrolling silver script. It read:

Archibald 'Archy' Chadwick Lawrence Jr.

Level 1

Health Points: Two out of three

Focus Points: Zero

Endurance: Three

I cried out in fear, shaking my hands as if I could fling the text away. The text that had floated out before me vanished in an instant. The suddenness of it made me jump, causing me to lose my balance and fall onto some of the glowing fungi.

Brightshrooms!

The word echoed in my ears as my hand sunk into the squishy mushrooms.

Brightshrooms are a common item used for crafting and potions.
Just don't eat them raw. They can explode on impact!
Do you want to add to your inventory?

Two words appeared, floating before my eyes:

Yes! No…

I screamed.

Item added to Back Left Pocket
+3 Brightshrooms
Brightshrooms are used for crafting and potions.
If put into direct sunlight, Brightshrooms combust into a small flame.

I had hit my head too hard and was clearly losing my mind.

"Archy!" Georgia's shout brought me out of my spiraling confusion and panic.

The words flashed away as I lifted my hand from the smooshed mushrooms. I began to crawl toward my friend, hoping beyond hope she was alright and not seeing what I was seeing.

"Archy! There are words, EVERYWHERE! And I'm... I'm blinking. Why am I blinking?" Georgia cried out, panic overtaking her words as she stumbled around on the ground.

Oh no. She was seeing them too?

I looked about, frantically searching for any sign of what could be causing it. Could it be the mushrooms? I had never messed around with any of that stuff, but my friends online had said they went on some wild trips before. Maybe that was what was happening. The question was, did I tell Georgia I was seeing the same? Would that make it better or worse? Then I remembered I was a terrible liar. We needed to be open with each other about what was going on if we wanted out of here.

"I see them too," I said, trying my best to keep the hysteria out of my voice. I was failing miserably. I sounded like a dog's used squeaker-toy. I cleared my throat. "It's okay. We're okay. I was a Boy Scout."

"A Boy Scout? I think I broke my leg," Georgia said with bitter cynicism, her voice tight with pain.

When I got to her, I could see the twisted way her leg lay, bent at an unnatural angle. Just the sight of it made me queasy, and I almost extricated my lunch all over the cavern floor.

"That bad?" Georgia said, a hand against her sweaty brow. She had laid back down, seemingly unable to hold herself up in a seated position.

"It's going to be okay," I said shakily. "I'll just call..."

I had been reaching into my pocket in an attempt to pull

out my phone. What I retrieved was a shattered and bent facsimile of what had once been my phone. My heart sank. I had been to one or two wilderness survival trips with Dad when I was eleven and twelve. He had wanted me to join the Boy Scouts. I had begrudgingly went for two years until Mom finally convinced Dad it wasn't for me.

"You have a phone?" I asked, shoving the mangled mess back into my pocket.

"My bag," grunted Georgia, unable to say much now. The little half-heart pulsated ominously. I tried to ignore it as I pulled open her backpack.

Suddenly, dozens of texts began to slide across my vision:

Inventory:
Flashlight. Batteries, 81%
Band-Aids, plus one to health, quantity: 6
Feminine Hygiene products
Earth technology communication device, broken, value - 0
Books, 3, value - undetermined

Consumables:
Canteen with raw-earth water, 61% full, bonus feature, none
Granola bar, plus one to endurance for 5 minutes x 3
Chocolate dipped granola bar, plus one quarter to health,
plus one to endurance for 5 minutes
Ham sandwich, plus one to health. Caution, short-life! Minus
two to health if spoiled.

Somehow, I consumed all this information at once. It was a dizzying experience, but strangely satisfying. I reached for the band aids, not sure what a tiny adhesive would do for a broken leg, but what else was I going to do? I had played video games my whole life; medpacks and healing flasks were common there and this just oddly made sense in the moment.

"My leg is broken, not scraped!" Georgia said when she saw my hurriedly trying to open the little bandage.

"Just, I need to try something," I said as I finally got the stupid wrapper off. I moved quickly at first, but then stopped suddenly. Georgia was wearing shorts, and I was... well, it felt weird for me to touch her bare leg. "Can I—"

"Just put the stupid bandaid on, Boy Scout!"

I dropped down to my knees and placed the adhesive to her skin randomly. What happened next made my eyes go wide. There was a subtle *blip* noise followed by a chime. One of Georgia's dull hearts flashed vibrant once more. Elated, I rushed back to the backpack without uttering a word.

Inventory:
Flashlight. Batteries, 81%
Bandages , plus one to health, quantity: 5
Feminine Hygiene products
Earth technology communication device, broken, value - 0

"Go away," I grunted, and the inventory disappeared from before my vision. I retrieved another bandage and hurried back over to Georgia's leg. I did not even attempt to ask permission this time, just opened the adhesive and pushed it onto her.

Blip. Chime.

"What was that?" Georgia asked, sitting up suddenly. As she did so, her leg kind of snapped back into place as a second dull heart flashed into bright red.

"OH My god," I uttered under my breath. "I think we're in a video game."

Georgia burst out laughing.

I did not. I wasn't kidding, but I realized Georgia thought I was. I needed to figure out more before I brought it up again.

Chapter Five:
I Survive an Encounter

THE NEXT FIFTEEN minutes or so was spent ambling around our newfound cave. Like the moss and water, everything was just a little brighter than I felt it should have been. Veins of crystal protruded through parts of the cavern wall, every bit of the selenite glowing like a dim lightbulb. It was eerie, but extremely helpful. All of the light allowed us to see far better than we would have normally.

While the shock of it all had yet to wear off, the memory of what had caused me to descend into this place returned. Dad. I needed to find him. Eventually we found an exit, following the stream until we came to the mouth of the cave. The view that met my eyes froze me in place.

Trees, tall as the redwoods, reached high into the star-strewn sky. However, the trees appeared to have emeralds for needles and bronze for bark. But it was the sky that caused my head to spin. Two moons sat heavy in the night sky, one far larger than the moon I had come to know and love, and the other a pale blue and a third of the size.

"Well, I never. . ." Georgia's statement had been the first uttered words since those Bandages had miraculously healed her leg. Neither of us had had words to spend. Now, it didn't seem like I could keep all of them inside.

"Two moons?" I gawked. "There are two moons! And the stars, they're all wrong. No Ursa Major. Nope. Don't know these ones. And the trees, did you see? They are sparkling. Trees aren't supposed to sparkle."

I could feel my mind begin to break, like a glass plate that had been dropped onto a tile floor. My hold on reality slipped, and I quickly found myself falling to my rear-end.

"Pawpaw would lose his ever-loving mind."

"Your Pawpaw? *I* am losing my mind! Are you not seeing this?" Unable to fathom how Georgia hadn't begun to spiral like I currently was. This was not earth, not the earth I knew.

"Come on, Archy, look around you! Isn't it amazing?" Georgia's voice was filled with excitement and awe.

I was filled with existential dread. Where were we? How did we get here? Could we get home? Who was playing that stupid music?

"Uh, Archy?" All of the excitement and awe that had been present in Georgia's voice was gone, replaced with terror.

I looked up from between my knees and saw what had to be more confusing than the giant trees and the two moons. A man, dressed like he was going to a purple-themed Renaissance fair, was ambling forward while playing some musical contraption I had seen others play on YouTube videos. It was a large, one-man-band apparatus, and the sound it produced was downright haunting. He had painted face, like that of a jester, and wore a goofy-looking hat on his balding pate, barely held up by long, pointed ears.

Ding!

"Watch out!"

"What was that?" I whirled about, searching for the source of that noise, but couldn't see anything save for a strange zip of blue light.

Silverly text flashed before my eyes, being read aloud by some unseen being of female nature:

Field Boss!
The Bleating Bard
Level 5 Half-Elf Bard

A long, red bar appeared over the man's morose head, though only the left quarter was bright, the rest dull. He began to twist the crank on his music box wildly, emitting a fast-paced tune that made my skin crawl.

"Ho-ly crap..." I muttered under my breath. "Is this a fight?"

"What are you saying?" Georgia asked, clearly confused.

"I think this is a fight..."

Suddenly, one of the cymbals sprang to life, hurtling towards me, emitting a tail of blue, sparkling mist in its wake. I cried out in fright, barely dodging the brass plate as it whizzed into the mouth of the cave, vanishing from sight. The rumpled half-elf let out a cry of derision, revealing four rows of razor-sharp teeth.

"What the heck is going on?" Georgia screamed as I scrambled back to my feet.

"Georgia, I can't explain how, but I think we're in a game or something," I said, my words jumbling as I looked about wildly for anything I could use to block another attack. "It says Level 5. You're a 2 and I'm a 1—"

"You're a 1? Why am I a 2?"

"Not important right now," I cried out as I pushed her just in time to keep a shimmering lute from smashing us.

Inventory:
Flashlight. Batteries, 81%
Bandages, plus one to health, quantity: 5
Feminine Hygiene products

I thrust my hand into Georgia's backpack, pulling out the 3-D Maglite. As quick as I could, I pressed the button at the base of the flashlight, pointing it right into the face of the deranged musician, just as he began to wind his music box for a third time.

The creature emitted a terrible cry as he dropped his music box onto the ground in an attempt to shield his eyes from the bright beams of the light. When the box struck the ground a loud *CRACK!* reverberated through the trees, followed by a terrible scream. When I clicked the light back off, I could see the momentarily blinded bard on his knees, fumbling about for the cracked box, which was emitting a faint, blue light.

I didn't know if what I did next was due to me utterly succumbing to hysteria or if I experienced courage for the first time in my life. I found myself rushing toward the music box, Maglite held like a club. I swung with all my meager might, slamming the flashlight into the box, which burst into thousands of tiny pieces, leaving nothing intact save for the hand crank.

The music in the forest stopped. Everything got weird. Like really, really weird. The half-elf bard let out a keening wail, thrusting his hands up into the sky. Slowly, just like in an old-school video game, the creature began to disintegrate into pixels of black and purple until all that was left was his stupid little hat and something that looked like a tennis ball that was totally consumed by yellow fire.

Winner!

The word both scrolled across my vision and was proclaimed by the same female voice I had heard earlier. I had no idea where any of it was coming from.

The ball of light surged forward, striking me in the chest. To my surprise—because man did I let out a scream as it hit me—it did not hurt. Actually, it felt really good. Like a warm bath after playing out in the cold or sliding into a hot tub on a winter's night.

One Yellow Soulfire - Soulfire of the Defeated Bard + 5 XP.

Level Up!
Winner!
Achievement Unlocked!

I blinked, utterly dumbfounded.

Health Points - 4!
Focus Points - 1
Endurance - 4

Strength - 2

Dexterity - 2

Esoteric - 1

Speed - 3

Charisma - 1

Winner!

Defeat a Field Boss. Bonus action - win with Running Strike.

+ 1 Strength

+ Dexterity

Achievement Unlocked!

Saved your life!

Saved a friendly from harm.

+1 Charisma

"Archy, are you alright?" Georgia asked, stumbling forward, eyes wild and darting about, as if she couldn't believe what she had just seen.

To be fair, I couldn't believe what I had just seen, either.

"I think so," I said, voice more level than I would have expected. "Actually, I feel really good."

"You're glowing."

"I mean—"

"Archy, why are you glowing?"

I looked down at my hands, willing away all of the silver text in front of my face. Georgia was right. My skin was glowing a faint white. That calm, warm feeling vanished as suddenly as it had overtaken me.

"And what the heck did you do to that guy? He is just gone!"

"I don't know. I just broke the music box," I said, eyes searching about wildly until they fell upon the hand crank, which also glowed. However, the crank shone with that ghostly blue, and when my hand hovered over it:

Ghostly Item
Dangerous item!
Crank of the Bleating Bard.
This item's description cannot be read until placed into one's inventory.

No Room! You have no inventory space.

"What's that?" asked Georgia, swooping down and picking up the hand crank. As soon as she did so, it vanished. She blinked twice, like a speck of dust had flown into her eye. Then said, "It's a ghostly item used to fuse a soul to a magical item of level four or lower. It's in my backpack now, but I only have fourteen more slots."

She stopped suddenly, a shudder running through her body.

"Holy crap! How did I know that? What happened? What is going on?"

There it was. There was the fear and dread I had been feeling. I guess it had only taken a half-elf magical bard throwing ghost instruments at us to get her to realize we were in way, way over our heads.

"Oh, and I leveled up something called Esoteric, I am now a five instead of three."

"What? How?" I guffawed. How was she a five? How

did these stat-points work? And most importantly, what in the heck was going on?

"I can't see yours, only your level and your health. You're a two now, like me. But your green bar is about twice as long as mine, though it looks like it's almost empty right now."

"Endurance, I think. Mine is four, it's my best stat, well, and health," I answered blankly, unable to focus on anything. The reality that someone, or something, had just died in front of me was hitting me like a ton of bricks. I couldn't help it. Before I said my next stat, I puked.

"Easy does it," said Georgia as she placed a consoling hand on my back, rubbing gently.

"I think I'm okay now," I answered. I could feel the heat rising to my cheeks as she rubbed my back. My moment of reprieve was cut short.

Squawk!

Georgia and my heads shot upward, seeking out the source of that horrid noise. And I don't know if it was my wits frayed to their very end or pure exhaustion setting in, but when I saw the gigantic, turquoise pelican plummeting toward us. He wore on his head the most ridiculous cap and goggles I had ever seen.

I could not keep the laughter from spilling from my lips.

"*Squawk!* Welcome, travelers, to Neverwhere!" the spoon-billed behemoth bellowed in a voice so loud that it seemed to shake the trees. "I have been sent to bring you to the Court of Erle'em Ud'din Nidlahm, Lord of the Wood Elves and Once-Sovereign King of Neverwhere. Glory be to his name!"

What did one say to that? It really did feel like I was in a video game now. My head spun, but some part of me was enthralled by this. I loved gaming. But, when I looked at what I could only conceive as my stat-list, I was missing half a heart and my knees wobbled. I never physically hurt when playing in my room, unless I drank too much soda before a big quest and had to hold it in. This was different. Very different. And if I was going to be thrust into some quest, I needed answers, and fast.

I knew how these tutorials went. You entered a world and were placed up against some low-level boss so you could understand your move set and skills. I unfortunately did not have any real skills and my move sets were that of a lanky teen who was currently in the throes of puberty. My first question sprung to my lips before I could stop it.

"What is going on?"

I am not proud of how manic my voice sounded, but I needed that answered before anything else. Though I doubted I would get a straight answer. I didn't.

"You are in Neverwhere and have been summoned to the Court of Erle'em Ud'din Nidlahm, Lord of the Wood Elves and Once-Sovereign King of Neverwhere. Glory be to his name!"

"I get that," I called up to the bird, who was preening his wings, which, outstretched, were long enough to cover the side of a school bus. "But why are we here? Or, how did we get here?"

"*Squawk!* You have been summoned to the Court of Erle'em Ud'din Nidlahm, Lord of the Wood Elves and Once-Sovereign King of Neverwhere. Glory be to his name!"

I let out a heavy sigh. I knew where this was going. This bird was like an NPC—a Non-Playable Character—and in most games, they had a set of pre-defined lines and could not deviate from them. I was not giving up that easily. There had to be something I could get out of this towering waterbird.

"What is Neverwhere? I am from Earth. Is it the same place? A parallel dimension?" I pressed hopefully.

"*Squawk!* Neverwhere is the realm of the Court of Erle'em Ud'din Nidlahm, overseen by Erle'em Ud'din Nidlahm, Lord of the Wood Elves and Once-Sovereign King of Neverwhere. Glory be to his name!"

That . . . that wasn't even grammatically correct, was it? My head was beginning to spin and that spark of hope was beginning to fizzle out. Fine. We would do it this bird's way.

"How does one get to the Court of . . . um, Lord of the Wood Elves?"

"*Squawk!* I have been summoned to bring you to the Court of Erle'em Ud'din Nidlahm, overseen by Erle'em Ud'din Nidlahm, Lord of the Wood Elves and Once-Sovereign King of Neverwhere. Glory be to his name!"

"Do you have to keep repeating yourself?" I groaned aloud, unable to keep my frustrations sealed up any longer. I was queasy, lost, tired and probably a little mentally damaged due to just destroying some half-elf bard thing... even if all I did was break his music box.

"*Squawk!* Option one: Climb on to my back and fly to the Court of Erle'em Ud'din Nidlahm, overseen by Erle'em Ud'din Nidlahm, Lord of the Wood Elves and Once-Sovereign King of Neverwhere. Glory be to his name!" the spoon-billed bird squawked. "Option two: walk! Choice is yours. I would not advise option three: meandering through the Emerald Forest. It is dangerous to go alone through these trees. Dark creatures dwell here, changed creatures. *Squawk!*"

Something above the bird's head appeared in that silver scroll-work text:

10

9

8

"Oh no!"

"Archy, what is that?"

3

2

"Ride! We chose ride!" I cried out.

"*Squawk!* Excellent choice!" The bird said triumphantly. "Climb onto my back."

As the bird lowered its gigantic wing, a saddle appeared on its back. Or at least, I thought it did, as I did not recall seeing it when it had first landed before us. Well, saddle was a massive understatement. It looked like a tent atop a gilded, framework, strapped down with leather straps, with room for four people inside. Georgia and I did not wait to debate at this point, but clambered up into the structure silently. Inside, it was opulent and surprisingly warm. Cushioned benches sat on either side of the tent and in the center was a small table fashioned out of lightly colored wood.

"*Squawk!* Off we go to the Court of Erle'em Ud'din Nidlahm, overseen by Erle'em Ud'din Nidlahm, Lord of the Wood Elves and Once-Sovereign King of Neverwhere. Glory be to his name!"

PART TWO
THE ADVENTURE BEGINS

Chapter Six:
I Find A Hallowed Glade

Archy Lawerence Jr.

~Classless~

Level 2

Health Points - 4

Focus Points - 1

Endurance - 4

Strength - 3

Dexterity - 3

Esoteric - 1

Speed - 3

Charisma - 2

I HAD FLOWN dozens of times in my life, both on commercial airlines and in private jets. Never before had I experienced anything like the flight of the gigantic, spoon-billed pelican we rode upon now. The bird introduced himself as Briggaforth Darethal Gimongus Longerbeak, but preferred to be called Brigg for short, for which I was utterly grateful. And like many first-touch NPCs, his role seemed to be integral in getting us from our 'loading zone' and into the greater world of Neverwhere. What I didn't expect was the length, or lack thereof, of time we spent inside the carrier.

No sooner did we get situated and Brigg leaped up into the sky than I found my stomach lurching as we plummeted, landing far softer than expected upon the ground. My head spun a little and my eyes could not quite focus, my vision having gone fuzzy for about ten seconds. When I finally could see straight, I noticed that Georgia too was holding her head and looking woozy.

"*Squawk!* We have arrived at our destination, Kandarian Forest, Court of Erle'em, home of Erle'em Ud'din Nidlahm, Lord of the Wood Elves and Once-Sovereign King of Neverwhere. Glory be to his name!"

"I swear, if Brigg says that one more time, I am going to lose my mind," whispered Georgia as she leaned toward me, uttering aloud what I had been thinking in that moment. "And, did your eyes go all fuzzy? What was that about?"

"This is going to sound really nerdy," I said, trying to speak quickly before the tent flaps would magically open or we were just booted out of our tent. "I think we're in a video game. I mean. I don't know how, but what else could it be? I can see your...um, stats."

Georgia's face reddened a little bit, and she reflexively scooted away.

"No, I mean, uh—"

I was cut short as music began to swell: soothing, harp

music accompanied by that of a flute. The tent doors rolled into themself, allowing beams of golden light to fill the tent. It was so bright, I could not see outside of the tent, even with my hand up, blocking the direct rays. Unsure what else to do, I got up from my sent, proffered a shrug to Georgia, and stepped out into the light. The whole time thinking to myself, *what in the world is going on?*

The moment I stepped off the bird's back, the whole world came into focus in an instant. The rays of golden sun fell behind towering trees of emerald and white, veined with glittering gold. The ground upon which we stood was grass, so perfectly manicured it looked fake. We were in a glade, that much was clear, but it was not all natural. A pergola overgrown with bright blossoms and vibrant ivy stood before us, and inside, seated upon a throne of opulent gold, sat the most glorious being I had ever laid eyes on.

The man was tall. Like, really tall, and slender. He had an angular face and long, straight hair the color of ivy. His eyes were green too, something that kind of shocked me. He had a crown of holly on his head and wore layered robes of gold with emerald stitching. And when I say lots of gold, I mean, a lot of gold. He had gold jewelry, gold shoes, gold, gold, gold. It was, if I was being honest with myself, a little much.

"Wow." I heard Georgia gasp as she gazed upon him. I felt a little pang of jealousy at that. Though I knew it was not fair to feel so, as I too was gawking at the towering, pointed-eared, green-eyed man.

"I am Erle'em, welcome to my Court."

The elf's voice was like a midsummer's dream and I could not help but feel entranced by the melodic under-tones. As he rose from his seat, his robes moved like water cascading over a fall, fluid and perfect. A waft of honey-suckle and spring rain rushed through the glade. I could not help it, I felt my lips curl up into a smile as a calming balm fell over me, removing the stress and worry I had held so tightly since my father had disappeared. I was realizing more and more that the disappearance was probably even stranger, and worse, than what it had originally seemed. But I did not have time to worry about that right now. I needed to hear what this glorious king had to say.

"I am Georgia," said Georgia, stepping forward quickly, a big grin plastered across her face. She extended her hand, saying, "Pleasure to meet you."

I felt a sudden and acute flurry of emotion. I knew first hand how awkward I was when greeting people, but my mom had spent countless hours instructing me how to introduce myself to different people. And while I can honestly say I had never met Elven Royalty before, or any royalty for that matter, I had met plenty of wealthy, powerful people, governors and mayors, and other such offi-cials. And if they had all had one thing in common, in a more intimate setting like this, none of them enjoyed casual greetings and shaking hands with teenagers.

Erle'em, however, smiled warmly and reached his own hand out, taking Georgia's in his. It looked like a father holding a toddler's hand, so much larger was he. My eyes widened further as he crouched down and shook her hand saying, "It is indeed a pleasure to meet you, Georgia of Earth."

"Of Earth?" I could not help it. I blurted out the ques-tion, or statement, or whatever it was, utterly ruining the mystical moment.

Erle'em let out a laugh that could have granted angels'

wings before he rose back to his full stature and said, "Of course. Or am I mistaken? I have only met a few humans in my time. You are of the Upperworld, called Earth, are you not?"

"Yep, yes were are," Georgia said, her voice a mixture of frustrated embarrassment and eager excitement. Her hands were gripping the straps of her backpack so fiercely, her knuckles had gone white. "I am from Arkansas, I live with my Meemaw and Pawpaw. Excuse my friend here, he gets a little nervous when introduced to new folks."

Despite my fear and my confusion, my mind began to race. A thousand question cascaded like an overwhelming avalanche of possibilities and idiosyncrasies until my dam burst and I began pepper the lustrous elf-king with questions.

"How do you know about Earth? Is this a part of Earth? You know about humans? Have you met our kind before?" I did not have time to get the next question out—have you seen my father, and another human—when the kindly king raised a hand.

I felt a chilling calm wash over me, causing my questions to dissipate into irrelevance. All I wanted to do was hear whatever Lord Erle'em had to say next.

"So many questions, excellent questions, young traveler." His voice, so rich and smooth, was like a summer rain, refreshing and sweet. "I will do my best to answer them all. But first, let me start with this."

Lord Erle'em reached into his robes and retrieved an ivory box with golden hinges. His opened it without fanfare, though Brigg let out a not-so-subtle *squawk* as the contents were revealed. My breath caught in my throat. A jade figurine sat inside. A figurine just like the ones my father had kept, only much larger. I wanted to say something. The words practically beat at the back of my teeth to break free. But before I could speak, Lord Erle'em began to monologue.

"Years ago, before I lost my throne as the Sovereign of Neverwhere, before even my own birth, when the two worlds were one, my people, the Elves, lived in harmony with the Five Forces. Air, Water, Earth, Spirit, and Fire. Eventually, humans and the beings of the wyld—the Lights Elves, the Seafolk called the Gilla, the Granus of the Floating Mountains, the Ungas of Deep Jungle, and many others—became contentious. Some worshipped the Five Forces, others loathed them. In the end, it did not matter.

"A terrible war broke out, splintering the tethers that held the two realms together. The Five Forces, unable to intervene directly, sealed a portion of their souls, tethered to us within five separate Totems, just as I hold here.

"My grandfather, Lord of all Neverwhere, made a pact with each of the higher sentient species of the wyld, giving each kingdom a Totem containing one of the Five Forces, keeping Light within our house.

"So had it been for decade upon decade and millennia upon millennia. Peace and prosperity lavished the lands of Neverwhere. But in our grandeur, we lost our vigilance. We had, in our naivety, believed that all the bridges between the realms had been broken. One remained. This truth was hard learned. Three of our most sacred treasures were stolen from us, taken to a foreign land. Your land. The realm of Earth. And when they returned, they were corrupted. Tainted by some otherworldly darkness.

"Thus we come to you two." As Lord Erle'em concluded, he snapped the box shut, hiding away the green figurine. His eyes fell expectantly upon us, as if we were two kids caught stealing cookies.

"Umm, sir, I've never seen anything like those little guys before," Georgia said, somehow able to find words in this mess of confusion and craziness.

"And you," Lord Erle'em asked of me, "What was your name again?"

I felt my throat go suddenly dry and my heart skip a beat. I had a decision in front of me, though this time there was no silver scrollwork letting me know my options. I knew them well. I could either tell this person I had never met before in my life that my dad had three of those stones hidden away in his office; at least he had three of them as they had gone missing with him. Or I could play ignorant.

Well, I had already been staring stupidly long enough, might as well keep it up.

"Archy, my name is Archy," I said, unable to keep the wavering from my voice.

The Elf cocked an eyebrow, studying me as if he knew I was hiding something, holding back some piece of the puzzle that made up who I was and why I was here. However, he did not hold the stare long, his smile returning as he said, "Well, Archy of Earth, I wish I could say that all was well in my kingdom and that I could show you about. There is but one problem. All of the magic of Neverwhere is inverted now. I am unable to physically leave this glade. For three hundred years I have been trapped here. For three hundred years I have grown separate from the Five Kingdoms. When the three stones were stolen, it caused a ripple effect that we feel deeply to this day, and unfortunately you are caught up in the tidal wave it has produced. For only lower-sentient beings of the wyld and those not from this place can travel between the Five Kingdoms. And none can leave until the stones are returned to me."

Wait? None could leave? He didn't mean—

"Are you saying we're stuck here too, now?" Georgia blurted out, her Southern accent causing her words to jumble together in her fright.

"Unfortunately, yes," Lord Erle'em said as his shoulders dropped. "For three hundred years I have been rooted in place, unable to go as I would. I fear it shall be the same for you, that the portal from whence you came is only a one-way looking glass. That, until this curse is broken, and the stones brought back to me, you will be unable to return to your world, to your families."

Lord Erle'em's words struck like a bell and hung heavy in the air. No one spoke for a long time. And in that silence, my mind began to turn.

If this was like a game, then this was the quest. It made sense to me. I needed to complete the trials, figure out the puzzle. I needed to complete the quest if I were to escape. The only differences between the games I played, and this were quite simple. Firstly, I was a lanky teen with suboptimal social skills and a brain that like to freeze up in tense situations. Next, in the video games, I played a hero with magic weapons and powerful spells. I was neither a wizard nor warrior. And lastly, I was human! This could not be happening.

I pinched my arm as hard as I could.

"Ouch!" I cried out, fingers still latched to flesh.

"Archy, are you alright?" Georgia asked.

I guess my dad's advice didn't work if I wasn't actually asleep.

Oh no...oh no, no, no, no! What if I wasn't dreaming?

What if this was all really happening? No...it couldn't be. Could it?

"I, uh, sorry," I muttered, finally allowing my hand to fall from my arm, where a little red mark remained.

"I know it is a lot to take in," said Lord Erle'em. "But if you were to assist me, help return the Totems to me, I could help you get home. I could use my Light Magic once more and return you to Earth."

"My dad," I said after a moment, trying to force myself to understand the incomprehensible. "I lost my dad."

"Your dad?" Lord Erle'em asked, his voice softening.

"I think he came here, like us, or at least, he must have," I said, slowly building confidence as I spoke. "Can you help us find him?"

Lord Erle'em stepped back, raising a finger to his chin, pondering something for a long moment. After a short bit of time passed, as smile spread across his lips. "I think, we have, mutual need of one another. You return the Totems to me, allow me to cleanse them and return their light, and I shall do everything in my power to find your father and reunite you to him. How does that sound?"

"Where would we even start? What could we even do?" I said, head still reeling with the idea that all of this was actually happening. "We're not warriors."

"True, true," said Lord Erle'em as his face brightened and his smile widened. "But you are well on your way to becoming one. Here in Neverwhere, as you may have noticed, guests operate under different rules, so that we may know their intentions and powers. It was the final gift of the Five Forces to us who remained loyal to them, so that we may always know what we're up against. I can see your health and strength. I can tell what kind of weapon you hold if you were to take up arms against me. But the spell was two-sided; it works for outlanders as well, unless were are in a Safe Space, such as this Hallowed Glade or any place where Light shines in purity."

"That doesn't help me suddenly know how to fight," I said, not understanding why this was so important. It really did feel like I was in a tutorial phase of a game and just getting exposition-dumped on right now. It was making my head hurt, the jumping back and forth between the oddity and the mind-breaking preposterousness of it all.

I blinked.

"I don't think preposterousness is a word," said Georgia.

"Me either." I answered, as if she had read my mind.

I stopped short, turning my head slowly to face her. Her eyes were wide as saucers and she looked as if she had seen a ghost.

"How..."

"What..."

"Calmly now," said Lord Erle'em as he raised his hands in a soothing gesture. "It appears that Georgia's special skill activated. Insightful Glance. This skill allows the wielder the ability to read a person's thoughts once a day per level. It does also show that the skill can be upgrade three times, adding further benefits."

"What? You mean, are you saying, Georgia can read minds?" I blurted out as my face flushed.

"Once a day per level, so twice a day, as she is level two right now," Lord Erle'em said as he stepped forward toward her. He took hold of one of the many rings that hung from his pointed ears. He unfastened it and handed the golden loop to Georgia saying, "This will increase your skill ability to level two. This is different from your character level."

"My character level?" asked Georgia, sounding just as confused and uncertain as I was. Though, her confusion did not stop her from taking the ring.

The ring suddenly appeared on her ear, affixing itself without her raising a hand.

Skill Level increased!

+ 1 to Insightful Glance
Wilder of this arcane earring received a +1 Skill Level to Insightful Glace
Caster may now glimpse into the mind of most Sentient Beings.

Warning!
This comes with a risk.
Sentient Beings do not like their sentience being prodded in.
If caught, negative repercussions might ensue.

+2 to Focus
This arcane earring adds +2 to Focus

10% increase to Esoteric power
You are becoming quite the little enchantress
Warning! Those whose Esoteric Stat reaches 100 must either join a Coven of Light or Nature, or face the wrath of the Bedlam Queen of Arcane Witchcraft.

"Wow! Holy heck!" Georgia exclaimed, stepping back.

Lord Erle'em let out a long peel of laughter, causing a myriad of birds to fly out from the canopy. He raised his hand to his chin, as if pondering some deep question. As if struck by some magnificent idea, he reached out and plucked a branch from a tree. He whispered something into the branch, causing the wood to glow with a pale light. "Take this, Georgia of Earth."

As soon as she extended her hand, I saw the silver scroll-work declare:

Character has Leveled Up!
Character has received an enchanted item!
Character has chosen the Mage Class.

"Wait! Hold on," Georgia stammered. "I didn't mean to..."

"It is alright, Georgia of Earth." Lord Erle'em's voice remained calm and tranquil. "If you wish to change your preferred class, once every ten levels, you can go to a Spirit Well and cast a Do-Over coin. This will allow you to re-arrange any of your Status Points and change your elected Class. This will, however, wash away any special skills or item leveling you have tied to the Class you were at the time of Do-Over. That being said, Mage is fine starting class. It will allow you learn up to three unique spells and two common ones. I can teach you your first spell. It is the one I use to keep this Hallowed Glade alive. That is 'Heal'. The higher your level and the more you level the spell, the more powerful it becomes."

Georgia's eyes widened with excitement at Lord Erle'em's words. I could see it there, written in her face. She wanted to learn that spell, though I could not understand why she was so excited. I would learn why soon enough.

I did not see how he showed her. To my eyes, one moment she was holding her new wand out, the next she was panting, eyes dilated and sweat beading at her brow. But the triumph plastered across her grin was all I needed to see to know she had succeeded. I felt my heart do a little flip when that smile beamed onto me.

"Now, Archy of Earth, let me take a look at you," Lord Erle'em said as he walked over toward me. "Hmmm, you sir have the beginnings of a true warrior."

I couldn't help it. I laughed out loud, long and wild. Me? A warrior? Dad was a fencer, which really wasn't actual fighting. But me? No, no, no...

"Your *Running Strike* skill has already been leveled, though your weapon of choice is, how should I put this? Less than optimal."

I looked down at my hand. Somehow, without me pulling it out myself, the 3-Cell black Maglite sat heavy in my right hand. I wanted to drop it, but found I could not unlatch my fingers from around its cool surface.

"What you need is a weapon befitting the quest you are about to embark upon," proclaimed Lord Erle'em in triumphant tones.

I had yet to agree upon said quest. But, if I was being honest with myself—after seeing Georgia level up and gain two really cool items—I wanted to see what I was going to be offered next.

Lord Erle'em reached into his robes and pulled out a comically large halberd. Now, if you don't know what a halberd is, let me explain it real quick. It is kind of like a spear, but with a small axehead on one side and a spike on the other. Most are about five or six foot long. This was around ten foot tall and the head on it was as large as my whole torso. Strange black smoke rose ominously off of the polearm. Lord Erle'em looked at the weapon for no more than two seconds before thrusting it back into his robes and rummaging about until retrieving a mace with a head that looked like the moon, or at least, the moon one could see from earth. He replaced this one with the same nonchalance as he had the halberd.

I felt my eyes grow wider and wider as he pulled item after item. Flaming swords, ice-coated spears, a pair of actual bear arms, claws included, and two or three bows. At long last he came upon a rather unassuming sword. My dad had two or three like this in his old study. I knew them as English Arming Swords, though this one was leaf-bladed and the pommel looked like an acorn. The blade itself was polished to a shine, and the hilt was wrapped in green wire. The cross guard and pommel were both brushed bronze. It looked like something an elf would have. And, for the time being, I forgot about all of the other strange, mystical weapons the Elf Lord had pulled out of nowhere and shoved back into the same place.

"Ah, so this one draws your eye," said Lord Erle'em with a sad smile. "As it should. It was the sword of my elder brother. He died long, long ago. He fell prey to Longing, and I lost him. Perhaps this sword will treat you better than he."

Lord Erle'em presented me the sword, hilt first. At first, I was not sure if I could take the weapon up. But then the reality of what I was facing, of what this place was, came crashing over me. I remembered the look of that deranged half-elf bard and I recalled how I had wished for anything to defend myself with, to defend Georgia with. So, placing the Maglite in my pocket, I took hold of the sword.

As I did so, the text scrolled across my vision:

Inventory Slot - Right Pocket
Full
Maglite 76%

New Weapon!
Sword of the Promised Elven Lord, Level 2 - Legendary Item
This sword is a split-damage type weapon
This sword is a melee weapon
This sword is imbued with Slicing Edge
This blade has experienced a traumatic event
This blade needs to be restored to reach its proper power-level

New Skill Unlocked!
Slicing Edge

Slicing Edge allows the wielder to charge their attack for 1 FP Charged attack sends a slicing edge outward, attacking all enemies in a 130-degree angle. Enemies caught in this attack are inflicted with the hemorrhage debuff, causing them to lose 5% health every second. This sword can be upgraded using a gemstone imbued with any of the Five Forces. Only one level can be added per Force. This Sword is currently imbued with the Forces of: Light.

"This is a very powerful weapon. For as not all that glitters is gold, so too is this weapon. While unassuming and plain in make, this sword, if wielded by one with a true heart, can change the world. Or so the legends tell," said Lord Erle'em reverently.

"I, I don't know what to say," I stammered, utterly lost for words.

"Your skill, *Running Strike* has now been added to the sword's memory. This sword can hold seven skills. It currently holds two," said Erle'em. "But, your personal skill set is low. Allow me a moment, as did your friend, Georgia, to teach you the ways of the blade."

The whole world shimmered.

Chapter Seven:
I Learn to Swing a Sword

Archy Lawerence Jr.

~Classless~

Level 2

Health Points - 4

Focus Points - 1

Endurance - 4

Strength - 3

Dexterity - 3

Esoteric - 1

Speed - 3

Charisma - 2

I was no longer standing in the Hallowed Glade. Georgia was near, though it looked like I was looking at her from under water. The sky was grey and the ground upon which we stood was barren. Lord Erle'em wore a sleeveless tunic now, showing off lean, muscular arms covered in emerald tattoos. His head was crowned with antlers sprouting from his hair, like those of a deer. He had a tail that swished behind him, not dissimilar to that of a lion. He looked at me with cat-like eyes, bright yellow.

"We are in the Wyrd," he said, his voice now deep and feral. "He we can train and not risk true harm. Here we are our truest selves."

I looked at my hands. I looked the same. Just a human boy with pale skin and thin arms. The only thing I had was the sword Lord Erle'em had given me and my grandpa's watch that dad had left with me. The little rubies shone extra bright against the dower grey of the Wyrd.

Lord Erle'em reached out his hand, as if trying to grasp something I could not see. Mist swirled about his fingers for a few seconds. A loud *crack* sounded as a spear with a sheath over its head materialized. "This will keep you safe, for though no true and lasting harm can come upon us in this place, I do not wish suffer in the moments of my tutelage beyond that which is necessary."

If the Elven Lord was trying to inspire a sense of calm, he was doing a terrible job at it. Despite the leather that covered the head of the golden-hafted spear, I was almost certain that thing would hurt, badly, if it struck me.

Ready!

A male proclaimed, the thunderous voice echoing through the ether.

A health bar appeared over Lord Erle'em's head. Except, instead of green at its full length, it was a dull grey with a white border over the whole meter. I looked to my own floating four hearts, and they looked the same.

"We do not take real damage here," Erle'em said once again, noting how my eyes flashed back and forth. "Also, you need to learn how to hide your display. It will distract you, blocking your field of vision."

"You can hide it?" I asked, my heart beginning to race as panic at the imminent battle gnawed at my crumbling resolve.

"I am not going to hurt you," said Erle'em. "I am here to help you. Relax. Clear your mind."

I tried to do what he said. I took a deep breath and closed my eyes. I exhaled, long and slow. When I opened my eyes once more, all the stats and silver writings were gone. The only thing I could see was Lord Erle'em, smiling proudly.

"Good," he said. This made my heart warm, melting away all of the fear and trepidation. His smile turned mischievous. "I am going to attack you. Listen to your body, listen to the sword. Defend yourself."

I did not defend myself well...at all.

Crack! Snap! Whap!

I slid across the barren earthy as my sword slid away from me. My head, chest, and side throbbed with an ache. I was pretty sure I had been struck by a truck. And a bull. And perhaps even lightning. Whatever it was. I just wanted to lie down and never move again. Ever.

"That was...suboptimal," said Lord Erle'em as he crouched over me, extending a hand. His face had a smile as bright as the summer sun, but I thought I could see something in his eyes, a glint of fire. "I am sorry. It has been a very,

very long time since I have wielded my spear. I was too aggressive."

I looked at my stats, pulling them up reflexively. All of my hearts were whole. They were still greyed out. But they were whole. And despite the beating I had just taken, I was already feeling whole.

"This is weird," I groaned as I took Lord Erle'em's hand, allowing him to pull me to my feet.

"You cannot be hurt here, not truly, but I will check myself moving forward," Lord Erle'em said with acquiescence in his voice, which was strange. I still hadn't come to grips with the bestial form he had taken on here in this place of shadow and mist.

Who am I kidding? I hadn't come to grips with any of the events of the day. Not the portal Georgia and I had fallen through. Not the magic and silver scrollwork. None of it, least of all some high elf lord, made any sense at all. But I took up my new sword once more, the sensation of 'rightness' tingling through my skin as I gripped the hilt.

"Listen to the blade, hear its memories," Lord Erle'em said, encouragement ripe within his voice. "Give over to the power that resides within."

I did what he said, opening my mind the best I could. I could see something, a light, a power, thrumming somewhere deep in my imagination. It was like trying to recall a long-forgotten dream. Pieces were there, and I tugged at those strands calling upon all the forces of my mind in doing so.

"Ready yourself."

I raised my blade in a position I did not understand, but that somehow felt 'right'.

Ting!

Crack! Snap! Whap!
Beep beep!
Beep beep!

I blinked away the flashing stars in my eyes. My little grey heart containers now only held one true light. And the beeping in my ears was more than that ringing sensation you get when you aren't paying attention and accidentally walk into a pole. No, this was coming from some external source, one which I could not see or understand.

"Better!" cried out Lord Erle'em. His face was absolutely beaming, which, given the elongated teeth that gave him a tiger-like appearance, was a little terrifying. "You managed to block my first strike. Well done, well done indeed!"

"I am going be sick," I groaned as I held onto my stomach.

"Your health is nearly depleted. You need to drink from a healing flask."

"A what?"

"Ah! How could I have forgotten!" Lord Erle'em said, placing a palm to his antlered head. He then rotated his hands, causing the air to warp in a purple blur. When the mist cleared, he held a bandolier with four, bulbous glass bottles affixed to it. Two of them held a bright, crimson liquid. One held a green so bright it looked like highlighter fluid, and the final was filled with a royal blue so brilliantly delicious looking my body craved it in an instant. "I have two healing flasks, one stamina flask, and a focus-boosting flask. There are spaces for more along the bandolier, but I unfortunately do not have any other at my disposal. These can be refilled by mixing various tonics at an alchemy table or via purchasing at shops located throughout the differing cities and townships of Neverwhere, though at your current level, you can only hold four."

"Wait? My level decides how many bottles I can attach to the bandolier? How does that even work? How does it know?" I asked, confusion at the ludicrous nature of that statement. I hadn't even come to grip with the fact that I could even have a level or what that even meant.

"When the Five Forces—" Lord Erle'em's voice cut off as a shadow of consternation passed over his face. He regained his composure quickly though, eyes hardening in determination. "Another stone has been captured. Listen to me, Archy of Earth. It is unfair of me to ask any of this of you, to place this burden onto your shoulders. But you are, quite literally, my only hope. Without you, everything breaks. I know my world is different from yours, vastly so. It will be confusing at times, but it is not without its perks. As you develop your skills and abilities, you will grow far stronger, become more formidable, than you ever could in your world. Please, take this, it will help."

Lord Erle'em extended the bandolier with a heartfelt expression. Reluctance slowed my hand, but determination to find my father, to help and be useful for once, moved it forward. I took hold of the bandolier and draped the leather harness over my shoulder. It immediately adjusted itself to my body.

Bandit's Bandolier of Recovery Flasks - Rare Item

Inventory Slots - 8

Available Slots - 4

Level 3 Required to access Slots 5 & 6

Available Flasks

Health Flasks - 2

Stamina Flask - 1

Focus Flask - 1

I pulled one of the spherical glass bottles from the bandolier, popping the cork that affixed flask with ease. The aroma of sweet cherry candies filled my nostrils, and when I say sweet, it was sickeningly sweet. I raised the bottle to my lips and drank deeply. The warmth that rushed through my body was breathtaking. I felt as if every pain, ache, and discomfort that I had was washed away in an instant.

Beep, beep, beep!

The sound chimed in my ears as I swallowed, each one higher pitched than the last. When I looked back at my HUD to see my stats, my heart containers were all filled to the brim, though still dulled do to whatever supernatural forces were at place in this mirror world.

"That was... refreshing!" I said, unable to keep the smile from my face and the excitement out of my voice.

"A Flask of Healing can recover up to six hearts. You can upgrade your flasks with Blessed Dewdrops, which can be found in places visited by the Five Forces or where a sacrifice of love has been made," said Lord Erle'em as he pulled out a small, golden drop of liquid glass. "It takes three Dewdrops to upgrade a flask type. I only have one to give. But, if you find others, make sure to collect them. But, be warned, these are quite valuable and many creatures across Never-where are constantly seeking them out. Do not take them out of your inventory at night unless you are ready to face great perils."

"Okay," I answered, awestruck while taking the Blessed Dewdrop from Lord Elre'em. It was warm to the touch and shone with a gentle brightness that captivated me. As I slid it

into the pocket of my khakis, another scrollwork notification flashed:

Inventory Slot - Left Pocket - Full
Blessed Dewdrop - rare item; upgrade item
Blessed Dewdrops are an uncommon item found throughout
Neverwhere that are used to upgrade sacred items, potions,
and flasks. Once used, they cannot be reused. If consumed,
untold concerns and/or changes may arise.
Do Not Ingest Directly!
1 of 3 recovered for upgrading.
1 of 12 known Blessed Dewdrops found.

"Wow!" I said, "that's a lot of information."

"I will help you refill this back at my glade, but for now,
let us focus upon the task at hand," Lord Erle'em said as he
raised his covered spear once more.

I looked at the Elf Lord, once again perplexed at the situation. Unable to do anything about it, I raised my sword and
did as he had instructed, opening myself to the connection
within the blade.

Memories—or hints of memories—wound their way
from the grip of the sword and up my arm. I felt them
moving subtly beneath my skin, infusing themselves into my
very muscles. It was really weird, and yet oddly satisfying.

This time, when Lord Erle'em rushed forward, spear tip
pointed toward my torso, I felt my mind open and I heard a
voice whisper.

Roll!

I did just that, dodging beneath the leather cover of the
spear.

Upward strike!

I used my momentum to push myself from the ground, swinging my sword as I did so. The action caused me to pop up like a corkscrew. A loud *crack!* followed by a painful reverberation through my hand followed the action. The next thing I saw was the bright smile of Lord Erle'em as he held his spear to the side. I had knocked it off its course.

Impaling Thrust!

I pulled back, fear of what that meant creeping in from nowhere. He was standing there, chest exposed. I could see how I could have closed the distance and pierced him through the heart. But I couldn't do it. Even if he had said that we could not actually get hurt here. I just could not do it.

Lord Erle'em's smile sharped as he whipped his spear about, driving the butt of it toward my head.

Guard Counter!

I raised my blade, placing my left hand against the flat, knocking the spear to the side once more. This time, I closed the distance. A thrum of energy flowed from the pommel of the sword and into my arm. I rushed in and drove my shoulder into his body.

It felt like I had ran into a brick wall.

I fell backward, landing on my rear.

"Very good!" exclaimed Lord Erle'em as he thrust the butt of his spear into the earth, leaving the spear pointing upward. He then stepped forward and extended a hand once more. "You are quite the natural. What was it you said your father did again?"

"He was an art appraiser," I answered, still a little dazed. I did not miss that I was missing a quarter heart from my greyed out container. Thankfully there was no obnoxious beeping noise.

"Well, you surely must have the blood of a warrior in you!" he said, smiling brightly. "I think we have done enough here. As you continue to train your skills, your connection to the sword will strength, unlocking new and better skills. For now though, I believe you have enough. Let us return to your friend."

The earth warped around us, the mist swirling into an orb that turned bright white right before vanishing. I covered my eyes with my hand to shield them for the bright light. When I blinked again, I was standing back in the glade, Georgia appearing frozen in place.

Pop!

"And if I can train my—" Georgia stopped talking and furrowed her brow at me. "Why are you all sweaty? Wait! Did he take you and teach you some weird stuff in some old school looking place?"

"No, Georgia of Earth," Lord Erle'em said with a melodic laugh. "I took him to the Wyrding World, to train where the ancient masters did so atop the Lake of Memories. Where you went was the Archive of Endless Tomes, where the mystical secrets of Neverwhere are stored."

I found it hard to breathe, and my head was really spinning now. I had the sudden urge to take a long nap or eat a whole pizza and then nap. Either way, I was utterly exhausted. And that exhaustion came on without warning or mercy. And before I knew it, I found myself sagging to my knees.

Level Up!

Achievement Unlocked!
Parry this you filthy normie!

You have parried someone ten times your level or more!

+2 Endurance
+1 Strength
+2 Dexterity

"Perhaps it is time for a meal," Lord Erle'em said with a warm smile. "While we eat, I can answer more of your questions. And give you one final gift before your journey truly begins."

Chapter Eight: I Learn About Totems

THE TABLE that had literally sprouted up out of the ground mere seconds ago was now set with various fruits that grew off of vines directly from the living wood. The seats were so comfortable, I nearly fell asleep the moment I plopped down into the leafy-green structure. It was all vines and moss, making the cushions extra spongy. I let out an unexpected, but very welcome, sigh of contentment.

Lord Erle'em began talking about his family once more, expounding upon the many lands and journeyings of his lineage before the Sundering. For the most part I zoned in and out. Part of me was fascinated by it all—the game-like reality of this Neverwhere, the vibrant colors and wild visuals—yet the greater part of me was utterly exhausted and mentally tapped out. So I spaced out, focusing on a bright purplish-pink dragon fruit and shutting my brain down before I could spiral into a panic attack.

I stayed this way for a while. Honestly, I have no idea how long. All I know is that I nearly jumped out of my skin when Lord Erle'em asked, rather loudly, "Archy of Earth, are you alright?"

My eyes darted about the table. Georgia looked concerned. Lord Erle'em perplexed. A strange little gnome-like creature that looked to be made of living stone and wearing a red, pointed hat with the words, *Gerald, Floating Mountain Gnome or Granus, NPC*—wait.

Where did he come from?

Where did all of these people, or, um, creatures come from?

Aside from the gnome in bright blue overalls and a white beard that covered its entire face, save his gemstone-green eyes, there were four other creatures I did not recognize. A female fish-person who sat in a tub and held a dainty tea cup in her webbed fingers. She had a silver tiara on her head and skinsuit like a surfer would wear, except instead of neoprene it looked to be made of silver and blue liquid metal, flowing about her body in mesmerizing patterns. Above her head the following text scrolled across my vision, each word appearing with a splash, *Princess Xiadiaphrina, Gilla Folk, NPC.* What looked like a bundle of multi-colored rags with a misty-black hole where the face should be sat silently, two oversized swords hanging from its back. The clump of rags sat upon a floating carpet, like from the Aladdin cartoon my parents used to have me watch. They always raved about that movie, saying it was one of the best from their own childhood. In a scrollwork of silver that was far more crude, the following appeared, floating over the being's head, *Tgnkakl, Golden Desert Nomad, Level 55.* Next was Brigg, sitting in a nest of sorts, happily chortling along. And lastly, a bronze monkey creature sat. Like, actually made of bronze. And you know what, that wasn't even the strangest part. The creature had two sets of arms. In each hand a varying fruit was held, and it looked as if it were about to gorge itself before Lord Erle'em had said something. Over its head the following text formed, *Luk Luk Ci Ci, Tribal Elder of the Jungle of Unga.*

My head spun as I tried to read all of the words at once while my eyes darted from one oddity to the next. Thankfully, I was saved further humiliation and confusion, when Georgia loudly said, "Don't look at me like that, they all popped in here like a bag of Orville Redenbacher without any warning whatsoever!"

"Now, now," said Lord Erle'em with a little sigh of exasperation. "I informed the both of you that I was summoning these fine delegates from across the realms of Neverwhere. Though, they are not truly here, only in spirit. They each stand upon a Lightcaster, which emits their presences from great distances."

"Now what in the tarnation are we all get'n up to? Its been a right long time since you've asked us all here!" Gerald the Floating Mountain Gnome practically screeched in a voice that reminded me of a cartoon prospector.

"Wow dude," said Princess Xiadiaphrina, just like a surfer girl. She turned her head when she spoke and what looked like strands of hair braided with seashells clattered loudly when she did so. "You need to chill my man."

"Chill? Chill!" The little gnome-like creature proceeded to pull out a pickaxe from nowhere and pointed toward the bathing princess. "I'll shove this pickaxe where the sun don't shine, little lady!"

"Hey man, you need to check yourself," Princess Xiadiaphrina sighed, taking a sip from her tea cup and setting it down. "It is that kind of attitude that got your Totem lost. You are too high-strung, my man."

"Does the Princess of Gilla mean to say that those who lost their Totems did so in an act of frivolous behavior?" Tgnkakl said, his voice like grinding stone and smoke.

"*Squawk!* Here ye, here ye!" bleated Brigg, flapping his massive wings. He, unlike the other delegates, was present in the glade. So this sent billowing gusts of wind across the table, blasting my face with air and particles of dust, along with various fruits. "This is not a place of accusation or dismay! We are in the Court of Erle'em Ud'din Nidlahm, overseen by Erle'em Ud'din Nidlahm, Lord of the Wood Elves and Once-Sovereign King of Neverwhere. Glory be to his name! We will behave as such."

Everyone burst into a slurry of insults, taunts, and jabs. Fins and fingers were pointed, dishes were overturned, and disarray ensued. Which was really confusing to me, because I was just told they were all Lightcast, which I had assumed meant they were not physically there. The splat of a purple fruit that looked like a fist-sized grape upon my chest told me otherwise. The only two beings that were not flailing about or casting insults were Lord Erle'em and the bronze monkey guy.

What was up with this place?

"I'll use y'er feathers for me nephew's pillow, y'er oversize turkey!" shouted Gerald.

"You are all a disgrace!" grunted the floating bundle of colorful rags. He then proceeded to spiral into a litany of rambling, though I could not understand a single word the thing uttered.

At this point, my brain was really starting to hurt, and the panic I felt on the inside must have been evident upon my face, because when Lord Erle'em's attention fell on me, he rose up from his seat and thundered, "Silence!"

As if a magic spell had been cast, all the squawking and arguing and name calling stopped instantaneously.

"Friends, fellow dignitaries of Neverwhere," Lord Erle'em continued, forcing a calm to his voice that reminded me of Mom whenever Dad announced we would be having guests over without at least a week's heads up for her to prepare. "We must put aside petty differences and come together. The magic of Neverwhere is fading. We have all felt it. In the night, strange creatures lurk and loom. During the day, disarray and disorder abound. We, the last leaders of the Sentient Wyld must stand together. We must collect the lost Totems and reunite the Golden Sun."

All eyes turned to Lord Erle'em. Gerald, who had still been pointing his pickaxe at Brigg, dropped the tool to the ground. It clattered loudly in the now silent glade.

"Long has been since the Golden Sun was raised heavenward," said Tgnkakl in a mystic tone, his deep voice reverberating through the trees. "Our forefathers found wisdom in granting each of the kingdoms their own piece, seeing the power for any one person to hold a threat too great, a burden too heavy, to bare."

"It is totally unsafe to like, you know, bring those together," said Princess Xiadiaphrina, her words filled with hesitation. "Last time that happened, it was like, really bad. That is why we separated the realms, my guy."

"I know, but the risk is worth the reward," said Lord Erle'em solemnly. "For if we do not, all could be lost."

"Listen hear, y'er overstuffed turnip," Gerald barked, still standing on his seat just so he face poked over the edge of the table. "I ain't gonna have any one of you-uns hold'n all that there power. Ain't gonna have it no how!"

"I am ashamed to admit that I agree with rock eater on this matter," grumbled Tgnkakl as he produced a long, fluted pipe from his rags. He inhaled slowly from the pipe and the blew out a shimmering bout of multi-colored smoke. "No one person should hold the Five Totems. It was wisdom in the gods that they were separated."

"My friends," Lord Erle'em, noticeably trying to keep the frustration from rising in his voice. "If we do not act, we will be forever frozen in such a manner as we are now. Never growing, never expanding. Trapped forever in our own realms, unable to travel this wild world we call home."

"And what about the rails? They do work," said Gerald, folding his stubby arms across his bushy beard. "Why do I need to go t'er the desert for? Or worse, the sea?"

"Hey man, that is like, not cool," Princess Xiadiaphrina said. "My shores are vast and like, totally rad."

"The rails work for transporting goods, but none of our

people can leave their homelands. Tell me in truth, do you not yearn to see the glittering caves of the endless deserts?" Lord Erle'em asked of Gerald. The small gnome's gemstone-eyes widened with unrequited desire. Lord Erle'em's eyes drifted to the others as he continued, focusing on the individual as he spoke. "Princess Xiadiaphrina, when was the last time one of the Gilla swam in the sapphire waters of Lake Shillah? Or honored Tgnkakl, how long has it been since one of the Ir has tested their skill against a true opponent. And what of your kin, Luk Luk Ci Ci? You have been oddly silent this day."

"Hmmmm," sighed the elderly, four-armed bronze monkey. "Jungle of Unga is vast, but Luk Luk Ci Ci no know of peace. Our great Chieftain, Ta'Boom has darkness in his mind. Luk Luk Ci Ci would hear how the forest man would help the Unga."

Lord Erle'em's surprised delight was palpable. I watched as his eyes glinted with excitement and he leaned toward the bronze tribal elder and said, "My friend. If you were to just lend us your Totem, I would be able to return your jungle to the way it was before. Where your kin could move freely through the trees and sing your songs of glee. It was for this reason I believe our new friends were sent to us, an answer to prayers sent to the FIve Forces, who have not abandoned us. For these two can travel freely across the realm of Neverwhere."

All eyes turned on Georgia and me. I felt my mouth go dry.

"Luk Luk Ci Ci would welcome them to his home, but dark is our temple. Dark is the heart of the Mighty Chieftain. If little squishy ones come to Jungle Unga, Luk Luk Ci Ci no think they walk away without a splat."

I swallowed hard. I did not like the sound of that. Suddenly, the thought of actually going out into the wyld made no sense at all. What was I doing? I had taken a sword and strapped it to my belt. I wasn't a warrior or a fighter. I played video games and watched movies. I broke out with rashes if I got to sweaty. And what about Georgia, there was no way that—

"It is a pleasure to meet you, Mr. Ci Ci," Georgia beamed, laying it on thick with all of her Southern charm, something I had always heard of but never witnessed myself until now. "Archy and I would be more than happy to help y'all!"

What was she doing? How could she say that?

"Now I like her!" piped up Gerald. "She got herself some spunk!"

"Easy, you old codger," said Princess Xiadiaphrina. "You are like, going to scar her for life, little dude. Now, we Gilla, are pretty chill. Do you even know what you're like signing up for, my girl?"

This could not be happening.

This wasn't happening, was it?

I pinched myself again...and yelped.

"You need to stop doing that," whispered Georgia under her breath. "People are gonna start thinking you're weird."

"Friends," interjected Lord Erle'em. "If Georgia and Archy of Earth are able to collect the Totem from Unga Jungle and I were then to break the shadow curse that hangs upon that realm, would you agree to reconvene? To speak further on this matter?"

"If? That is a very large if," said Tgnkakl hesitantly. He then drew in another puff and blew out a colorful wisp of smoke. The silver scrollwork over his head changed just before he spoke again:

Master Tgnkakl of the Golden Desert Nomads

"If you are successful in retrieving the Totem of Earth from the Jungle and Lord Erle'em is able to break the Shadow Curse over the Jungle Unga, then will my people agree to same. Only then. But know, Jungle Unga is not the only realm plagued. Our Great Oasis is spoiled and our temple, besmirched. One will not walk idly across the golden sands. Though, we will hold to our word and do what we can, if you prove successful."

Before Lord Erle'em, or anyone else could speak, Master Tgnkakl of the Golden Desert Nomads vanished from sight in a crackle of light.

"I agree with the pile of rags," grunted Gerald as he bent down and picked up his pickaxe, shoving it into the bib of his overalls. It slid in and disappeared like Vegas magic trick. I do not know why that surprised me, but I found myself blinking in shock at the causal nature of it. "Until then, y'er two keep y'er heads on. Them monkey folk ain't no joke. Ha! And watch out Chomper Vines, right nasty buggers." And with a pop and crackle, Gerald, the Floating Mountain Granus vanished from sight.

"Gilla is still totally fine," sighed Princess Xiadiaphrina. "But if we can help the world, the Gillafolk will rise to it. We will be there when you need us. May the goddess of the waves watch over you, little Earthlings. Peace out." When Princess Xiadiaphrina vanished, it made a splashing sound as her body disappeared like an old tv being turned off.

"Luk Luk Ci Ci will wait with excitement and hope for

our new friends," the monkey elder said. "Long time since there was hope in Unga Jungle. Prepare yourself well. You will need it. I meet you at Kah'Boom Village." And he was gone, just like that.

All that were left around the table were Brigg, Lord Erle'em, Georgia and myself.

"Well, now that it is settle, we must prepare you for your journey," said Lord Erle'em. "There is still much to do."

I did not feel like eating anymore.

Chapter Nine:
I Meet Some Faeries

Archy Lawerence Jr.

~Classless~

Level 2

Health Points - 4

Focus Points - 1

Endurance - 4

Strength - 3

Dexterity - 3

Esoteric - 1

Speed - 3

Charisma - 2

DESPITE MY RESERVATIONS, hunger finally won out. I had sat in silence for a while before I began to eat. But once I started, I could not help but stuff my mouth with the multitudes of new and exciting fruits that covered the table. And while I was truly coming to grips with the fact that this was not a dream—and no, I did not try pinching myself again—I could not help but feel overwhelmed with disbelief. Everything was so vibrant and delicious. The flavors were super sweet or super sour, or just, everything was so, unique! Before I realized it, my stomach was full and my eyes were heavy.

How long had it been since I had slept? I felt utterly exhausted.

As if he could read my thoughts, Lord Erle'em rose from the table and said, "While I cannot leave my Hallowed Glade, I would invite you to journey just south, there you will find the small village of Eldalar. Briggaforth can fly you there. Take this token with you. This will give you access to Oaktree Inn; there you can rest and recovery. Once you have found sufficient rest, call for Briggaforth with this whistle," Lord Erle'em handed me a silver whistle that looked a lot like a piccolo. "He will find you and bring you where you wish to go as long as it is not within the borders of a Corrupted Territory."

"What do you mean, Corrupted Territory?" Georgia asked, taking the question straight from my mouth.

"Places where their Sacred Totems have been removed, there Briggaforth cannot go. Darkness lurks there, and only those such as yourself can enter."

Briggaforth rose up next and stretched out his wide, colorful wings. "*Squawk!* Hop up little hopes of the realm, it is my great honor to carry you to and fro."

We climbed aboard Brigg's back, Georgia first and then

me. I sat quietly; my mind unable to take in anything else. It was all too strange. I had hit the maximum amount of new and strange for me to be able to digest. At this point, if a twelve-foot-tall purple sasquatch walked out playing a ukulele, I would not even bat an eye. My brain felt like I had not slept in two weeks and all I wanted to do was close my eyes and drift away.

With two massive beats of his wings, and *clomp, clomp, clomp* of running feet, Briggaforth shot up into the sky. As we rose higher and higher, I realized just how very dark it was. The Hallowed Glade had an ethereal light to it. Now, despite the two moons and the brilliant stars, it was so dark.

"Archy?" Georgia said in a hushed voice, which surprised me, because wind was whipping past my ears and still I could hear her clear as could be. "Do you think we can do this?"

"Do what?" I asked, my brain feeling like pea soup.

"Any of it? I want to go home. And the elf king said we had to get these totems to get back. But, Archy, we're sixteen...we're not real explorers or adventures. I'm scared."

"I'm scared too, Georgia. But, we're in this together. No matter what, we stick together."

We were silent for a long time. I worried I had said something wrong, but then felt a strange rush as Georgia kind of leaned back into me. I was not sure what to do, and I found myself holding my breath, as if taking a single breath was would ruin everything. So I just sat there, motionless, as we flew over the canopy of trees.

After what seemed like a far too short of time to have spanned the distance we had, Briggaforth squawked out, "Eldalar below! Hold tight as I prepare to descend!"

My heart leapt into my throat and my arms instinctively

tightened around Georgia's waist as Brigg plummeted out of the sky. I heard screaming, and I was not sure if it was mine alone or if Georgia had joined in with me as the tiny, twinkling lights below us rapidly formed into buildings and fairy-lit pathways. Just before we crashed into the ground, Brigg's enormous wings snapped out and we landed light as a feather upon a colorful perch made just for him.

"Welcome to Eldalar."

Silver text, far larger than any I had ever seen, scrolled across my vision as I looked over magical town reading:

Eldalar Village. Home of the Light Elves.

The shops and buildings were all grown, mostly from enormous mushrooms and trees. Tiny balls of multi-colored lights danced about the midnight sky. The tranquil trickle of a small stream that cut through the center of the quant village brought a soothing calm to my nerves. Somewhere, a harp was being played, the melodic sound mixing effortlessly with that of the stream's song. At the far side of the village, a large house made up of six toadstools sat atop a gentle hill.

"*Squawk!* The hour is late. You should retire to Oaktree Inn, it is just over there," Brigg said as he pointed his wing to what looked like a tree stump with a door hinged to it and two small, circular windows. "Once you sleep, we can meet here in the morning. Good evening."

Georgia and I moved wordlessly through the tranquil village. I felt so enamored by what I saw, heard, and smelled. There was an overwhelming sensation of peace here, and not just calm and quiet, but actual peace and kindness. So much so that I feared stepping on anything that could be considered living as I walked the earthen path to Oaktree Inn.

Air Sprites. Magical Creatures.
Tiny, Friendly Humanoids.
Can cause mischief, do not leave socks alone near these little
pixies.

Will-o'-the-wisp or 'Wisp'.
Friends of the sprites and in the pixie family, Wisps are known
for helping others find their truth or purpose. Whatever that
means.

Toadstool
This is a toadstool.
It's a mushroom.
That is all.

"Are you seeing this?" whispered Georgia into my ear, eyes wide with wonderment.

"Yeah," I muttered. "I am. It doesn't seem real."

"It is just like in Narnia," she said back, her voice filled with excitement. "I can't believe this is happening."

I couldn't either. But it was not excitement I felt, but a sense of existential dread. This was impossible. This couldn't be real. I needed sleep. I would go to bed and wake back up, probably with a knot on my head, in the bottom of that cave Georgia and I had explored up on Hawkin's land.

Despite this sudden onslaught of dread, I could not help but feel a strange sense of familiarity with the blue wisp that was dancing about on the breeze. I couldn't put my finger on it, but there was something about it that made me feel...safe? Maybe that wasn't the right word, but there was something about it. Georgia did not seem to feel one way or the other about the dancing faeries, but pulled me excitedly toward the inn, her eyes wide with excitement.

Inside the Oaktree Inn, a tall, ethereal woman stood behind a desk. She had long, ivory hair and her skin was stripped like a zebra. Her ears were pointed and eyes looked just slightly too large. But when we walked in, the smile that slid across her face nearly took my breath away.

Aela Lyn Shadowleaf
Nymph: Dryad family.
NPC.
Proprietor of the Oaktree Inn

"Welcome travelers," Aela said in a singsong voice, "to the Oaktree inn. Would you like a room?"

"Two," Georgia said as she dug her elbow into my ribs for some reason. "Lord Erle'em gave us a token to pay."

Aela's unnaturally large eyes grew even wider and excitement filled her airy voice. "You have spoken to the Lord of Lights?"

"Um, yeah," I said, the weight of everything that had transpired fully falling on me now. It took everything I had to just keep my eyes open.

"No one has seen him in an age," Aela said, an edge of pain revealing itself in her voice now. "How does our lord fare?"

"He seems to be doing fine," said Georgia with a yawn. "But, he does want out of that glade he's trapped in. We're hoping to fix that."

"Is that..." Aela's eyes flashed toward the acorn-pommeled sword that hung at my side. "It cannot be, but it is. The Sword of the Promised Elven Lord."

"Yeah," I said, rubbing at the back of my head. "He kind of just gave it to me."

"Please, no need to pay," Aela said, voice filled with deference. "Haella! Quick, girl!"

"It is fine, we're happy to pay. We got this coin and everything, just for this," Georgia said without relenting one bit, flashing that knowing grin that made a dimple appear on her left cheek.

"As you wish," Aela said, taking the coin into her hand. "Haella, girl, where are you?"

"Coming!" came a voice from up the stairs, followed by an elf I first mistook for a girl of six or seven, only realize that she was probably older than me, simply much smaller with large pointed ears. "Humans?" she gasped as her large eyes darted between Georgia, myself, and Aela.

"Don't be rude," Aela snapped. "Show our guests to our finest rooms."

"Separate," Georgia echoed.

"As you wish," Haella piped in a musical tone. "This way!"

Our rooms were adjacent to one another, though from the quick glance inside Georgia's room, and the others we passed on the way up the stairs, I could see that each held a unique theme. Hers was amber and brown, her quilt looked like something a grandma from an old movie would have hand made for their granddaughter. My room was vibrant green and gold, with fairy lights dancing on the ceiling.

"Clap twice to turn the lights out," Haella said as she closed the door behind herself. "They'll leave out the window."

I looked up once more, and sure enough, it was not magic lights, but dozens of fireflies that lit the room. The room itself was circular with a round bed in the middle that looked much like a toadstool. The sheets looked natural and earthy, but as I ran a hand across them, they were soft and smooth. The scent of fresh pines and tinkling streams filled the room, and that of steeped lemon-and-honey tea.

The weariness that had followed me throughout the day seemed to pounce on me all at once. I felt dizzy and weak. My stomach, somehow forgetting that I had just consumed more fruit than I believe I had ever seen in my life, growled loudly.

Welcome to Oaktree Inn

Food options

Wheat bread, honey, and salted butter
Crackle razzleberry jam on toast
Banana and oat soup
Green tea and sprig gelatin surprise

"What in the world?" I jumped, startled at the voice that rang out as the silvery text scrolled across my vision. Despite everything, moments like these still took me by surprise. I was just going to have to get used to it if I was going to keep my wits about me.

I studied the list, my curiosity getting the better of me. "What is banana and oat soup?"

You have selected banana and oat soup.

"No, no! What is banana and oat soup?"

Two orders of banana and oat soup, coming right up.

There was fanfare of whimsical music followed by a flash of light. Upon the small table next to my bed, two wooden bowls of banana and oat soup clattered for a second and then went still.

"What am I supposed to do with two bowls of this stuff?"

Inventory Space
4 open slots
Open slot: back pocket
Do you wish to store one helping of - Banana and oat soup - in, back pocket?
Yes! Or no…

An image of the mushy, tan sludge leaking through my back pocket made my skin crawl with discomfort. "No! I do not wish to store that in my pocket! That is disgusting!"

Inventory Space
4 open slots
Open slot: front left pocket
Do you wish to store one helping of - Banana and oat soup - in, front left pocket?
Yes! Or no…

"I do not want to store it at all," I said, flailing my hands at the text before my eyes. "Go away!"

The text disappeared once more, vanishing as if it had never been there. I let out a breath of frustration and anxiety. I had to get this under control. Of all the things I had experienced in this wacky new world, the text appearing out of nowhere was by far the most disconcerting. It seemed so real. So, there.

I walked over to the table, my appetite abated due to the events.

"What am I—" I cut myself off, silencing the question I was about rehash out. "Do you guys like banana and oat soup?" I asked up at the dancing fireflies.

The swarm descended down from above and land on the edge of the bowls of soup. They did not, however, partake of any of it.

"I don't blame you," I said as I looked at the mush. "It doesn't look too appetizing to me either." I had a thing with textures, and I knew this would put me over the edge.

"Can I get some of that jam on toast?" I asked up to the ceiling, feeling a little ridiculous in the process. To my surprise, the bowls of banana and oat soup vanished in a puff of smoke, replaced with plate of toast spread with vibrant pink jam along with an additional fanfare. "Thank you!"

The toast was what I needed, soothing over the strange pit of hunger in my stomach. As I ate, I got a new notification.

Stamina replenished.

My little green bar was filled up once more. I had not noticed that it had almost emptied. That wasn't good. I needed to keep an eye on that. When I was back home, I often went hours, if not a day or two, without eating more than a bite here or there. Then I would gorge myself with anything and everything I could find. It drove Mom crazy.

Mom. I missed her. I missed her, and I missed Dad. I hoped they were alright and weren't worrying too much. I would get back quickly. I just needed to get those totems so that Lord Erle'em could fix this. It was with those thoughts in my head that I drifted off to sleep, fully clothed, fireflies still dancing.

Chapter Ten:
I Set Out on an Adventure

Archy Lawerence Jr.
Level 3
Health Points - 4
Focus Points - 1
Endurance - 6
Strength - 4
Dexterity - 5
Esoteric - 1
Speed - 3
Charisma - 2

I AWOKE to the call of songbirds and the soft glow of the
morning sun. I don't believe I had ever slept so soundly in all
my life. I had almost forgotten I was no longer sleeping in

my own bed in my own world until I looked over the bed and came eye to eye with a walking pile of, if I was being honest, cutesy rocks. I nearly jumped out of my skin in startlement.

"Good morning," piped the pile of rocks in a voice that was far more pleasant and gentle than I would have expected from something like this. "I'm Clatterclomp. Ms. Aela sent me to wake you. But I've never seen a human before, I was just watching. Hope you don't mind."

My eyes darted between the locked door and stone creature with her mossy 'hair' up in a sprig of side pony. "Trolls can move through natural matter." She said it so matter-of-factly that I felt I was the one crazy for not know that something could just walk through a wall or up through a floor.

I met Georgia in the main room in the downstairs of the Oaktree Inn. To my surprise, it wasn't hiking shorts, super-hero t-shirt, and an oversized flannel she was wearing, but some kind of get up that looked a cross between Assassins Creed and medieval mage. It was sleek, a mix forest colors, with sleeves embroidered with golden markings that must be the written language of the elves.

"Looks crazy, right?" Georgia asked as she tucked an errant strand of hair behind her ear, hair that was not up in double pompoms, but French braided.

I felt a rush in my gut as I looked at her and could not help but smile as I said, "Wow! You look amazing. Where did you get those?"

The words came out before I could stop them, and for the briefest moment, I felt as if time froze solid and I wished I could reach out snatch them out of thin air. That is until I saw her face light up.

"They were on my nightstand," Georgia said as she

turned about, her backpack still on. And despite it clashing with the outfit, I couldn't picture her without it. "I thought it was a little much. It's too much, isn't it? Why didn't you get an outfit?"

"I don't know?" I said, blushing and rubbing at the back of my neck.

"Well, these gave me a +2 to Esoteric, +1 to FP, and another point to Charisma," Georgia said proudly. "And it comes with a nifty wand holder in the sleeve for fast casting." She flipped her wrist at this and her wand shot out from her cuff and into her hand. "Still not much use, don't have that many spells. But, Aela was telling me there are grimoires you can find scattered throughout the Wylds. I want one that casts offensive spells. I didn't like being useless against that bard thing. That was awful."

I was, yet again, taken aback at how well she was taking all this. I was still mentally reeling at all this newness. But maybe that was just me. I always struggled in new situations.

"Oh, and did you try the banana and oat soup? It gave me an extra heart!" Georgia said with excitement.

I blinked, turning on my HUD, and I could see another heart container floating over her head. "I wonder why we have hearts and bosses have meters? Seems inconsistent."

"What are you talking about?" Georgia asked, her smile diminishing slightly as her brow crinkled.

"Never mind," I said, waving away my HUD in embarrassment. It felt weird to see the various bars and stats floating over her, almost like a violation of privacy.

"You look..." Georgia started, cocking her head slightly before stepping forward, eyeing me up and down. "Bigger."

"Huh?" I asked, taken aback.

Georgia's checks reddened. "Not in a bad way, you just, I think you were a lot skinnier yesterday."

"It is an effect of leveling up strength and endurance," came the voice of Aela. "Have you been extra hungry lately?"

As a matter of fact, I had been.

"It's not bad," Georgia butted in quickly. "You're just a little more full, that's all."

I turned my attention from Georgia to the Innkeeper. She was draped in robes of brilliant white and soft, mossy blue-green. Her hair was done in at least a dozen braids, each tied with golden thread.

"You better make sure to eat or you'll deplete you stamina," Aela continued, studying me with querying eyes.

I recalled a standing mirror in the foyer of the inn and I could not help but hurry over to it. And, sure as day, I was bigger. Not a lot. If you didn't know me, you probably wouldn't have noticed. But, for someone who had spent too much time staring at the mirror, wishing and wanting to be different, to look more manly like Dad, seeing a few extra pounds put confidence in me for perhaps the first time. And for a moment, I could see him staring back at me, except with Mom's eyes.

"Easy there, Arnold, don't let it go to your head," Georgia said with a smirk and I blushed deeply.

"I need to go take care of something in the kitchens," Aela said with a knowing smile that did not help my embarrassment. But, depart she did, leaving Georgia and I alone in the sitting room.

"Crazy, isn't it?" said Georgia after realizing I wasn't going to be starting any conversations any time soon.

"Yeah, it really is," I mumbled back, scratching at the

back of my neck. My shirt did feel a little tighter around my chest and arms. This was all just too much, but my brain kept making it make sense to me in terms of videogame logic. But this was real. I was here.

"You know, my Pawpaw always said if I wasn't careful I'd end up somewhere strange. Never really thought it'd be a place with gemstone trees and evil musical elves," Georgia said with a laugh.

I joined in her laughter, feeling some of the awkwardness wash away. Maybe she wasn't taking this quite as in stride as it had looked from my perspective. "Right? Next time I fall through a cave into some magic land, it better be filled with chocolate rivers, not one-man-bands intent on...well, whatever he was intent on."

"We're going to find your dad, Archy," said Georgia, her voice growing more serious. "I know this is all wild and strange, but I promise, we'll find him and get back home."

My heart did a little flip at her words, and I couldn't help but feel a measure of hope and confidence at hearing her conviction. "How are you so certain all the time?"

"Well, when Pawpaw and Meemaw took me in, they always told me to live life to the fullest, because you never know how long you're gonna get."

"Yeah," I said awkwardly. I hadn't really dug into the reasons why she had lived with her grandparents, and I wasn't confident in my ability to comfort her right now.

"So, we take this day by day. So what? We're in a world that exists opposite to our own. There is magic, there are rules, and we have some kind of interaction with the forces that control everything, allowing us to travel where the rest can't."

"Right, and we have abilities that can level as we fight

monsters. You're clearly a caster and have magic abilities. And a Class."

"Yeah, and you got a sword and some manly muscles," she said with a wink, bringing my blush back.

"It's just a part of the world's magic—"

"*Squawk!*" Brigg's honking call caused Georgia and I both to whirl about. The enormous bird's head was poking through one of the window, flight cap still on with a rolled bit of parchment around his neck affixed by a leather strap. "Lord Erle'em Ud'din Nidlahm, Lord of the Wood Elves and Once-Sovereign King of Neverwhere, has sent to you a parcel and bids you make haste on your journey!"

With that the leather strap unclasped from Brigg's neck and the parchment dropped to the ground and rolled directly into my feet. Brigg did not move from his spot, but watched us with wide, impatient eyes.

I leaned over and picked up the paper and slide my finger along the waxen seal that held it shut. My eyes did not recognize a single symbol or character on the page.

"Umm, I can't read this," I said, holding up the paper with confusion.

"Oh? Oh! That is right, you are not from these lands," said Aela, popping back in from the kitchen at an uncomfortably convenient timing. She disappeared again before returning with two small marbles. "You'll need to ingest these, it will help with translations."

I took the multi-colored ball, which was surprisingly warm. I had expected it to feel like glass. I could not have been more wrong. It was like jelly, filled with gritty sand. My stomach lurched at the thought of swallowing it, but I popped it into my mouth before I could get too worked up over it.

"Wait!" Aela cried out.

It was too late.

"You needed to crack it first," Aela said with a shake of her head, a rueful smile spreading across her lips. "It will take a while for your stomach acid to break down the shell now. Georgia, dear, make sure you crack yours open first so at least one of you can read and understand what is going on."

"Right," Georgia said with a smirk as she cracked the little orb. A smell like spicy honey wafted from the ball, much stronger than I would have thought possible from something so small. Yet, there was something else, a malodorous undertone that I caught just before Georgia raised the cracked orb to her mouth. "Bottoms up!"

Georgia slurped the liquid down. Her smirk vanished in an instant.

"Perhaps young Archy was the luckier of the two," Aela continued as she handed a kerchief to Georgia, who looked as if she were about to be sick. "It is an acquired taste, tonguefruit. You can find them growing in the coral reefs of Gilla Bay. But they normally work for a few weeks at a time."

"It tastes like rancid fish dipped in honey..." choked Georgia as she wiped her mouth with the embroidered cloth proffered her.

"To the Gillafolk, it is a delicacy," Aella said in measured tones, as if she were fighting back a chortle. "To the rest of the world, a helpful, if rather distasteful tool for both inter-species and multilingual communications."

"Let me see the dang note," grunted Georgia, reaching her hand to mine. All the humor that had been on her face had vanished, and I thought I saw something strange on the sides of her neck, almost like tiny scales forming.

Georgia cleared her throat as she held up the paper, reading aloud:

To the brave adventures,

I wanted to leave with you a few final notes before you set off into the Wyld.

Firstly, your dedication and desire to help restore the light to Neverwhere is beyond admirable. I truly thank you for your willingness to help those to whom you owe no allegiances.

Second, you are both new to this world, and while I did what I could to get you started, it is imperative that you spend time every day training and increasing your abilities. The lands of Neverwhere are not made for the faint of heart or the weak of wills, neither of which I would say describe either of you. That being said, several of the foes you may encounter are very dangerous. Please continue to invest in yourself so that you may come off conqueror.

Third, and this ties into my second point, as you seek to level up, look for enemies with Soulfires. You have defeated one such being, though it was only a White. Soulfires come in the following types:

White, most common and will afford a small amount XP.

Yellow, also common, but slightly less so, these have a chance to drop a rare ability along with a small amount of XP.

Blue, less common, found mostly in the souls of powerful field and mini-bosses, drops uncommon items and a decent amount of XP.

Red, abnormal, found in the souls of Esoteric, no XP drop, but a chance for a new spell or spell slot increase.

Green, rare, vast amount of XP, chance for random stat increases outside of leveling.

Orange, Very Rare, unique drops and random XP boosts, along with chances of percentile health increases.

Purple, extraordinarily rare, only found amongst the most challenging of foes

Note, the only other thing to keep a watch out for are Corrupted Soulfires. These will be tinged with inky black. Do not consume these. While the positives are tremendous, the risk of Soul Corruption far outweighs these perceived benefits.

Lastly, always be on the lookout for the unusual and bizarre. My world, the Wyld, is a world of beauty and wonder. It is also filled with unique tools and consumables that may help you on your way. Georgia's backpack can hold almost anything, so don't worry about overloading your-selves. Archy, you're limited for now, so I would advise finding some manner of enchanted container or carrying case if you can.

Best of luck and may the Grace of Light abide within you,

Your Friend and Guide, the Lord Lights

"So, guess we need to go experience grinding?" I said as I mentally took stock of everything Georgia had just read, thinking about how scared I was facing off a simple Yellow and how it had only been dumb luck that had saved us in the end.

"It has been an age since any have traversed outside of these trees," Aela said solemnly. "I would offer you two things before you depart."

"We would gladly take them, ma'am!" Georgia said wish

excitement as she slid her backpack over her shoulder and deposited the note inside.

Aela let out a soft chuckle before saying, "You two are quite possibly the most interesting beings I have ever met."

"Sorry," I said sheepishly. "We're just nervous, that's all."

"There is no need to apologize. As you venture into the Wylds, oddity will be your constant. Perhaps that is why the Lord of Lights has chosen you. That being said, allow me to give you one piece of advice as well as something from my husband, who long ago ventured off to Jungle Unga in hopes of breaking the curse upon our land," Aela said was a sad smile as she walked once more to her desk. She bent over and began to work at something. There was an audible *click* as a lock was opened. When she rose back up, she held in her hand a round, painted wooden shield with an iron boss in the middle. "This was his first shield, my dear husband's. I pray that it will protect you and keep you well on your journey." Aela handed me the shield and as she did so, silver text appeared:

New Item!

Wooden Shield of the Adventurer

Blocks 75% of all physical damage

Blocks 50% of esoteric damage
Blocks 35% of spectral damage
Is weak to fire damage
Is weak to lightning damage
Is weak to lava-type enemies
Is weak to fire-type enemies

Is weak to lightning-type enemies
Is strong against plant and Cretaceous types
Special attack against plant and Cretaceous types - Shield
Strike!

This was a common item
This item belonged to Venlin Shadowleaf and was hand
painted by his then fiancée, Aela Shadowleaf as a gesture of
her devotion and love

This item requires 2 strength to wield and can be used in
either hand, but works best as a blocking and parrying tool

This items does not require an inventory slot at the moment
Do you wish to store this item on your back or place it in your
left hand?

Yes! Or No...

I mentally selected to store the item for later. This would come in handy, though the number of weaknesses concerned me. But something was better than nothing.

"As for the advice," Aela said once she saw the shield vanish and then reappear on my back. "Georgia, while I am no mistress of the esoteric, I can sense a great power within you. Many dark creatures will seek to take that light from within you. You must never fall prey to the temptations they may offer, regardless of what lies they may spew from their corrupted lips. Your Soulfire already burns bright; I do not wish it extinguished. Do you understand me, child?"

"Yes, ma'am," Georgia answered, though I could tell that the usage of child niggled at her pride. But the advice was good. I hadn't thought of about Georgia and I were leveling and changing all that much. But we were. I was getting physically stronger, but she was changing more so on the inside.

"*Squawk!* We must make haste to the rail station! Come young adventurers, we must depart at once!" Brigg said with a loud honk.

We said a short set of goodbyes, and upon the insistence of Aela, took several wrapped meals which Georgia shoved into her seemingly endless backpack. When I opened the door, I was yet again taken aback at the scenic views of the quaint town and wished for a moment I could linger a little longer here, where it was peaceful and quiet. Those thoughts fled quickly as I thought of my own missing father and the worry that must be deepening my Mom's heart. I needed to get home, no matter what. I needed to get back home.

"*Squawk!* Off to Woodland Railstation," Briggaforth called out as we climbed aboard. "Let us hope it has not fallen."

"What do you mean, fallen?" I asked. But it was too late. Brigg beat his mighty wings, and we soared high into the air.

Time and vision muddled into a blur of lights and dizziness, but before I could truly become queasy, I felt Brigg rapidly slow and descend. We landed upon a perch that seemed made just for the gigantic bird, but it looked in desperate need of repair. The smell of distant smoke hung heavy on the air and the feeling that something was not quite right loomed over us as we descended from Brigg's back and steadied ourselves upon the platform.

Outskirts of Woodland Railstation

The silver text appeared over the whole of the region,

hovering just over my line of sight as I looked about crumbling outpost. Directly behind us rose the trees of the forest from whence we had come. As I scanned the trees, another silver text hovered:

Kandarian Forest

"Woodland Railstation is due south. This is where I must leave you! Glory be to the Lord of Lights! *Squawk!*" Brigg honked as he launched himself high into the air, leaving Georgia and I standing alone.

"Now what?" Georgia said after a protracted moment of awkward silence.

I could literally feel the danger coming from the direction of the Woodland Railstation. But I knew what I needed to do. Besides, it was like Dad was always saying, we Lawrences do not bow. I was not about to bow out now, not on my first sign of danger. "We go on an adventure."

"Lead the way, big guy," said Georgia with a smirk that turned into a somewhat sulky grimace. "Not like I am going to be much help. All I can do is read minds and make a light beam," as she said this her wand dropped into her hand from her cuff. She flicked her wrist a little orb of light hovered over our heads.

"Well, at least we won't have to worry about the dark," I said with a shrug.

"I am going to need to find a grimoire or a tome with an attack spell if I am going to be of any help," Georgia said, flicking her wrist and dismissing both her wand and the orb of light.

"We'll make a deal. If we see any Red Soulfires, those can

be yours," I said with a shrug. "I can't use it much any ways with my sword and shield."

Georgia....jumped down from the landing platform. Though it was only a few feet, I was surprised at how easily she landed. When I leapt down beside her, I barely even felt the impact when I landed.

"Weird," I muttered.

"Archy, you're going to just have to get used to the fact that everything is strange and weird," Georgia said as she elbowed me in the side before she started marching purposefully toward the rail station.

"How can you say that?" I asked, running to catch up to her. "We felt through a portal and are in a world with magic, and elves, and glowing mushrooms."

"Earth has glowing mushrooms," Georgia said without looking back.

"Not like these, and that's beside the point," I pressed.

"Listen," Georgia said as she stopped. "I lost my mom when I was a baby. My dad, who knows where he is. I love my grandparents, but we don't have money or time to adventure, Archy. I'm not like you. This might be the only thing I ever get to do. I am not going to squander it away wishing and wanting. I want to experience this, and if we can do some good in the processes, all the more reason to do it."

Her words cut me deep. I felt shame spread through me like hot water. I had been missing Mom and Dad so much I hadn't stopped to think much about Georgia's home life.

"I didn't mean—" I began.

"Don't worry about it," Georgia said, turning to face me with a grin, but I could see the red at the edges of her eyes and the quiver to her forced smile. "Now, let's go kick some monster butt and level up!"

Woodland Railstation

Woodland Railstation, what once must have been a bustling hub of commerce and transportation, was a dumpster fire of crumbling buildings, smoldering campfires, and stinky refuse. I stared down at the buildings that looked like they had been pulled from a Western movie mixed with ancient buildings of heavy stones. The streets were in a grid pattern and a gigantic water tower was erected in the middle of the settlement. Dozens of pig-faced little creatures in barbarian styled furs walked about carrying the most ridiculous looking types of weapons.

"What's your plan?" Georgia asked in a whisper.

We were laying down next to each other, spying from a vantage point atop a hill just outside the crumbling, mossy walls of the settlement.

"Plan?" I gulped.

"Yeah," Georgia groaned. "Don't you have a plan?"

"Well, I didn't think there were going to be like fifty goblins in there!"

"Well, there are. So, what are we going to do about it?" Georgia asked.

I lay there, looking over the city, mind racing. Everything I had dealt with so far had led me to believe that this world operated like a video game, if that logic held, this would be a stealth mission. We just needed to—

"I see the station!" I said, unable to keep the excitement from my voice. Georgia was right, this was an adventure, and I needed to start treating it like one. "We need to make our way to the east end of town, past the water tower and down that backstreet there. Looks like most of the goblins are massing near the gates, so we'll need a distraction."

"What about a stupid ball of light?" Georgia asked as she too began to smile.

"Yeah, that would work," I said, plotting out my next steps. "If you can get them to focus over there, I think I see the trick to this whole thing."

"Trick?" Georgia asked.

"Yeah," I said as I took one final look at the settlement. "There are little barrels all around, they are red and have big black Xs on them. Now, I am no munitions expert, but I bet you those make a pretty loud boom. We need to clear out the town and gain XP. Neither of us have every really fought before. But, if we can get those goblins to get away from the tower, I could move a few barrels and blow it down. That should do the trick and make a large enough distraction to get onto the train."

"But my notification says to clear the settlement," said Georgia, a bit of concern started to spread now at hearing my plan. "And what if you go down there and get caught?"

"Well, I got this," I answered as I awkwardly pulled out the sword from its scabbard. Apparently this action did not inspire the type of reaction I was hoping for.

"If you get cornered, just yell and I'll figure something out," Georgia said with a shrug. "Besides, they all have little Level 1 signs floating over them. How hard could they be to take out?"

Turns out? Very hard.

I had only just gotten to the city wall right as Georgia sent up a signal flair. There was a tumultuous riot of grunts and piggy-like squeals as around two dozen goblins began rushing toward the opposite side of the settlement. That being said, three of the little buggers were still walking around aimlessly, one wearing what looked like a boot on their head. All three wore nothing but simple loincloths and dangly necklaces that looked to be strewn bones.

Level One Gibblin Sounder

I nearly lept out of my skin as the text scrolled across my vision, an action that caught the attention of the three... Gibblins?

One let out a high-pitch squeal, point at me with a hand that only had three fingers on it. The other held a large stick. Each of the three Gibblins had a *Level One* sign over their head and health bar that was so short I could barely see it. I let out a deep breath as I tried to stop my hand from shaking.

What on earth had I been thinking?

The three Gibblins charged.

Chapter Eleven:
I Find Something That Goes BOOM!

Archy Lawerence Jr.
Level 3
Health Points - 4
Focus Points - 1
Endurance - 6
Strength - 4
Dexterity - 5
Esoteric - 1
Speed - 3
Charisma - 2

Now, I am by no means an expert, and I'm not trying to make this sound morbid or anything. But these waist-high, pig-faced Gibblins were not good at fighting, at all. I mean, I am bad. But they were really bad. I moved through a few of the forms Lord Erle'em had taught me, side stepping and swiping my blade into them. And, just as Lord Erle'em had said, as my sword moved through them, they fell into pixe-lated piles on the ground. Three tiny white balls of fire where all that remained of the Gibblins.

+1 XP

+1 XP

+1 XP

Loot Drop!
Dirty Boot.
Do you wish to store this in your inventory?
Yes! Or No…

I quickly selected no and hurried away from the piles of ash. As I ran toward the first enormous red barrel, I tried to calm my nerves. I had just fought something and won! Not like the half-elf bard, but an actual attacking foe. And, to my surprise, I was not utterly distraught at the act of violence. These were creatures made out of darkness. They weren't actual living things. Or so I was told. I held onto that thought as I skidded to a stop next to an old-timey saloon.

Gibblin BoomBoom Oil!
This product is UNSTABLE!
This is an explosive device. Do you wish to place this in your inventory?
**Unstable devices CAN still explode while being stored.*
Yes! or no…

BoomBoom Oil? That sounded useful.

I glanced around, making sure no other Gibblins were near. When I saw that the coast was clear, I attempted to add the large, red barrel to my inventory.

Uh-oh!
Item not storable!
This item requires a Bomb Bag to carry.
You do not have a Bomb Bag to be able to carry unstable explosives.
You need to find a Bomb Bag if you want to carry unstable explosives.

"Dang it!" I said aloud. I immediately regretted that outburst. From around the corner of three different buildings came a horde of pig-faced goblins, only, that is not what they were called in this place.

Gibblin Sounder!
A group of feral Gibblins.

Gibblin Chief!
Level 3 Field Boss

A fat Gibblin with a crown of what looked like chicken bones tied together with flaxen cord, waddled to the front of the sounder. He had at least six chins and a pimply belly that nearly dragged on the ground. His stubby legs were as thick as they were long, juxtaposing his flabby, but twig-like lengthy arms. His fingers were covered in rings and capped with yellow, cracked fingernails.

Music began to swell, several of the Gibblins beating

little drums and playing on pipes, as the chef slammed the butt of a spear into the ground and bellowed out a loud: "Battle time!"

I did not have time to think about the oddity of it all, the sheer lunacy, because six of the pig-faced Gibblins were running full boar at me, heads lowered and spears angled for spitting.

I felt a tingle of power move through the handle of my sword, like magic lightning dancing along my fingertips. I wasn't sure where it came from, but I felt as if the sword itself cried out, *Slicing Edge!*

I moved in an instant, my arm arcing laterally. The edge of my blade shone with light as I saw my FP bar decrease entirely to nothing and I felt a jolt of energy leave my body. The light that danced along my blade shot out in a semi-circle around me, cleaving through the approaching Gibblins.

They all fell into little heaps of pixilated ash, tiny +1 XP's rising up over them. Small Soulfire orbs of white were all else that remained. The Gibblin chef let out a cry of fury, stomping his stubby legs back and forth in a tantrum.

Achievement Unlocked!
Defeat three or more opponents at once with a special attack!

I waived my arms frantically, trying to get the silver text to disappear. Half a dozen other Gibblins, along with their bulbous chief, were already making their way toward me.

"Slicing Edge!" I shouted, slashed my sword in a perfect replica of the last motion.

No FP!
Slicing Edge requires 1FP.
You currently have, 0 XP
Would you like to drink a Blue Flask?
Yes! Or, no…

"Yes!" I cried out as I stumbled backward away from the oncoming enemy. Just as I said it, I felt the blue flask loosen.

Don't ask me how I knew it had loosened, I just did. I reached up and pulled it free, drinking the azure liquid. I drank quick and deep, allowing the potion to fill my mouth and coat my tastebuds. The flavor was a mixture of melted blue raspberry Jolly Ranchers and southern rain. It sent the hairs on my arms erect and my eyes fluttering. Suddenly, I felt as if I could run a marathon without breaking a sweat.

I shoved the flask back into the bandolier, which seemed to envelop it without any effort on my part, including sealing the spout with its golden stopper. I watched as, in the blink of an eye, my Focus Points meter refilled entirely. An errant thought popped into my mind as I ready my sword once more. I was going to need to level up FP, and fast. One attack per flask was untenable.

I raised my hand, but before I could say the words, I caught two more enemies form the corner of my eye, coming from the left. The slash would not catch them all. I needed another plan.

Quick as I could, I pulled the shield from my back as I stepped slowly toward the building that looked an ill-fitted western saloon. The Gibblins squalled and squealed, each moving slowly after seeing three of their brood hacked to pixilated ash.

"I'm warning you," I said, trying to force any semblance of confidence I could muster into my voice. "I have a magic sword! I'll cut you all to dust!"

"You have stinky sword! We have many! Gibblins will crush puny elf man!" the Chef Gibblin said with a deep-throated laugh, though I could see the fear in his too-close-together eyes.

He was just as scared as me. I didn't know if that made me feel better or worse. And I wasn't an elf. These things really must not be able to see well, or smell. All the elves I had met smelled so fresh. I am pretty sure I needed a new stick of deodorant, and was almost certain Neverwhere didn't sell that.

"Last chance!" I said, feeling my back brush into the swinging doors.

"Go!" Roared the Gibblin Chef, pointing at me with a meaty finger.

They all charged at once. I only had one shot at this, and I was not certain it was going to work.

I dove backwards, and as I did so, I opened my inventory.

Inventory
Right Pocket - Full
Left Pocket - Full
Back Right Pocket - Full
Back Left Pocket - Full

Back Left! I thought as I seemed to fall in slow motion.

+3 Brightshrooms
How many - Brightshrooms - would you like to retrieve?

One! I thought as the ground rapidly approached my back. The blue mushroom appeared in my hand in an instant, and I threw it as hard as I could out of the saloon and toward the unstable barrel of Gibblin BoomBoom oil.

The sound that permeated the settlement was deafening. The concussive blast that followed the little mushroom bouncing into the red barrel sent my head spinning. The heat and force that followed it picked me up and flung me even further. Darkness took my vision from me as my ears were flooded with silence.

"Archy!" a voice cried out from far away. "Archy, where you?"

You have taken a Critical Hit!
Your HP is below ½ a heart.
Your HP is critically low.

A low, obnoxious beeping filled my ears. My HUD had turned fully on as well. When I blinked, the whole world looked like I was looking through binoculars with lenses covered in red mist. I coughed. Something smelled absolutely awful. And then the notifications started rolling in. Ding after horrid ding.

Enemy Defeated!

Sounder Defeated!

Boss Defeated!
+1 Point to award of your own choosing

"Archy! Archy, there you are!" I heard Georgia crying out as she rushed up beside me. She had a scared look on her face and as she knelt down beside me, I could see her hands were trembling. "Are you okay?"

"Just a sec—" I mumbled. My mouth hurt and my throat felt like it was on fire. I mentally released a crimson flask from my bandolier, but couldn't raise my arm up.

Georgia, apparently noticing the vial springing lose, quickly grabbed it and shoved it to my lips. Instantly, the overwhelmingly sweet taste of cherries filled my mouth. As I drank, I watched as she used her other hand to swing her backpack around and retrieve a bandage. She promptly placed the bandage on my right arm.

I let out a cry, nearly spitting up the red liquid. My arm snapped around with a sickening *crack!* Suddenly, I realized just how bad off I must have been. But, just like in the cave with Georgia's leg, my arm was healed in an instant and my hearts began to slowly fill as the healing flask did its work.

Georgia sat back, taking in steadying breaths. She was dirty, covered in ash and mud. She had a scrap above her right brow and another one on her leg. It was then I was realizing she wasn't wearing her dress, but back in her khaki shorts and oversize flannel and t-shirt.

"You changed?" I said, my voice still sounding strained, despite me trying to sound nonchalant.

She raised her eyebrows. "Did you like the dress better?"

"You're scuffed up, what happened?" I asked, trying to steer the question away from an awkward one.

"Oh? What happened?" Georgia asked, looked at me with bewilderment. "Well, let's see...what did happen? Oh yeah, I climbed up a hill and sent a signal flare up so that someone could go and blow up a water tower. Turns out, he missed. Do you know how many Gibblins rushed that hill? Twelve! Twelve of them!"

"How did you survive?" I asked, both impressed and mortified that I had put her at risk.

"Turns out," Georgia said with excitement, "Esoteric items can be turned in for a new spell!"

"What can be what?" I asked, confused, my brain still muddled from the explosion.

"Well, I turned in the dress Lord Erle'em had sent for me and got a new spell, Golden Needle!" Georgia said, her excitement compounding. "When I cast it, it used up all my FP, but created this giant golden needle that shot out of thin air, and I could direct it with my mind for ten whole seconds. What's even better, if I can level it up, I can do it for fifteen and even thirty if I can a second time!"

"So, where did your dress go?" I asked, trying to keep up with all of it.

Georgia blushed deeply. "Away."

"Oh," I said. "OH! Oh, I didn't mean, I, uh..."

"It's okay, Boy Scout, it's fine," Georgia said with a shrug, apparently relieved that I was more embarrassed than she was about it. "I had my change in my back pack. I am going to miss that dress though. It was really nice. Oh! And I leveled up like three times because of it and picked up a couple weird things we gotta look at. Having a back pack that is bottomless is kind of nifty. Speaking of leveling up, you have a lot of Soulfire out there to collect and a couple items you might want to grab."

"Why didn't you take them?" I asked.

She looked down, "Well, turns out, if you're not the one to score the kill, you don't get to share in the loot."

"Weird," I said as I laid my head back. "That's really weird."

"You think that is weird?" Georgia said with a laugh that nearly turned to a cry. She sniffed and then said, "I miss worrying about how hard Mr. Highfield's exams were."

"I thought you were excited about being here?" I asked, picking myself up gingerly from the ground. My arm was feeling much better, but my whole body felt a little weak. Looking up at my HUD I could see I had three and three-quarters hearts filled. I wasn't about to waist a flask on a quarter heart.

"It's not like I don't miss my home, Archy," Georgia said as she too rose up, cinching down the straps of her trusty backpack. "I just don't have as much to go back to as you. Doesn't mean I want to get exploded by pig-faced goblins in this place."

Ouch.

"I didn't mean anything like that," I said, voice low. "I just meant, I thought you were excited for this kind of thing."

"I guess I didn't realize how real it was going to feel, you know, fighting and...killing," Georgia muttered as she kicked a loose bit of debris.

"Well, I don't think it is really killing, not like from our world," I said as I thought back on the fight. "They all just turn into ash that looks too pixilated to be like dying. Maybe it is a mechanic of this world, or maybe it's because we're not from here, but I don't think we're actually killing anything."

Ding!

"You are in fact not killing anything."

I whirled around, eyes wide with fear, searching for the source of the words. To my surprise, floating in the air, right over Georgia's shoulder, was one of the two faeries from Eldalar. She was currently a soft blue hue and barely more that ball of light with wings.

"I am Treoirael, but you can call me Treo," the blue faerie chimed brightly. *"And what you're doing is not killing. These will return each time our second moon turns red, like last night and most likely tonight. Then, for a few days, she will stay pale."*

I blinked in confusion.

"How did you find us?" Georgia asked, clearly as surprised as me to find this faerie fluttering over her shoulder. "Did Lord Erle'em send you?"

... *"No."*

"Well, how did you find us then?" I asked.

"This world is very old. I am born of nature's heart, a child of the wyld. My mother is the moon and my father the deep roots of the trees. I am wind and wild, and all things esoteric. I was sent by my nature to guide you."

"I saw you in Eldalar, floating by Oaktree Inn," I interjected, feeling almost sorry for breaking the rhythmic way in which she was speaking.

Her tinkling stop and she let out a low, *"Oh..."*

"Are you supposed to be here?" Georgia asked.

"No more than you are," Treo shot back, and I swear I could hear her fold her arms and tut at us.

"Well, we're here to help him find his dad," Georgia said matter-of-factly. "And if you're willing to help, well, the more the merrier."

At those words, Treo let out a loud *ding!* and began to flutter all around, leaving trails of sparkling light in the air behind her.

"Wait," I said suddenly. "I thought you couldn't leave your particular regions?"

"I am a Glider, a Guider, a Will-o-the-Whisp. My kind can move through all planes and realms, unimpeded. Though, we lack the traditional magical skills some of our cousins posses. So no wishes or flying for you two," Treo said gleefully. *"But I can help guide and answer questions to the best of my ability!"*

"Let me get this straight," Georgia said. "You can travel about Neverwhere because you're a Whisp? And you can help tell us about different things and places we encounter?"

"This is a truth," chimed Treo. *"Ask away, ask away! I will answer whatever you say!"*

"Are all of the Gibblins gone?" I asked, peaking out of the saloon and down the street. Several White Soulfires burned, along with a singular Yellow. "Are we in danger?"

"Questions are like snowflakes, so varied in make. One you ask, I can make no mistake. Gibblins are gone, turned back into gloomy mist," Treo said as she bobbed up and down. *"But danger is ever near, never far!"*

"Well that is ominous," I said, stepping back into the saloon. "Listen, I am going to run out there and collect those Soulfires, then I'll come back in here. Georgia, see if you can't find anything in this place we can use. And if you see something called a Bomb Bag, grab it. I can't take Boom-Boom Oil without it."

"Bomb Bag?" Georgia asked with a raise of her eyebrows.

"Yeah, something to carry explosives with," I answered as I stepped into the street.

"You will need to level up! You have gained much experi-

ence, Archy!" Treo said in my ear, apparently choosing to follow me rather than stay near Georgia for the time being.

"I will, I just want to gather these Soulfires first, so I don't have to do this over and over again," I answered.

"Have you tried, Select All, Gather All, on your Drop Tasks?" Treo asked, as if it was the most common sense question of all time.

"I have never even heard of that," I said as I mentally pulled my HUD fully up and began to look about. In the bottom right, I noticed a golden circle, kind of like a compass. As a looked at it, it moved to the center of my view. Instead of North, West, East, and South the words: Armor, Crafting, Spells, and Consumables appeared.

Select Consumables!

You have selected Consumables
Do you wish to:
Gather All Consumables
Gather Unique Consumables
Gather Like Consumables
Gather Rare Consumables

I selected 'Gather All Consumables'.

No sooner had I done so, all the Soulfires in the area rushed toward me at once, and as they struck my person, small notification charms went off.

+17 XP
+6 ember of flame
+37 Gibblin tooth
+12 Gibblin horn

+14 broken stone

+9 Ear of Gibblin

+1 eye of Gibblin

+3 fetid meat

Level 3 Field Boss, Defeated!

+3 XP

+1 Strength

You defeated a Chief!

+1 Charisma

Achievement Unlocked!

Double Kill! Overkilled! Kill-a-jaBoom!

You have taken out ten or more foe's with an explosion.

+10 XP

Boo-yah! Botanist

You used natural fungi to exterminate a foe!

+1 Point to award of your own choosing

Lucky-ki-yay, Cowboy!

You narrowly survived a devastating blast YOU caused

You used a saloon to save your life

+1 to Dexterity

Inventory is full!

Do you wish to discard:

+37 Gibblin tooth

+12 Gibblin horn

+14 broken stone

+9 Ear of Gibblin

+1 eye of Gibblin
+3 fetid meat

I nearly fell over due to the onslaught of information. My head felt as if a kettle had been placed over it and someone had struck it repeatedly with a wooden ladle. Despite this, I began to work through the information as efficiently as possible. I went to the inventory tab under the Consumable section and selected, *Discard.*

A pile formed directly in front of me, a stinking heap of Gibblins parts and bits, along with some chunks of stone that had been destroyed in the blast. Georgia could gather all this at once now I had discarded it. I would let her decide what she did and did not want to keep. I was far more interested in my current leveling.

I had gained enough experience to level up three different times, and had a few spare points to add where I pleased. The first thing I did was move two points to FP. I did not want to be limited to one special attack a fight. Next, I moved to HP and dropped a point there. My Charisma had increased, though I did not really see the value in that right now. It took me a few seconds where to decide to place my final point before I finally settled on Speed. It had literally saved my life, being able to move the way I had into the saloon. If I were against a wall again, I wanted to be able to get out of the way and quick.

As soon as I made my decisions, I could see my HUD changing before my eyes. My XP bar tripled in length and an additional heart container formed, which had the side effect of filling them all to the max. I felt a little dumb for using a crimson flask. I could have just leveled up to restore myself to full health. I would need to remember that. What I hadn't expected was the strange sensation as both my Dexterity and Speed increased.

It was not that the world had actually slowed down, I just seemed to notice more movement with far more clarity. I could sense the change in the wind by the slightest turn of the air, I could see dust moving and fall of a leaf from nearly thirty meters away.

"Weird," I gasped in surprise, unable to keep the stupid grin from spreading across my lips.

"Everything alright?" That was Georgia. I could hear her walking, the dust grinding under her hiking boots. I was going to need to learn how to focus or I was going to go insane.

"Yeah! Better! I took my Dexterity and Speed up a level, and something changed, like a lot," I said, whirling about to face her.

"Yeah, turns out, the more you level a particular trait, it compounds it," Georgia said with equal excitement. "My Esoteric is at 9 now with the additional bonuses. Hey, did your Charisma go up?"

"Yeah, why?" I asked, a little befuddled at her question.

"You just seem a little more confident," Georgia answered me, scanning me up and down, as if she were studying me.

With my HUD fully open, I could see Georgia now with her full stats. I nearly fell over. How on earth had she gained so many points in such a short period of time? Like, I knew Lord Erle'em had given her a few things, but really?

Silver text read the following:

Georgia Stoddard
Level 8 ~ Human Mage

Health Points - 5
Focus Points - 5
Endurance - 3
Strength - 3
Dexterity - 4
Esoteric - 9
Speed - 4
Charisma - 7

"Crazy, right?" Georgia said with a mixture of pride and excitement. "I mean, you have a lot more Strength and Endurance, but I really am coming into this whole magic thing!"

"How come yours says, 'Human Mage'? Does mine say anything?" I asked.

"Your's just says, 'Archy Lawrence Jr.' and lists your stats," answered Georgia. "Maybe it's because you haven't really specialized in anything yet."

"I mean, I have a sword and shield, so a knight or warrior would be cool," I muttered, feeling a little embarrassed at myself. But it was unfair. She got extra points and a cool title and created her own magic spell. I just kept narrowly escaping death.

Ding!

"You should gather the Consumables. They will vanish if they are not collected in a timely manner. Also, it is growing later in the afternoon and if you wish to get the steam train running, you must hurry."

"Treo is right," said Georgia. Her eyes kind of lost focus for about three seconds and then suddenly all of the stinking pile of consumables vanished.

"Wait, is that what I look like when I am in my HUD?" I asked.

"Like what?" Georgia asked back.

"You went all vacant for a second or two, like you weren't here."

"Well, I mean, I was moving through my options, but it felt a little longer than a second or two. I have to get used to the new compass feature."

"You have that too?" I asked, excited.

"Yeah, it just kind of showed up once we left Eldalar Village," said Georgia. "It is where I could trade in my Esoteric items to form new spells."

"Wait, what did you mean about getting the steam train running?" I asked.

"Do you know how to operate a steam engine? Treo asked with excitement.

"Well, no," I answered.

"Then you will need to figure it out and fast! You do not wish to be trapped here. While the monsters will reset at night, the barrels of BoomBoom oil will not. Oh, and one more thing, fallen enemies might be able to remember prior encounters. So, best not to attack the same ones over and over again, as their rewards will be less and their difficulty will increase exponentially."

"Anything else we should know" I asked incredulously. "Because that seemed like it would have been good to know before we were sent out."

"Of course! All you have to do is ask!" chimed Treo happily.

"Thank you," said Georgia as she forcefully took me by the arm and pulled me toward the train tracks. She then stood up on her tiptoes and whispered, rather sharply, "Let's not offend the one person in this settlement that is actually trying to help us."

I was chagrined at the reprimand, but it was warranted. I was being ungrateful toward the little sprite. But did she have to be so obnoxious with her incessant dinging and flittering about? And her voice was so high pitched.

"Now, let's go find the train," said Georgia with a brighter tone, aloud for me and Treoirael to hear.

Chapter Twelve: I Get in a Fight

THE TRAIN STATION WAS, like the majority of the settlement, overgrown and broken down. Yet, the train itself seemed entirely alien. It was jade and bronze, and the patterning reminded me of the clockwork automaton ape, Luk Luk Ci Ci we had met in the Hallowed Glade. The tracks were not what I expected either. Instead of iron rails, blocks of ancient stone with jade clusters formed a trail that the steam engine hovered over.

"Well I never," said Georgia as we both looked on in astonishment.

"Don't you have trains in your world?" asked Treo, her little voice sounding confused.

"Yeah, but they don't hover like that," said Georgia.

"Maglev trains run on something similar, but they aren't steam powered," I said without thinking, just staring in wonderment at the bricks. They looked as if they could move if pushed or directed. But they had to weigh a metric ton a piece.

"Know-it-all," sighed Georgia. "What I meant was, I don't think we have magic trains the are powered by arcane gemstone."

I reddened and rubbed at the back of my neck, "I guess that makes more sense."

"This train require five jade Powerstones. Powerstones can be found scattered throughout the Floating Mountains and amongst the ruins of many of the ancient cities of Neverwhere."

"Okay, so we have to find these jade Powerstones to get the train moving?"

"Be careful though, Powerstones are not good for human skin," Treo said brightly. *"The source of power within them with scorches the flesh straight off the bone."*

I blanched at the brightness in Treo's voice as much as the imagery that was conjured in my mind at the description. "So, how do we move them?"

"Well, how am I supposed to know? I am three inches tall! I can't do everything." The little sprite chimed in a huff of exasperation.

"Well excuse me if I don't want to have the meat cooked of my bones!"

"Will the two of you just stop?" Georgia cut in, sounding as annoyed as I felt, her Southern accent turning to dastardly levels of hick. "Y'all are worse that two possums fighting over a McDonald's wrapper in a trash bin, good Lord Almighty!"

"Sorry..." I muttered under my breath, feeling wholly chastised.

"Thank you," Georgia said with a sigh. "Now, looks like there are some carts lying about. I'll look around for something to lift the super-rocks. You two can go find at least one cart that is usable, and while y'all are at it, figure out whatever 'this is'." She said that last bit with a flippant wave of her hand. "I can't stand arguing."

To my surprise, Treoirael chimed in delight and began bobbing near my head, as if she were itching to go exploring.

"You sure you're going to be alight?" I asked, looking around as if another Gibblin might pop out of thin air.

"I'm fine, Boy Scout," Georgia said with a wink. "Y'all get yourselves figured out and get me a cart. Sure as day I'll jimmy up a way to move them rocks in a jiffy."

"If you see or hear anything, just shout, okay?" I said, still feeling unease separating after such a traumatic fight. Which, in hindsight, I had fared far less optimally than she had. As far as I could tell, all she had lost was a dress. I had nearly lost my life, with only dumb luck and accidentally storing some Brightshrooms saving me.

"I'll be fine," she pressed as she drew her straps tight

once more on her backpack. "Now, off with you. Sun's a burnin'!"

The next several minutes were spent in near-silence as I walked about the settlement, searching for a cart that wasn't utterly busted. You'd think there would be several, but I couldn't find a single one. And though she wasn't speaking, Treoirael's little wings would make a chiming sound here and there as she fluttered beside me.

"Okay, listen, I am sorry I was short with you," I said after I exited my fifteenth or sixteenth build without a cart in working order. "It's been a long day."

"Huh?" piped Treo.

"I said I am sorry," I reiterated, trying my hardest to keep my annoyance down. I had always struggled with apologizing when I felt like I hadn't done wrong or was justified in my actions. Mom said it was a tick. Dad said I was just stubborn. Either way, it had cost me a friend or two and several weekend trips or hours of video games. "I did not mean to offend you if I did."

"Oh! That is quite alright...I had forgotten all about it already!" Treo said brightly. *"Do not even concern yourself with it."*

"Oh," I mumbled, a little taken aback. "So, no hard feelings?"

"Of course not," she chimed.

"So, we're good?" I asked one last time. "I was kind of rude."

"You are silly! I chose to come here to help. You do not know the ways of the Wyld, and I do not understand you, but that

does not mean we cannot work together. Besides, it is not in the nature of Wisps to hold grudges."

For some reason, this made me feel even worse for how I had snapped at the little ball of light. Events of the day aside, I had been rude. I went to reiterate this point, but just before I could, Treo zoomed off in a jet stream of glitter sparkles. Confused and intrigued, I ran after her.

I ran through a maze of right-angled streets, hoping over broken stone and ruins, surprised at the relative ease at which I was moving. My whole life I had been pretty wimpy, unable to do many of the physical activities my peers were involved in. But now...now I was hurtling over walls that were waist high as if it were nothing, running without becoming overly winded, and pulling myself up without breaking a sweat. I could not contain the laughter as it began to roll from my mouth. To my surprise, Treo joined in with my laughing, her tinkling voice mixing in with my own. And for perhaps the first time since arriving in this place, I found myself actually allowing myself to enjoy it.

After a while, Treo pulled up and began bouncing around what appeared to be an old storage shed. The door was composed of decaying wood and the walls were painted after a manner not too dissimilar to that of ancient Mayan art style.

Something bright glinted into my eye, nearly blinding me. It was an old mirror, like one my grandma had in her house, a full-body thing on a swivel. The sun was getting lower and the light that bounced off the glass caused me to stumble a little.

"A little sunlight never hurt anyone," laughed Treo at my unfortunate stumble.

Not wanting to give her the satisfaction of how much

the light had hurt my eyes, I shrugged, and I walked up to the door of the shed, placing a hand on it and pushing it open. The hinges squealed as I did so, one of them crumbling into a rusty pile of dust. A stairwell loomed before me, descending into the dark room below. Unease crept its way up my spine as I peered down into the lightless abyss.

"I believe you will find what you need down there." Treo beamed. *"I can sense something whole. But, be warned. I can also sense something else. Do you have a source of light with you?"*

Just as she asked, silver scrollwork text appeared before my eyes, just over the blackness that was the stairwell's depths:

Do you wish to retrieve your - Flashlight - 71%?
Yes! Or, no...

I mentally selected yes, pulling the too large light from my pocket. I also drew my sword, holding it in my right hand. When I clicked the light on, the beam pointing down the stairs, half a dozen bat-like creatures cried out in unison before flight up and out of the storage shed. I let out a yelp of fear and surprise as they one-eyed rats with wings zoomed past me in a flurry of wings and screeches.

Common Skreets!

Skreets are cycloptic, winged vermin that typically consume fruit and or insects. They are nocturnal and hate the light. While they might be small, beware their teeth. They inflect a +1 poison, nauseating bite that compounds with every attack. These are weak to light, slash, and bludgeoning. Different regions have caused these vermin to evolve into fire, ice, electric, and cyclone types. Common Skreets are the most prevalent and pose little to no threat on their own. However, if you anger a nest, you could be in for a rough time.

"Oooooo," crooned Treo. *"You should stay away from those! They sound nasty!"*

"Yeah," I grunted, trying my best to steady myself. "I'll do my best."

After a second thought, I returned my sword to its sheath, moved the flashlight to my right hand, and pulled my shield off my back. I figured it would be easier to knock these little rats with wings out of the sky with my shield or protect myself with it than a sword.

"Shall we?" I said, trying my best to project an air of confidence.

"Down, down, down, into the darkness to save the realm. Down we go in hopes of finding a wheeled cart!" sang Treo as she danced around my shoulder.

The steps were large and shallow, making it awkward for me to walk down, as I was far more used to human steps in the human world. And why shouldn't I be? Well, every step only dropped us about six inches, so it took a fairly long period of time to reach the bottom, not that I was in too much of a hurry to get down their anyways. The problem was, with every step, the passage way grew darker than it should have, as if the light was being strangled away by some unseen force. With everything I had encountered so far, I was almost certain that was the case.

When I finally stepped onto the floor at the bottom of the steps, a chill ran up my spine. The air smelled bad. Like, really bad. To make matters worse, I could hear the rustling and moving of small creatures. Unfortunately, my HUD gave me no indication that there were any enemies nearby.

"Treo," I whispered up at the tiny ball of light. "Why aren't I get notifications of what is near me? I can hear stuff moving."

"You need to be able to see it, silly," laughed Treo as she leaned close and whispered back into my ear, conspiratorially.

You Have Entered a Cave

"Aren't you scared?" I asked, a bit of frustration mingled with fear putting a sharper edge on my words than I had meant.

"Why would I be? I have you here, and you're a hero!"

Oh no...this little faerie thought I was a hero. A pit formed in my stomach. That was why she followed us. That was her reason. It was like in the stories Mom used to read me. But I wasn't a hero. I was just trying to get my dad back.

Something big moved next to me, knocking over what sounded like a bunch of tools. My heart nearly leapt into my throat. I whirled around, pointing my light in the direction of the ruckus. What I saw dropped my heart from my throat all the way down to my toes.

Chapter Thirteen:
I Meet a Troll

Archy Lawerence Jr.
Level 4
Health Points - 4
Focus Points - 3
Endurance - 6
Strength - 5
Dexterity - 6
Esoteric - 1
Speed - 4
Charisma - 3

Level 8 Hill Troll!

Hill Trolls are big, stinky, hoarding, buffoons! They are fiercely territorial, but extremely lazy. They have a tendency to move into other creatures' homes, forcing them out or eating them for their supper. With an IQ lower than the room temperature, don't expect a philosophical debate or try talking your way out of this one. These are barely even considered sentient beings in Neverwhere. Pigeons have a larger brain than these ugly, slimy, mossy omnivores. The only thing they enjoy more than hoarding other people's stuff, is smashing said other people with their meaty fists.

THE DISPLAY HAD JUST FINISHED READING in my mind when another dozen or so Skreets burst past me. I swung my shield about wildly as they did so, strike one out of mid-air. The bat-like fiend struck the opposite wall with a sickening crack and a single XP point floated over it while a White Soulfire burned in the pile of ash.

Lucky Strike!
Achievement Unlocked

Not right now!

Strike a flying type out of mid air through pure luck!
+5% to Dexterity in jumping attacks

Okay, that was actually helpful.

"Who go there?" roared the Hill Troll in a broken—if I wasn't mistaken—poorly formed, Cockney accent. He stepped forward, holding something in his hand. I couldn't really make it out. I did, however, catch the glint of a key hanging around his neck. Before I could ponder on that oddity, he bellowed, "I grind your bones to bread!"

Something clipped the edge of my shield, which I had barely enough time to raise to guard my face, whirling me about. Agony shot through my arm and one of the hearts over my head depleted by half. I grunted in both frustration and pain as I tried to steady myself.

That chunk of something hadn't even directly struck me and it took half a heart?

I sized up the ugly troll once more. This was going to be far more dangerous than I had thought.

Just as I was about to make a move, another voice caught my attention. This one, however, was not that of the tinkling wisp nor the Cockney troll. It was that of an overly dramatized miner, just like Gerald.

"For Pete's sake, get me out of this kerfuffle!"

My eyes darted around the dark room until they landed on what looked like a birdcage made out of blackened iron bars. And on the inside, stripped down to his red union suit, was another gem-eyed gnome.

"What in the tarnation are ya waitin' on? The sun to rise?" the little bearded man shouted.

"I smash and make bread from two tiny ones, hehe," grunted the troll. "Now hold still little man, let me smash you good for bread."

I jumped as the lumbering behemoth chucked another handful of spare cart parts at me, this time what I realized as it smashed into the wall behind me, was an axle.

"You must act swiftly," Treo said in a panic. *"Trolls are vile creatures that become stronger the longer they're allowed to rage."*

"I'm trying," I answered as I looked around for a means to outwit the troll. What I saw was less than heartening.

The basement was held up by four—well, now three—pillars. The majority of the fourth was currently being used as the troll's club. I had an idea, but it would cost me the only whole cart I had seen.

"Treo, how fast are trolls?" I asked quickly.

"Trolls become progressively faster as they run," Treo started, sounding as if she were reciting something from a book. *"Be careful. They are not agile beasts and can be rather brutish. They tend to bowl over things in their way."*

I was counting on just that. I would have to find another cart elsewhere.

"Hey you, Stinky!" I called out, waiving my arms. "You missed me!"

"Oye, that's not very nice," the troll said, heavy brows furrowing on his pencil head. "I'll smash your bones for bread!"

"You have to catch me first, Stumpy!"

"Urg!" roared the troll as he barreled forward, running directly at me.

I leapt out of the way, just as he smashed headlong into the pillar I had been standing in front of. The enormous health bar over his head went down barely a sliver as the wooden beam shattered like a toothpick. And as dust rained down from the ceiling, I felt my heart skip a beat as a new realization dawned on me. But, before I could action on that thought, the troll ran at me again.

Tossing all sensibility to the side, I ran toward the troll. Apparently, he had not been expecting my action either because his eyes widened and he tripped over his feet. I raised my sword toward the cord about his neck holding the key.

My blade bounced off of the troll's thick grey skin, but not before catching under the rope. The key sailed through the air as the troll careened into the third pillar. This time, more than dust and dirt fell from the ceiling, as several boards, old lamps, and a myriad of nicknacks were knocked free.

"Ouch!" groaned the troll. "You tried to kill me!"

Dazed, I looked about the ground in a tizzy, searching frantically for the key. I wasn't even certain that the troll would need to knock down the final pillar for this whole thing to come tumbling down. But I couldn't leave the little Granus to be crushed.

"I'm going to crush—"

"Stop with the bread!" I shouted as my hands thrashed about in the rubble. I did not know what had come over me, but I had about had it with near-death experiences for one day. "Come up with a new thing."

"Hey! That's not very nice!" the troll said, scratching at his pin-head. "I'll make you into bread for that."

"Finally!" Relief washed over me as I felt my fingers slide over the hard edges of the iron key. As quickly as I could, I opened my inventory, seeking out the now familiar blue mushrooms.

"Oh, look at that!" I cried out as I selected the object I was looking for.

Brightshroom!

I hurled the bioluminescent mushroom across the room, a comet tail of dazzling light following the arcing fungi. The mushroom landed with a splat, wholly taking the troll's attention, just as I had hoped.

I rushed toward the cage where the Granus was imprisoned, trying my best to be as quiet as possible. Thankfully, the troll was just far enough away that when I turned the lock and mechanism clinked in release, that I had the time to grab the gnome by his red union suit and dash out of the way just as a club came crashing down on the cage.

"Missed me, you great oaf!" I shouted, as I rushed sideways.

"What are y'er doin'?" cried out the Granus as we dashed not toward the stairwell that led to safety, but to the final pillar.

"I have a plan!"

"Y'er gonna get me kur-splatted!"

I did not have time to respond. It happened in slow motion, just as it had been when I blew up the BoomBoom oil. I could feel my stamina bar depleting as I ran up the side of the pillar and sprang off in a near perfect backflip, like one of those parkour guys you see on Youtube. I did this just as the troll brought his club swinging horizontally, my shaggy hair clipping the weapon as it whizzed past me and into the pillar I had just ran up. All the while, the little Granus was yowling like a soaked cat.

Crash!

"Uh-oh," muttered the troll.

Uh-oh indeed.

The whole roof gave way as I rolled across the ground and sprang to the base of the stairwell. The last bit of my stamina vanished away, leaving a blinking, empty bar hovering in my very warped and distorted vision. Dust and debris filled the air as the whole world shook around me.

The silence that followed was deafening. It was not like when the BoomBoom Oil had blown. This was very different. I could tell that my hearing was fine. It was just silent.

That silence only lasted a few seconds before a second shifting in the rubble caused my heart to leap into my throat.

I felt someone tugging on my shirt collar, followed by a heavily accented, "Laddie, we got to get up them there stairs!"

"Bread..." a weak voice groaned. "Bones for bread."

No way...there was no way that troll had survived.

Level 8 - Skewered Hill Troll
Mini-boss from the destruction you caused.
Defeat him, or he'll turn your bones to bread.

I pried my eyes open, my HUD was coming back into focus. A tiny amount of stamina had been replenished, but not enough for me to feel any level of confidence in taking on a Level 8 Mini-boss. I needed time or a distraction, but was clearly out of both. So, doing the only thing I could think of in the moment, I began to force my body up the stairs.

"Hurry, laddie! You've done did ticked 'em off!" the Granus bellowed in my ear as he continued to try and help me up the stairs.

"Archy," Treo said, buzzing in my ear. *"The Granus is right, we need to get up and into the light. Trolls can't abide the light."*

I had just dropped a house on this thing; how was a little light going to hurt the beast? But then I recalled a story about a wizard and some dwarves on an adventure, and how the sun had turned three ugly trolls into stone.

I gritted my teeth and continued to pull myself upward as I heard the rubble shift and tumble as the Hill Troll attempted to clear a path. Despite my fear, I had done a substantial amount of damage to the beast. His health bar was down to the deepest shade of red. It was really the only thing I could see of the creature from my vantage point. Yet, as I climbed higher and higher, I could feel my strength returning, my stamina bar ever so slowly filling.

At last, I spotted the entryway into the stairwell and the glorious, warm rays of sunlight marking the exit to the abyssal dump I had found myself in. Why had I thought it a good idea to go looking down there in the first place?

I did not have time to ponder this thought as something went crashing into the wall next to me. I whirled my head about and found myself staring into the beady eyes of the troll, not more than ten feet away from me. The cry the tore from my lips was anything but manly, but the fear was just the boost I needed to make it the last few feet up and into the light.

"I - am - turn - bones - bread!" the troll grunted as it pulled its mangled body up, up, up after me. To my horror, the troll looked far worse than he had before. His lip was swelled up and drooping, causing the slur in his words, and his left eye was a mass of bruised flesh. But that was not the worst of it. A massive chunk of ceiling had, as his new title name had indicated, skewered him through and through. In all honesty, I had no idea how he was still walking.

"By the beard of Auruwae!" cried out the Granus in front of me. "That is mighty disturbing!"

"Get into the sun." My words came out nearly as broken and incoherent as the troll's own jumbled threat.

"Archy, hurry! The sun is setting!" Treo chimed, her voice filled with fear.

Oh, that was just great.

Mustering the last of my strength, and just as the troll

was picking up momentum, I pushed myself forward. I was not going to get the troll up the stairs before the sun was down. He was moving too slowly. Heck, he probably would not leave the shadows until the sun had totally set. And then what would I do? He would just attack again after sundown and then would make my bones into bread. That was, unless...

I stumbled forward, up and out of the shed, feet trudging to where the mirror had caused me such a mild irritation before stood. Twilight glanced off the silvery surface of the glass, bouncing onto a wall just a few feet away.

"Help me," I said to the Granus, whose name I had yet to ascertain.

"With what? We're free!" He sounded far too excited, already dancing about and punching at the air.

"The troll will get out as soon as the sun goes down," I said, looking up in terror as the twin moons were already rising into a sky that was turning dark far too fast. Time here must be very different. I pocketed that thought for when I wasn't fighting a troll in a cave. Right now was not the time for that, I needed to act and fast.

"So what are y'er proposing we do, drop a looking glass on 'em? Y'er dropped a house on it and it didn't do no good whatsoever. What's a glass gonna do?"

"Just help me move it!" I shouted in frustration.

To my surprise, the Granus didn't argue or fight with me, but grabbed the other side of the heavy, wooden frame that held the mirror on three legs, and lifted. We waddled and tottered as we rushed the mirror to the edge of the stairs. The sun was almost gone. I looked down, catching the dastardly smile that was spreading across the troll's haggard face.

"I am enjoy to going turning your bone to breads!" the troll rambled out, slurring the malformed threat.

"Enjoy this!" I said as I wrenched the mirror toward the troll's face, just catching the last rays of golden twilight on the glass surface.

"Not good!" cried out the troll as the light bounced off of the mirror, striking him in his hideous reflection.

Have you ever seen a water bottle instantly freeze? You know, when you get it so cold and then strike it suddenly and the whole thing just turns to ice almost instantaneously? Yeah, that is what this looked like, but instead of ice, it was white-grey rock. And no sooner did the troll turn into the rocky statue than did it tumble backwards and burst into countless pieces.

Victory Achieved!

You have slain a Hill Troll!

A Soulfire began to burn in the midst of the troll's remains, and to my utter surprise, it was a royal blue colored flame.

"Blue Soulfire..." gasped Treo as she landed on my shoulder with a dainty tingling of faerie wings. *"I've never seen Blue before."*

"By George! That was the wildest thing I ever did seen!" cackled the Granus, who I had honestly forgotten was there for a second. "Name's Herald! Pleasure to meet a Big Person who isn't the absolute worst! To be honest with y'er, I thought you was a pointed-eared, good-fir-nothin' elf boy for a minute."

I looked down at the little Granus, the tip of his bald

pate just above my knee, and said, "What's wrong with elves?"

"Oh, don't go and ruin the moment," said Herald, the word ruin having been pronounced with one or two too many r's. "Anyways, thank ye kindly fir gettin' me out of that there cage, that was wild as three coyotes singin' harmony at a Beltane Feast, I'll tell y'er what."

I was now utterly certain that everything this Granus had to say was lacking any coherent structure or prudent point. That being said, a thought came to me. "Why were you under there in the first place?"

"Well, that's pretty obvious, don't y'er think? I was captured by that stink'n troll prit near a fortnight ago. Been held up in that cage with nothin' to do other than listen to that thing talk about bread," Herald said with chagrin. "I was half tempted to ask him to eat me then and there."

"Why didn't he?" I asked, not even considering how rude it was to do so beforehand. I could almost hear Mom's voice lecturing me on how to talk to people, but I was curious, and I had just saved his life. It's not like he was going to get that mad at me...right?

"Hu? Oh, about that," laughed the little, bearded gnome. "He said he was expecting several others coming his way and wanted more to eat I reckon. Guess he bit off more than he could chew, didn't he? Ha!"

"Ya," I said flippantly, already losing interest in Hareld's ramblings, walking slowly toward the Blue Soulfire.

As I approached the fire, like it had with the bard, flew into my chest, sending off a slew of notifications scrolling across my vision.

Blue Soulfire Acquired!

You have defeated an enemy of impressive strength
+10 points to Experience

Mirror mirror on the wall, who is going to make these bad
guys fall?
You are!
You used a mirror to manipulate light to destroy a Noct-type
enemy
+5% to all light-based attacks

Then There Were Three
You have collected three different Soulfire Types
All enemies of White and Yellow type now take an additional
10% of damage
You receive a defensive buff of 20% against all White and
Yellow types

New Item!
Formed from the mangled, flabby skin of the fallen Hill Troll,
and held together by the string of his loin-cloth, you have
received a small-explosives Bomb Bag!

Bomb Bag: Base Level
This sack allows you to carry explosives like TNT sticks,
Bombblossoms, and other small munitions you may acquire.
The space is limited and so is the stability of this sack. You
will need to upgrade this item if you wish to carry larger, more
volatile explosives.

The wheel on my inventory section suddenly added a new circle, and in that golden ring, the most disgusting looking sack I had ever seen populated. And though I couldn't actually smell it, I had a revolting memory of just how nasty that troll had reeked assault me, nearly bringing the contents of my stomach up.

"That is a really nifty item! You'll be able to carry small explosives now, helping you get into hard-to-reach areas and breaking smaller stones and rubble," Treo said as she seemed to study my HUD.

"Can you see my display?" I asked, slightly confused. I hadn't been able to see Georgia's or she mine.

"Of course I can, silly," Treo said with a laugh. *"I am your wisp, aren't I? How else could I help you if I could not see how you were doing? And speaking of how you're doing, you seem to be leveling really well! You will have noticed by now, however, that it takes a lot more Experience Points to level each time."*

"Yeah, I got that," I said, still trying to piece all of this new information together. It really was just like a game. Maybe I needed to treat it more like one. I was still acting like I was just some teenager, but I had ran up that pillar and flipped over that troll's club. Archibald Lawerence Jr. could never have done that. But Archy, here in this place, he could do things. Be something more.

Something began to blossom in my chest, a burning sensation. Hope. Hope was forming that I might actually be able to save Dad and return back home again.

"Oye! I know this is all nice and stuff, you just staring at them there dusty bits of troll talkin' to y'erself," Herald said from behind me, breaking the moment like the troll before me. "But I have a train I need to get working so I can get on back to me home!"

"Wait a second." I whirled about on the tiny man, who was now actively looking about himself as if he had lost an item on his person. "You're the conductor?"

"A conductor," said the gem-eyed Granus with a wink. "There a lot of us folk out here, mostly in Granite Heights, at the base of the Floating Mountains, home to all my kinfolk."

"But you can drive the train?" I pressed, excitement welling up inside.

"Of course I can?" Herald scoffed. "Wouldn't be much of a conductor if I couldn't, would I? Only problem is, my train got hijacked by a bunch of smelly, good-for-nothin', gibblins right before that ol' troll clunked me in the noggin."

"The gibblins are all gone, but the train, it needs Powerstones," I said quickly, trying to get the words out as best I could.

"Well dadgum! What in the tarnation is the train doin' missin' her Powerstones? I had prit near twenty of them there stones all secured up. Lord Erle'em was needed them fir something or other. Oh shoot! I bet them gibblins stripped me train! Oh, if I had my pickaxe I'd break it off in the tail-end of one them thieving little-"

"Herald, I need you to focus," I said, squatting down and looking into the prismatic irises of the Granus, which still looked mostly like a gnome to me. But this close, I could see that even the bit of skin behind the beard was made up of stone. "We need that train so we can get to Unga Jungle. We can help you get enough Powerstones loaded up, if you promise to drive us there."

"Hmmmmm," Herald said as he tugged a stubby hand through his beard. "I don't see no reason no how to be going to Unga Jungle. That place is filled with too many green things, things that live but are rooted to the ground. Chomp'n flowers, stinging nettles, and swarming flies the size of me own fists. But you did save my life, anyhow. Oh, alright. If you help me find ten Powerstones, I'll take you to Unga Jungle. Deal?"

"It only takes five to drive the train?" I countered, looking at the hand of the Granus gnome.

"How do you know how many Powerstones it takes to drive a Powertrain?" Herald asked as he slowly lowered his hand and squinted his eyes at me, which only caused his eyebrows to mush into his beard and mustaches, utterly concealing his face in facial hair.

"I told him!" said Treo in a condescending tone.

"I might have known. And just when I was startin' to think you were a decent feller," Herald said with dismay. "You've done aligned yourself with the faefolk. That do be a Wisp or I'll pluck every hair from my beard."

"And so what if I am, Rocky?" Treo countered.

"Ain't got no use for your type," Herald spat. "Always tinkling about in other, decent folk's business."

"No use or no access?" Treo shot back.

"Okay, listen, I just fought a troll, Treo. and Herald, I just saved your life," I said as I rubbed my brow. "I need you two to get past whatever this is right now. It is getting dark and Georgia needs my help."

"Who is this Georgia?" asked Hareld as his squished-up eyebrows rose up high on his bald head.

"She is a human and a friend of the faeries," Treo said. *"Not your type, rock-eater."*

"Dust dancer!"

"Earth digger!"

"Sky farter!"

"That's not even—"

"Enough!" This time I actually shouted. Treo and Herald both looked at me with shock, and a little bit of concern. "Listen, it has been a long, long day. Now, we're going to go and find a cart, then go help Georgia. I am sure she is worried sick. Then, we're going to load up the train and you," I pointed a finger at Herald. "You are going to drive us to Unga Jungle, I don't care your preferences. Treo, I need you to be a little more helpful and a little less obnoxious."

"*Obnoxious?*" Treo huffed. "*If only—you know what, fine. I'll just be quiet.*"

With that, Treo turned fully into a ball of light and hovered a few inches above my head.

"Thank the stones!" said Herald.

"I can put you back in that cage," I said, pointing the down the stairs at the pile of rubble. "Treo already told me she could teach me to drive the train. I believe this way helps everyone out equally. But I won't have you talking that way toward someone who has been more than helpful to me. Understood?"

"Yeah, I understand," Herald answered sheepishly.

And though she didn't speak, I heard a small *ting* come from where Treo hovered over my head.

With that, I made my way past Herald and began searching for another cart. To my dismay, I saw a cart right behind where the shack had been. And for a moment, I thought to myself how much easier it would have been had I never walked down those stairs. That thought, to my own shame, only lingered for a second before I saw Herald make his way around the corner to find me. Had I not gone down there, for better or worse, Herald probably wouldn't have made it.

"It is getting dark," Herald said, his voice still sullen from my scolding.

"I have a light," I said, reaching mentally into my inventory as I pulled on the handles of the cart. I stopped suddenly.

Inventory:

Sword of the Promised Elven Lord, Level 2 - Legendary Item
Wooden Shield of the Adventurer
Brightshrooms (1)
Bomb Bag: Base Level

"What's wrong, lad?" Herald asked, his dower expression replaced with emanate concern. "Is something the matter?"

I looked at the pile of rubble as a ping of sadness struck me. "I just lost my flashlight, that's all."

"What's a flashlight? A blinking torch or something?" Herald asked, confused but visibly less concerned.

"Yeah, it's like a torch," I said, almost adding from my world, but thinking better of it. There was no reason to give out too much personal information, not yet.

"Well, hopefully this Georgia friend of yours has a light," Herald said as he sprung up into the air and landed in the cart with a loud *thud!* "I ain't much for walkin', hope you don't mind I sit a spell while you cart us to her."

Frustrated, and a little saddened about the loss of my flashlight, I didn't even argue with Herald. I just wheeled it around and began to head back to where I had left Georgia, mind racing with all of the events of the last two days.

Chapter Fourteen:
I Take a Ride in a Train

Archy Lawerence Jr.
Level 6
Health Points - 5
Focus Points - 3
Endurance - 6
Strength - 5
Dexterity - 6
Esoteric - 1
Speed – 4
Charisma - 3

"About time, Boy Scout!" called out Georgia as I came into view. She was covered in dirt and grime, and despite being up in the twin buns, her hair was disheveled.

In her hands was a large bit of board, which had a series of markings that, as I drew closer, recognized as a crude sort of map.

"You look terrible," Georgia said without missing a beat. "And you found a friend."

"I am Herald of the Granite Heights Line of the Granus Dynasty," Herald said with a bow. "You may call me Herald."

I nearly spat out in laughter, but was able to keep it contained, if only just barely. He had never acted like this before. The little Granus had even been able to subdue his heavy prospector's accent. Georgia, who first shot me a withering glare, smiled at the bowing gnome and said, "Well, it sure is a pleasure to meet you."

"The honor is mine," replied Herald. "Though, you'll have to pardon my lack of decency. I done lost my trousers to a dangum troll, I'll tell you what."

This did push Georgia over the edge, and though she raised a hand to cover her mouth, her laughter rang like a bell, making my stomach do a somersault. I laughed too, more out of embarrassment than anything else, hoping she wouldn't notice the color in my own cheeks or mistake it for embarrassment for Herald's lack of wardrobe.

"Anyhow, I got a spare pair in the caboose, I'll run and get them on while y'all get them Powerstones gathered," Herald said as he straightened up, not noticing Georgia's laughter or at least not taking offense to it that I could see. "Also, if y'er need, I got some extra gloves in the trunk to help'n pick them suckers up?"

"That would be awesome," said Georgia with a little too much enthusiasm.

"Don't tell me y'er tried to pick up one of them

confounded things, did y'er?" Herald asked with a raise of his eyebrows.

"Not my brightest moment," Georgia acquiesced with a shrug.

"How did y'er not get blown to smithereens?" Herald gaped at her as he rubbed the balded top of his head in utter bewilderment.

"I mean it shocked the fire out of me," Georgia answered. "But that's about it."

"By the Eternal Stone, y'er either the bravest dame I ever did meet, or the dimmest," said Herald with an air of amazement in his voice. "Come with me to get them gloves and it should solve a world of hurtin' for y'er."

Georgia followed the Granus back to the train while I took a seat, replenishing my stamina meter. It was frustrating how long it took to fill the green bar up. I hadn't really been exerting myself much, but apparently if I did a single action that depleted it, it took an ample amount of time to fill it back up. I recalled Lord Erle'em talking about other potions, so I asked Treoirael if she knew of a stamina filling recipe.

"There are many types of potions you can form that will replenish, refill, and redouble your stamina, health, and esoteric meters, and some that can do two at a time, though there is only one that can do all three. But that is a very rare and dangerous potion to make. In order to make a potion though, you must first find a recipe book. These can be found in shops or acquired from traveling merchants," Treo chimed. *"Once you have a recipe book, all you need are the proper ingredients, a cook pot, or for better, more potent results, an alchemical worktable, and a flask or bottle to place the contents in for storing."*

"Sounds about right," I said as I looked at my own flasks.

I was running low and needed to find some materials to replenish my stock. I only had two full flasks, one of healing and one for stamina. I wanted to smack my own forehead. I could have downed that stamina flask in the fight against the troll, but I had totally forgotten about it.

"Many of the necessary items can be found growing around the verdant fields of Neverwhere. I would suggest you spend this time searching and filling your inventory."

"Right."

I trudged off, looking about the settlement. Trees were different in this place than my own home, far fewer branches, the tops looking almost like ice cream scoops of leafy-green. I noticed several apples, bright red and delicious looking, hanging from one of the tree, but too far out of my reach. I had a thought, which seemed a little ridiculous at first, but I went with it.

Lowering my shoulder, I ran into the tree.

Thud!

The leafs rustled, followed by a *plop, plop, plop!*

Three apples landed on the ground right before my feet.

Ding!

Neverapples!
Fruit.
+¼ to health
Can be used as an ingredient for cooking meals, making tonics, and brewing potions.
Can also be thrown at enemies as a distraction or used as bait to lure away foes.

I scooped up the apples and placed them in the same

pocket as the Brightshrooms. Apparently, I could hold an infinite amount of any type of thing in any one inventory slot when it came to crafting and cooking items. However, when I saw an old knife lying on the ground, I could not store it in the same slot as my own sword. While it didn't actually make physiological sense, the mechanics seemed to fall in line with games I had played in my own world.

My own world. How strange it was to think about being in another place entirely.

Ding!

Volatile Lightning Bug!

The alert snapped my attention back to the here and now. However, what was at first instant dread, was replaced by a smile of wonderment. A firefly, quite a bit larger than the ones I had seen flying about Georgia's grandparent's house, was drifting on the evening air. It glowed bright blue, not yellow, and had wings more akin to dragonfly wings, which emitted little arcs of lightening about it.

"Oooo! Pretty," cooed Treo. *"Be careful though, those little buddies will shock you if you touch them."*

"I wonder," I mused, looking at the little bug as I grabbed an empty bottle from my bandolier. I popped the cork and swung it at the lightening bug.

Ding!

You have captured: Volatile Lightening Bug.
These little bugs are an excellent source of light and power.

They can also be used as a base ingredient for Stamina Recovery.
Caution!
Keep away from water!
Mixing electricity and water can have dangerous side effects.

I looked about, spotting several more of the fireflies drifting about here and there. I did not know exactly what I could use them for or how to brew a potion, but having lost my flashlight, having a source of light and power didn't seem like a bad idea to me. So, I began running about swinging my bottle and catching the little balls of light.

Treo danced about me as I ran here and there, and despite myself, I couldn't help but join in laughing with her as we captured half a dozen or so in an empty bottle. And when I finally stoppered up the flask to my bandolier, Treo landed on my shoulder and elbowed me in the jaw lightly, still laughing.

"I knew there was some fun in you," she chimed. *"Don't be so afraid to let that boy out here and there. I like him."*

I blinked, feeling something strange inside me. I had just had fun for the first time in days. I had allowed myself to just be me, with no concern of who was watch or what anyone else thought. I rarely allowed that, always trying to be the best version of me for Mom and Dad.

"Hey, Boy Scout!"

I nearly leapt out of my skin at the sound of Georgia's voice. I whirled about to see her ambling forward with a broad grin on her freckled face. "You look like you're having more fun than a pig in a wallow."

"I, uh, was catching some fireflies," I said sheepishly,

unable to keep my hand from reaching up to the back of my neck.

"I can tell," Georgia said as she moved closer and closer, her eyes wide as she stared at the bottle that glowed on my chest. "That's super neat. Anyways, Herald gave me these," she held up her gloved hands. "Said they should keep me from being shocked by the Powerstones. What do you say about get'n those stones loaded up and getting out of here? I am about ready to be on my way."

"Yeah, I think I am ready to get a move on too."

The Powerstones, which Georgia had already mapped out, were fairly easy to move now that we had the gloves and the cart to haul them in. It did not take long before we had gathered the five necessary crystalline geodes for operating the train and were making our way back to the station. All in all, it was surprisingly uneventful. That being said, Georgia and I didn't say much. I kept feeling the urge to bring up some of the changes I was experiencing and to see if she was feeling the same. But, every time I drew up enough courage to start the conversation, she would point out another Powerstone and would hurry off and grab it.

"Well, that looks like the last of them," Georgia said as she placed the final Powerstone into the cart. "It is crazy how strange they feel."

"What do you mean?" I asked. I hadn't touched a single one of them, being delegated to cart-boy.

"The current, can't you feel it surrounding them?" Georgia asked, looking up at me with a questioning expression.

In truth, I couldn't really sense anything. They just looked like jade-colored crystals to me. But, not wanting to sound ignorant, I answered, "Yeah, a little. But, not much."

"Wow," Georgia said as she ran a gloved hand over one of them. "It's like a living thing, with, not a heartbeat, but something like that."

Seeing this as an opportunity, I asked, "I wonder if it has to do with your Esoteric being so much higher. Maybe they're more magic than natural?"

"Ooooh, I didn't think about that," Georgia said as she snapped her fingers. "I bet you're right."

Without meaning to, my display popped open, showing Georgia's stats and figures. It felt slightly invasive, as if I was prying where I shouldn't be. Despite this, I could not help but stare at how strong she was there, but then I felt suddenly worried when I saw how low some of her other stats were.

"You alright, Boy Scout?" Georgia asked, crooking an eyebrow at me.

"No, yeah, I am fine," I stammered, mentally willing my HUD to go away.

"You sure?" said Georgia. "You went all distant there for a second."

"Yeah, it's just been a really long day," I answered. Which wasn't exactly a lie. I was really tired, and I had just survived two near-death experiences in the past two hours.

"Okay then," Georgia said with a shrug, though I could tell she was not totally letting the topic go. "Let's head back to the train."

We found Herald decked out in conductor blues, little hat included. He had a vest with a gold pocket watch attached, which he was staring at with a exasperated expression. "About time, confoundit! I've been waitin' so long I prit-near turned into a turnip, I'll tell ya what! Dangum Big Folk taken all the dangum time in the world. No thought for us. None at all."

"Oh, get off your high horse, Herald, we were getting the Powerstones as fast as we could," Georgia said with an over-the-top roll of her eyes.

"Could've fooled me," Herald grunted as he shoved the watch into his pocket. "Now, get them Powerstones loaded into the Engine and we'll get on our way."

"How do we do that?" I asked.

"How do you do what?" Herald looked at me as if I had just asked him how to breathe.

"How do we put the stones into the engine? I've never done any of this before," I said, unable to keep the biting edge of irritation out of my voice. I wanted to add something about saving his life and he should be more grateful, but I let it lie. I was tired, and I wanted to get a move on.

"Well, for starters, you put them in the engine," Herald said holding up a finger as if he were counting down the steps of a process. "Yep, that about sums it up."

The rush of anger that sprung up inside of me was utterly unexpected. I had never really been quick to anger or frustration, always trying to resolve issues with logic and reason. To be honest, I did not know where the aggression came from, but I could not stop it once that dam inside of me burst. I stepped forward, grabbing the Granus Engineer up from the ground and shook him so hard his hat went sailing away. "Why are you being so difficult?" I roared the words, something in me snapping.

Georgia, rather than shrieking it terror or gasping in shock, burst into laughter, Treo joining in beside her. Herald, whose eyes were rolling about in his head like two pinballs, was letting out a slew of what I guess were Granus swear words, though I didn't understand a one of them. Georgia did, however, manage to regain her composure enough to add, "Is there anything we need to do specifically, or do we just drop the Powerstones into the furnace?"

"Tell your friend to put me down this instant!" Herald shrieked, his gravelly, prospector voice sounding cracked and a little high-pitched.

Georgia didn't need to tell me anything. I sat Herald down, mortified by my actions. I went to apologize, but before I could get a single word out, Herald held up a hand and said, "Ya, y'er just open the furnace by turning the right handle counterclockwise until you hear three clicks, then turn the left clockwise two full rotation. After that, pull down and then out. Like I said, just put the stones in and I'll get the train of in a jiffy."

"Is that all?" I said. The apology died on my lips, replaced with sour apathy.

"Ya, that's all," Herald shot back as he snatched his hat from the ground and slammed it on his head. "I'll give y'er a pass, cause y'er save my life today. But if y'er ever pick me up again, I'll break my foot off in your tail end, y'er hear me?"

"Yeah, I hear you," I answered flippantly. "Come on, let's go and get this train rolling."

Chapter Fifteen:
I Meet a Witch

Archy Lawerence Jr.
Level 6
Health Points - 5
Focus Points - 3
Endurance - 6
Strength - 5
Dexterity - 6
Esoteric - 1
Speed - 4
Charisma - 3

THE TRAIN CAME to a rattling stop, steam bellowing out as a loud whistle sounded, jarring me awake. I had found a little cabin, fully furnished and ready, and hunkered down for the night. Georgia was in the one next to me, hopefully sleeping as soundly as I had. To be honest, I was rather surprised at how well I had slept, but thinking back on the events of yesterday, I had been utterly exhausted, both physically and mentally.

"*Good morning!*" chimed Treo, floating over my head and looking out the window.

"Morning," I said through a long yawn as I reached my arms out in an amazing stretch.

Gentle sunlight warmed the small cabin, casting an amber hue across the crushed velvet interior. Other than the small bed that I had slept on, there was a table of antique design, appearing to come from the late Ottoman era, and not for the first time I thought on how strange it was that Neverwhere and ancient Earth held so many similarities. That being said, it was early and my mind was still waking up, so I did not dwell on those thoughts, but turned my attention to toast and berry jam laid out on said table.

"Where did you come from?" I asked to nobody as I looked with hungry eyes on the vibrant purple jam and multi-grain toast.

"*Powertrains fuels Esoteric pathways with clockwork operating systems to run, staff, and support the functions of said train,*" Treo said as she, too, stretched. "*Ooo! It looks like we're about to arrive at Crossroads Station.*"

Taking the toast from the tray, after slathering on a healthy amount of jam, I looked out the window. I nearly dropped the toast. I could literally feel my jaw loosen and my mouth fall open. Never before had I seen anything at all like what I was look at now, and my mind could simply not believe it.

To the south of the railway that we zoomed down,

towering mountains jutted up into the sky. And above them. More mountains floated. Enormous chunks of earth and stone, some snowcapped and others barren, hung suspended in mid-air by some unseen force.

"Ah, the Floating Mountains of Neverwhere, such a spectacular sight," sighed Treo. *"Did you know that over a millennium ago, those mountains were all earthbound? Crazy right? I can't even imagine a world where some of the mountains don't reach up into the sky."*

"I...I thought it was a figure of speech," I finally muttered out, the toast in my hand all but forgotten.

"Of course it isn't, silly!" laughed Treo. *"Powerstones form an electromagnetic field between the ore of the floating mountains and the earthbound ones. The Granus spend their lives mining and crafting Powerstones into various products, along with harvesting precious gems and ores for other crafting and financial benefits."*

"But what is that?" I asked, staring up at the largest of the floating mountains, which had a sickly-looking fog hanging about it.

"That is the corruption of which Lord Erle'em spoke of," said Treo. *"With their Sacred Totem corrupted, darkness and decay falls upon the realm of the Granus. The same is true of the Mighty Ungaboom of Unga Jungle, and those of the Golden Sands Desert. You see why it is so important that you return them to Lord Erle'em, so he may wash away the darkness and return the Light of the Golden Sun to our lands?"*

Yeah, I could see why. The mist that clung to that floating mountain, it filled my heart with dread. There was something terribly wrong with the way it seemed to corrode what it touched. And not for the first time, I wondered how I was actually supposed to do anything about this.

Knock Knock!

"Hey, Archy, you awake?" Georgia called from the other side of my sliding door.

I shook myself out of my stupor, forcing a smile onto my face as I attempted to bury the thoughts of inadequacy and mounting dread that threatened to send me into a spiral. "Yeah, just a second."

I took a bite of the toast I had been holding, and oh my goodness, it was amazing. It was sweet and tart at the same time, bursting with flavors that made my mouth salivate even as I chewed into the warm, fresh bread.

The door slid open as I touched a panel, just as it had done the night before. Georgia had the biggest smile on her face, her hair done up again into two pompoms, though an errant strand hung over the side of her left eye. Her backpack was in her hand and she was ruffling through it with excitement.

"Archy! You'll never believe it!" she said with enthusiasm that I found refreshingly contagious.

"Believe what?" I asked, pushing my former thoughts farther away and shutting a mental door on them. I could worry about that later.

"So, you know how when we defeat monsters they leave behind Soulfire?" she said as she withdrew a strange-looking urn I hadn't seen before. It was purple and rimmed with silver. It looked like something you'd see in an Ancient Egyptian section of a museum, but the style of the characters did not. They were far too Malaysian in design. "I found this while we were in the settlement, and apparently, if I am not mistaken, it can help convert Soulfire into Esoteric Elixir when combined with Powerstones and the remains of certain insects and lizards found throughout Neverwhere!"

"That is really cool," I said, riding the high of excitement she was emanating. But, then a thought popped into my head, and I couldn't keep it from coming out. "How did you figure that out?"

"Oh," Georgia said, rolling her eyes as if that were silliest question on the planet. She shoved the urn back into the endless backpack that had once just housed comics and mystery novels, and now...who knew what all she had already collected. She then proceeded to pull out a massive purple leather book that looked older than dirt. It was wrapped with black chains and locked with three combination locks. "Lord Erle'em gave me this Tome of Esoteric Observations. I was up almost all night reading it. It is really cool what all can be done if one applies themselves to the Esoteric Arts."

"Oh," I said, embarrassed that I had just crashed out and slept all night.

"Yeah, it is wild. But have you seen outside?" Georgia pressed on, not paying any heed to my reddening cheeks. "Those mountains, that's crazy. I bet Pawpaw would lose his mind if he saw them just floating there. Beats all I ever did see."

"Yeah, it is crazy. I was just looking at them," I answered.

"You okay, Boy Scout? You're all starring and stuff? You not sleep either?" Georgia asked as she slung her backpack over she shoulder again.

"Huh? Oh, no," I stumbled. "I just, a lot to think about, that's all."

"You're tellin' me. I just can't stop lookin' at stuff," Georgia said, face bright as the sun. "I know it isn't all gonna be rainbows and sunshine, but this is really cool too. I never would have thought in a million years I'd be able to go and do something like this."

"Well, I mean, who would think they'd find themselves in a magical realm where mountains float and faeries talk?"

"Anyone with a brain, duh," said Treo, lighting on my shoulder as she butt into our conversation as naturally as ever. *"Oh wait, that's right, you're world is all shut off from the good stuff."*

"I mean, I guess you could call it that," I said as I shot a side eye at the little wisp, who was shifting from aqua blue to a light teal. "Saying disastrous ecological situations is a mouth full."

"Wait until you see Unga Jungle," smirked Treo before she shot off, a comet-like tail of azure sparkles trailing behind her, darting between what I now realize were little automaton beings of stone and bronze, with tiny little Powerstone cores that sent tech-like trails of bright green across their clockwork bodies.

"Weird ain't they?" said Georgia, noticing my furrowed brows and stare.

"Yeah," I answered, unable to look away from the both ancient and futurist looking beings.

"You stare a lot. It's pretty rude," Georgia said, knocking her elbow into me with a chuckle. "People will think you're weird."

A crackling, hissing noise emanated throughout the train, stopping Georgia and my conversation dead in its tracks. That sound was followed by a few sharp pops and bursts, and some faint white noise as a voice began to speak across an ancient intercom:

"Uh, good mornin' travelers." It was clearly Herald who was speaking, but he sounded as if he were doing his best pilot impersonation, which was jarring given the prospector nature of his accent. "We're about five minutes from Crossroads Station. We'll be stopping for a, uh, few moments so that the automatons can restock our, uh, Powestone levels, seeing as we were, uh, unable to load up any extras. Not that anyone mentioned we might needs those or anything. So, if, uh, you could be patient with us during our stop, that would be much appreciated. If you'd like, you can enjoy a stroll down the historic marketplace of Crossroads Station, where merchants have traveled from all across Neverwhere to sell their wares. Uh, that is all."

"You think he is a little bitter?" Georgia asked with a cocked eyebrow, as if she would like to give him a what-for if she could.

"Napoleon Syndrome," I said with a shrug and we both laughed.

Before we knew it, the train had come to a complete stop and Georgia and I found ourselves staring out of the bay onto the marketplace of Crossroads Station. While the last station was reminiscent of a Western town mixed with ancient Aztec architecture, Crossroads reminded me of a steampunk style arboretum. The entire station was domed with glass ceilings that bubbled between bronze beams that were mostly painted green. Gaslamps hung all about, as did vines, which drooped from bare beams, causing the whole to look like some strange amalgamation of industrialization and flora. Birds, bright and beautiful, flew in the vaulted space high above our heads while dozens of terral species walked about the neatly ordered streets, most of them wearing smart suits or fancy dresses.

"Every time I think that I've seen it all, something like this reveals itself," said Georgia with a shake of her head as she stepped off the platform and down onto the cast bronze cobblestone road. Rain pelted the top of the glass dome that encased the station, and lightning flashed, but all was well and dry inside.

I followed behind her, looking at awe at all the various shops and signs. To be honest, it was a little overwhelming. Granus in suits that made them look like bearded Monoploy men were running about with literal sacks money over their shoulders, while others were in their more traditional prospector outfits. Gillafolk walked about, wearing re-breathers with bulbous tanks over their gills. Not for the first time was I struck by the odd sense of beauty these sea crea-tures held. They seemed regal, but not like the elves, more mysterious and somewhat frightening. Speaking of elves, there seemed to be plenty of them, also dressed less like forest folk and more like Victorian business tycoons. There were several of the mysterious Golden Sands people, whose race I did not wholly understand. They were utterly unchanged in appearance, all dressing somewhat similarly to how Master Tgnkakl had at Lord Erle'em's counsel. And then there were the Unga primate types; their diversity was as varied as all others. Small lemur types with minimal bronze portions up two red orangutan and dark silverback gorilla types. Yet, all were selling and talking in relative harmony with each other here in Crossroads, other than the haggling that was loud and apparent.

My nose crinkled. The smell was...well, a bit much. If you could imagine all the best smelling sweets, foods, and flowers mixed in with the scent of hundreds of people, animals, and birds, then adding a dose of steam and sweat, that was Crossroads Station. It reminded me too much of Manhattan in the summer. A ping of homesickness struck, but I buried it quickly, trying my best to focus on the task at hand.

"I looted several of the Gibblins, and I have about fourteen bronze pieces and two silvers. You have anything?" Georgia asked.

"I didn't know they could have any money on them, but I did loot everything," I said, feeling a little bit dumb for not thinking of that.

"Oh yeah, shows up in a subset in their inventory if you got any sacks or bags. That is where I found mine, other than a few strays in pockets."

I quickly threw up my inventory system, mentally wheeling through to the items. I had dozens of nasty looking Gibblin clothes and other parts and bits. It was gross. But Georgia was right, I did have eight pieces of bronze and one silver coin. To my surprise, when I looked at where the troll's belongings were, I found something odd.

"Check this out," I said as I pulled out an orange gemstone from my inventory, the item just appearing in my hand from my back pocket. "Wonder what this is worth?"

"I don't know," said Georgia, her eyes going wide at the sight of the fist-sized jewel. "But it's gotta be worth something. I bet we can find a money changer here."

"I also have one of those golden coins left from Lord Erle'em," I said, seeing the item in a subsection I hadn't noticed before title, *Coin Pouch.*

"There is one over there, let's go there first," said Georgia, pointing to a large sign hanging off the front of a shop that various types of jewels and precious stones on one side and then an arrow pointing to stacks of coins on the other.

"Sounds like a plan to me."

The shop was small, a few tables for counting and sorting, and at the far side a chest-high counter with iron bars over the window. "Morning." said an elderly female voice from the other side of the counter.

"Good morning," Georgia answered brightly. "We'd like to do an exchange."

"Oh, and what would you like to exchange?" said the woman, her voice sounding somewhat crackling and overly curious.

As we drew closer, what I saw gave me the chills. It was not just a grandmotherly elf on the other side, nor was it a Gillafolk female. It was what I could only describe as a witch. She had a long, long nose with an enormous mole on it, sickly green skin, watery grey eyes, frizzy hair under a wide-brimmed hat with a crooked and pointed tip. She wore a black dress with a gigantic pendent of the most vibrant royal blue I had ever seen. Her breath was like ice and her teeth were yellowed. She sniffed twice, her gigantic schnoz wobbling as she did so.

"I smell, I smell...Ooooo! Hahaha! I smell a Citrine of impressive quality. Rare gemstones, those," the old lady cackled. "Come, let Baba Greenstockings take a little look-see. Don't worry, I don't bite."

My gut told me to run, but then, I always felt like running away from new people. And so what if she was a witch? I had just ridden a train with a stone gnome and had trained with an elven lord in a mirror realm. I swallowed my fear and stepped forward, producing the gemstone.

"Eeeek! Hahaha, it is, my pretty, it is!" Baba Greenstock-ings said, grabbing at her midsection and laughing. "So pretty! So bright! We must have it!"

Now, I was never really involved too much in Dad's side of the business when it came to appraisals. But I knew good and well that if he ever even lifted a brow in excitement at something of worth, private collectors would be screaming and throwing money at him. Or, colluding with each other to low-bid out and then they would have it amongst themselves for a steal. This second option never worked. Dad was far too shrewd, and I hoped I had inherited that from him today.

"What does the young lord want for the Citrine, my pretty? What would he trade, me thinks, four gold pieces?" Baba Greenstockings said, apparently talking to herself as much as me.

"Four?" I asked, furrowing my brow as if insulted. Again, this wasn't my cup of tea, but it also wasn't my first rodeo. I was from New York. I shoved the gemstone back into my pocket and turned away. "Come on, Georgia, let's go somewhere more respectable."

"Gah!" cried out Baba Greenstockings. "Eighteen! I'll do eighteen gold here and now! No questions asked, no paperwork. My pretty, please?"

I stopped, but did not look back. I had no idea how much a gold coin was worth. What was the exchange rate between bronze to silver and silver to gold? I knew this would not be the right place to ask, but I also did not want to lose out any more on what I had been offered. So, taking a risk, I said. "Twenty gold and it's yours."

"Deal!" Baba Greenstockings said with an exuberant amount of elation. "Twenty gold for my little lord and lady! Any other gems, have they my pretty? Any other things to trade? I see Volatile Lightning Bug, a copper for each. I smell, *sniff sniff,* I do smell gibblin toes! What do they have with toes, my pretty? Why do they have Gibblin parts? Are they naughty?"

"I only want to trade the Citrine today, Baba," I answered, swallowing my discomfort as I turned to face her. How could she smell what was in my inventory? As far as I could tell, it was all held in a literal pocket dimension.

"Fine, fine," said the crone as she waved gnarled fingers to beacon me forward. "Come, come, let Baba Greenstockings see. Let me see."

I walked up and placed the gemstone on the counter. The witch snatched it up with a cackle, licking and sniffing the stone in a manner I did not appreciate. After an awkward few moments, during which Baba Greenstockings seemed utterly oblivious to us, she looked down and squawked, "Take your gold and leave me be! I'm closed now! Here, take my pretty's gold and leave!"

She waved a hand, and a sack fell heavy on the counter in front of me, landing with a clinking sound. I snatched up the surprisingly heavy sack, not daring to count it in front of the witch, and left the shop, Georgia right on my heels.

"Well that was strange," Georgia said as I counted out twenty golden coins. Unlike the ones Lord Erle'em had given us, these each just had the stamp of a golden sun with five rays. "She was batty as a cave."

"Yeah, I think I could go my whole life without dealing with her type," I said ardently, still counting the coins.

Georgia didn't answer, but I really didn't notice. After I had recounted twice, I placed the bag of coins into my inventory pocket. "I am going to need to get a bag."

"Probably," Georgia said as she walked off toward another shop that touted a bronze inlayed placard depicting tomes and scrolls.

I followed behind.

Georgia picked up two or three different spell books, all

of which were locked with a chain, though one was wrapped with two chains of gold instead of iron. From there we found our way into a potion shop owned by a Gillafolk female in a wetsuit. She had a ray-like head and a serpentine body that was a little too curvy for my comfort. We bought Georgia her first bandolier of flasks, and she chose to only take one health potion, two FP, and one Esoteric, a dark purple liquid that looked almost like a lava lamp with the way it bubbled and moved.

After that shop, we made our way to a cobbler, replacing our Earth shoes with boots of quality make. Mine gave me a +10% to fortitude and a +15% to poison resistance, which was cool. Georgia selected a pair that were long and studded with gemstones, boosting her per-cast speed and giving her Fleet Foot skill for dodging. Next was a clothier, where we saw several types of clothing from jesters rags up to suites of armor to Victorian garments and ruffled collared shirts. Unfortunately, we were running pretty low on coins, so I wasn't able to get anything. Georgia, on the other hand, found a pair of trousers that she liked, claiming her hiking shorts left her exposed to what she assumed would be treacherous vines and stuff in the jungle. I couldn't argue this point. Seeing as I had jeans and hoodie, I felt fine for now. So, we grabbed up the pants, she changed into both the trousers and her new boots, and we set back off to the train, hoping the Powerstones would be reloaded.

To my relief, it looked like everything was ready, and when the doors opened, Georgia and I parted ways without saying much. She seemed to be a little upset about something, but I chalked it up to a day around some many people, and who could blame her with all the sights, sounds, and smells. It was overwhelming.

As for myself, I found myself not walking to my room, but down the aisle of the train. There were three different cars for carrying passengers, and three behind that for transporting ore and precious stone. We were in the last of the passenger carriages, which was themed with crushed red velvet with lots of antique-looking furniture. The second carriage, which had a small pathway with a chain guardrail on either side, looked a lot light a 1920s speakeasy. To my surprise, there were several passengers aboard this carriage, though to my understanding, none had been there before. Most of these passengers were Gillafolk, though an occasional Elf or Granus could be spotted walking about. The final carriage was sleek and silver, all angles and chrome. There was only one passenger here, a lone Nomad of the Golden Sands tribe. Whether the individual was male or female, I could not tell, for their colorful stitched rags kept every inch of them concealed. They were sitting behind a table, one of the automaton creatures serving them some kind of smoke from a bulbous vase with long coils and bubbling blue liquid.

I did not stop to introduce myself, but just let my feet carry me through the last door and into the locomotive's engine car. I had been here before. It was where the massive furnace sat. There was also a large panel with knobs, levers, pulleys, wheels, and other apertures which powered and steered the train, and it was behind that panel that Herald sat, eyeing his pocket watch and grumbling incoherently.

"Oye, what in the blazes are y'er doin'?" cried out the Granus as he whirled about on me.

Apparently he had not noticed my entrance into the engine and had nearly jumped out of his trousers when he did. His gemstone eyes were wide and his forehead was sweating beneath his cap.

"Is everything alright?" I stammered, trying to understand the reasoning behind his frustration while also trying to calm my own heart down after the scare.

"Alright? Alright?" Herald repeated, his voice growing more shrill as his eyes managed to widen even further. "Does it look like everything is alright?"

"Uhhh—"

"There was another rockslide near Granite Heights. I was supposed to drop you and your lady friend off, then head to Granite Heights, but the tracks are utterly ruined. I've heard it'll take weeks to get it sorted out," Herald said with dismay. "What am I supposed to do now?"

I looked at the Granus, all flustered and fretting, and did the only thing I could think of. I shrugged my shoulders and said, "I am sure it'll all work out."

"Work out? How in tarnation is this going to 'work out'?" Herald said as he waved his hands around his head like a cyclone. "I'm gonna get canned for this! Pushed down the river. Sent off! It's all over now!"

My discomfort grew more and more by the second as I looked for any out I could find to get out of this situation. Luckily, my back hit the handle of the door. I hadn't even realized I was backing up. But I used that as an excuse to turn around and leave without a word.

I walked quickly, doing all I could to avoid eye contact through the two carriages that separated me from my own. I could feel the heat of embarrassment blazing up the back of my neck as intrusive thoughts ate away at my mind. Why couldn't I have just offered condolences? Or what about providing some moral support? Nope, I just ran out, leaving the little guy alone with his problems, because what was I supposed to do?

I opened my own room too fast, the sliding door emitting a loud *thud* as it rammed into the frame. I winced, but didn't stop, rushing into my room and sliding the door shut behind me, albeit a lot more gently than I had opened it, before throwing myself onto the little bed and burying my face in the pillow. I wanted to scream. Why was I so broken? Other people could just listen and talk to people without being weird, why couldn't I? Georgia was a fantastic listener. Had she been here, she would have heard him out and provided a point or two, maybe even solved the problem.

But me? No...I had to go running out without a word.

I needed to go back and apologize. I could do that much, I thought. But before I could muster the strength to drag myself from my bed, the crackling sound of the intercom turning on sounded throughout the train.

"Uh, hello. This is your engineer speaking. It is 11:05, sunny skies and nice and warm out. Looks like we are good for launching. So, please, no walking between carts as we disembark from Crossroads Station," Herald said, either masking the distress he was clearly showing only five minutes ago or already moving past it. "Uh, we should be arriving at Unga Jungle Station by nightfall. There are, uh, as you know, only a few accommodations for hospitality at Unga Jungle Station, but we at Powerline Rails always advise our partners, Banana Hut Treehouses, as your place of lodging, where you can feel free to peel off your stress and hang around."

The system crackled and popped once more, then went silent. The next thing I knew, we were sliding out of the station, moving a break neck speed toward the jungle.

PART THREE
EARTH TOTEM

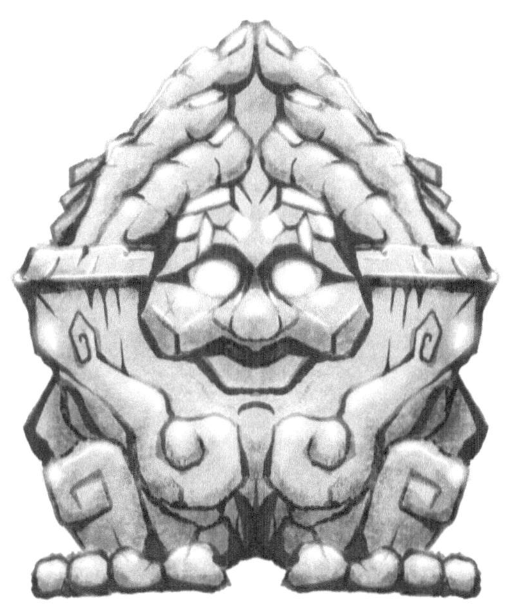

Chapter Sixteen: I Find a Ziggurat

GEORGIA DID NOT COME by the whole of the eight hour and twelve-minute drive, leaving me to ride alone in silence, staring at the ruby-encrusted hands of my Dad's watch. I had spent most of the time looking through my archive system, cataloging the items I had found, and learning how to quick swap between items in the ring section of my inventory title, Key Items. Currently I only had the shield, sword, and bomb bag there, and had three available rings that I could move between without needing to take up an actual slot in my pants pockets, which was nice, though I still wanted to find a bag or something like Georgia had. I also found that my sword could be attached to my bandolier, allowing me to leave it and my shield on my back.

After I felt confident in this method of swapping through my Key Items, I looked around my little room. I found an old trunk and swapped my old shoes out for the new boots I had purchased. It was an odd sensation, lacing up the new boots. I could feel my status change, the slight edge they gave me as I tied double knots in both my laces. I had to admit, I was getting more and more used to this place, these strange rules and mechanics, but moments like this, where I could feel a change take place within me, it was still weird.

As night began to fall and darkness began to set in, the train slowed to a stop, steam billowing up sides of the carriages. I looked out my window, staring at the dense flora that lay before me. Unlike Crossroads Station or even Woodland Railstation, Unga Jungle Station was lacking in the station portion of the name. There was technically a platform—a bunch of logs bound together with vines—and a swinging bridge that disappeared into a misty nothingness. That was it. Well, that wasn't entirely true; there were several torches burning that provided the only light other than the double moons and the stars above.

The now familiar crackle and pop of the intercoms reverberated through the train, followed by a short announcement from Herald letting us know we had arrived. Taking in a deep breath to steady myself, I rose up from my bed and walked off the train and onto the platform to face Unga Jungle.

Unga Jungle Station

The words scrolled across my vision as I looked over the barren pile of logs. A deep ravine was all that was before me. That and a particularly untrustworthy-looking rope bridge.

Unga Jungle is home to the Bronze Primates, whose arcane worship of the Mech God, Uulu'Bunga, has forged not only their society, but their physiology, blending flesh with machinery.
Be Warned.
Something dark lurks in this jungle.

New Quest!

Find out what is causing the darkness.

Would you like to track this Quest in your Quest Log?
Yes! Or, no...

I looked at Georgia, who mirrored my perplexed look. We hadn't received notifications of Quests before, or at least, I hadn't. When her eyes lost that distant stare and met my own, she just shrugged her shoulders and said, "It's why we're here, ain't it?"

"You sure about all this?" I asked, but I was already mentally pressing on the 'yes' button. I hadn't come this far to give up now.

"You can access your Quest Log under the Quest Tab, which should be loaded to your main display," Treo chimed in. *"You can see how many quests you have accepted, completed, and can even store hints to completing said quests."*

"That's useful," I said as I located the new feature on my HUD. I could also now see coins in the bottom left corn alongside an icon for what I assumed was my Bomb Bag, though there was a big 0 by it. "He wait, how did you know this? I didn't think you all saw it like this."

"What do you mean by 'you all'?" Treo asked, placing her hands on her hips. *"You think because I'm a Lesser Fae that I don't know how this world works? Hello! It is why I was called help you."*

"You said you chose this," I answered, recalling our conversation from, gosh, two days ago now. How did it seem like weeks?

"Of course I chose, but one has to be called to something to choose to do it, duh?" Treo said with a shake of her little head. *"You people from your world sure are dim."*

"Hey, that ain't very nice!" said Georgia, though her tone was more playful than hurt.

"Well, are we going to just talk or are we going to get Questing?" Treo asked with enthusiasm.

"Anything else we need to know before we go in there?" I asked, looking over the chasm that separated the train and the rest of the jungle.

The train chose that very moment to let out a bout of

steam and blast its whistle. I nearly jumped out of shoes in freight, a scene that caused Treo and Georgia to burst out in laughter. This, obviously, did not help my confidence, but it did build up enough angst for me to start off across the rope bridge with a huff, not waiting to see if the other two decided to follow.

Unfortunately for me, my fear of heights caught up to me about halfway across the swinging bridge. I gripped both sides of the vine handles with a death grip, barely noticing that it was not natural vine, but woven bronze that grew leafy greens. Every step was a colossal feat of will. My legs felt like lead and my stomach seemed to be practicing for the Olympic gymnastic team, doing cartwheels and tumbles the whole journey. I am pretty sure Georgia was having just as rough a time with it as me, because Treo hadn't come up and offered me any moral support, and the one time I deigned to look back, she was sitting on Georgia's shoulder head pressed against Georgia's chin. Georgia's eyes were screwed shut and her hands were as tightly wound around the handles as my own were.

When we both made it to the other side, we fell to our hands and knees upon solid ground. "I promise never to talk about it if you don't?" were the first words Georgia spoke, her voice still shaky.

"Deal." I answered with a weak laugh.

"Well, at least it can't get any worse than that," Georgia said, joining in my nervous laughter.

Don't ever say it can't get any worse.

Once we had gotten back on our feet, we saw that there was indeed a trail. There was even a large sign that read, in poorly written script, "Kah'Boom Village: 3 Miles Ahead". Georgia and I looked at the sign, then to each other, and lastly at the dark trail that cut through the dense, ominous jungle.

"I don't think I can run the whole way..." Georgia said after a long silence.

"Me either," I answered as I slowly reached to my bandolier and pulled out the flask filled with the Volatile Lightning Bugs. I gave the glass bottle a gentle shake, sending them into a tizzy of flashing lights. It wasn't much, but it did illuminate the path well enough for us to at least see a few yards at a time.

"I will try and warn you as quickly as possible if I notice anything lurking," Treo told us the first time we heard something go crunch in darkness. *"I still don't see anything,"* she said the fourth time.

At this point I didn't care anymore, I pulled my shield off my back and asked Georgia to prepare her wand. She only had the one offensive spell, and it took all her FP to cast it. That or Esoteric; I couldn't keep the two straight on what was cast a spell versus a special skill for her.

"Watch out!" cried Georgia as she moved in the blink of an eye to the left, her FP bar draining slightly as she did so. Her boots glowed with a faint light as my brain registered what had happened. She must have activated her Fleet Foot skill.

Where she had been, a three headed Venus Fly Trap had just clamped one of its drooling jaws with squelching *Snap!*

"Watch out!" Treo sounded as she turned from blue to red. *"That's a Viscous Venus Viscera! They are extremely venomous and have prehensile vines, but their chomping chompers are their main threat. Avoid contact, as their venom is both hallucinogenic and corrosive!"*

I raised my shield just in time to block a second bite, striking the watermelon-sized head of the creature with a sickening *thwap!* To my surprise, the shield took the head of the creature clean off.

Shield Strike!

My FP bar drained by one third. But the Viscous Venus Viscera was now reeling backwards, emitting a terrible squealing noise that was both natural and not. And where the third head had been, inky-black liquid was flowing, soaking the grass and trees with its putrid stench. Unfortunately, some of that goo splattered onto me.

"Aghk!" I cried out in pain as my right arm sizzled and burned.

"You have been hit struck with Viscous Venus Viscera Venom!" Treo sounded. *"You're skin is being dissolved! You need to cleanse the wound."*

"Hold on!" cried out Georgia as she rushed over. She pointed her wand and said something I couldn't quite make out. The whole jungle was turning this funny shade of purple and my tongue was going really numb. It tasted like wild strawberries and iron-toed shoes.

A bright, green light erupted from the tip of Georgia's wand, bathing my arm in warmth. The warmth spread from my arm to my chest and then my face, washing away the fuzzy sensation that had started to take hold of me. I did not even have the time to say thank you before I spotted the now two-headed plant making its way back toward us. And man, did it look mad for something that didn't actually have a face.

Leaving the jar of fireflies on the ground, I leapt to my

feet and drew the sword from its scabbard. The acorn pommel glistened, and the blade shone as I took up a defense stance, just as I had practiced with Lord Erle'em, and my dad before, back when he wanted me to be a fencer like him.

"Be careful!" Treo said, her coloring now yellow as she bounced around anxiously. *"That attack took two of your health away. You should drink a flask!"*

I did not have time. From the body of the plant, half a dozen or so vines erupted outward, thorny and dripping with green venom.

"Slicing Edge!" I cried out, not knowing why I said it as I swept my blade before me.

A beam of white light arched through the air, cleaving the reaching vines in half. The plant wailed again, but I did not give it time to react further. I rushed in, smacking the left head with my shield boss and hacking right behind the right head into the viney neck of the creature. It bucked and reeled, which caused the right head to snap off where I had chopped into the vine, again spewing the black ichor every-where. This time, however, I managed to avoid it. The left head, which had a dent in the side of its head, seemed to droop lifelessly. I raised my sword over my head, let out a war cry, and hacked down upon the thorny vine, severing the final head from the stock.

Viscous Venus Viscera, Defeated!

New Achievement!
Three heads are not better than one!
Defeat a multi-headed creature in combat.
+5% to dexterity based skills

Feat Unlocked!
Double Or Nothing
Two weapons at one time, taking out a foe!
+10% to stamina recovery

I blinked as the silvery scrollwork ran across my vision, and it was almost like I could hear them being read directly into my mind. I watched as my stamina bar began to refill. It was still slow, but I could tell a somewhat noticeable difference. I looked at where the giant stalk stood rooted into the ground.

What had once been lush and green, covered with oozing thorns, was now dead and decaying, just like the bodies of the Gibblins and the Hill Troll, turning to pixilated ash. In the middle of the pile, a strange-looking Soulfire burned.

"That's Esoteric!" Georgia exclaimed, rushing past me to the burning fire.

"I don't think you ca—"

Georgia picked up the deep red flame and pressed it to her chest. There was a *whoosh* of wind that lifted her hair and rustled her flannel shirt as she took in the flame. Her eyes flashed with a bright light as she let out an exclamation that was somewhere between excitement and pain, and I honestly couldn't tell which. When the light faded from her eyes, I noticed something in the iris of her right eye that hadn't been there before.

"The monster engaged with me first, and I guess since I healed you in combat, it counted toward me being there," Georgia said with an excited smile. "And with you not focused on Esoteric, I figured, why not take it?"

"Georgia," I said slowly. "What happened to your eye?"

"Oh!" she exclaimed, her face exuberant. "I got a jynx...

well, more like the opposite of a jynx. It's called, Lucky Glance. Says that I got this thanks to dodge a strike that should have either killed or seriously maimed me."

"What does it do?" I asked, more perplexed than anything.

"Says it takes on the form of a four-leaf clover, and allows me to ignore a fatal blow for every clover I have left, taking 80% health decrease instead, but granting me 50% attack increase on my next strike! Seems like a win / win to me!"

"Wow…" I muttered as I stepped a little closer, looking down into her eyes. It was strange, they had always looked green, but now they were even more vibrant. And that clover, it was so…real and detailed.

"Easy there, Boy Scout," said Georgia as she stepped back a little, tucking one of her errant strands of hair back behind her ear. "It's just a jynx mark. Nothing sinister."

"I'm sorry!" I blurted out as I too stepped backward. "I was just—it looks really cool."

Georgia's face brightened a little at that, her freckled cheeks turning a little red. I worried for a second I had said something wrong, but I didn't have time to even consider it before Treo darted off my shoulder, turning a stop-light color red and dinging wildly.

"Three creatures incoming! Prepare yourself!"

Georgia and I both whirled about, me raising my sword and shield and Georgia lifting her wand in preparation. What barreled out of the trees, nearly made me burst out into laughter at the relief.

Riding on what looked like massive, battle-armored corgis were three Unga Tribe automaton monkey beings, lead of which was none other than Luk Luk Ci Ci.

"Welcome, humans," the elderly chief said as he hopped off his adorable mount. "Welcome to Unga Jungle."

Luk Luk Ci CI led us from then on, talking constantly about the rich and vibrant culture of his tribe, the Kah'-Boom Tribe. At first I thought it was a joke, but when he and his fellow Bungas maintained an air of utmost sincerity and pride as he rambled on, I soon realized just how serious he was.

The journey took about an hour, and luckily for Georgia and I, they had brought two other giant corgis with them, Renlie and Rambo. They were surprisingly comfortable to ride, though the way they shook their rumps as they ambled forward began to churn my stomach by the end of the trip.

Kah'Boom Villiage

The silver scrollwork appeared just as we crested a hill and the Bunga village came into sight. And what a sight it was. The mixture of mechanism and nature, so perfectly intertwined, was breathtaking. I had expected huts or treehouses like a Donkey Kong game, but this was vastly different. A large wall, very indicative of ancient Mesopotamia, with a massive blue gate with golden effigies embossed on the surface included, surrounded the village. Guards in towering hats and holding spears stood sentry, each clacking hands against chests as we passed over a dry moat and into Kah'Boom Village.

Once inside, the smells of spices, fruits, and crackling energy assailed my nose, each fighting for dominance. Colorful tents were set up along the open walk of the village. All of the houses were in the manner of Mesopotamian architecture, only interwoven with the green light of Powerstone veins, the whole of the village seeming to draw power from a singular tower in the heart of the square. Vines and plants grew and flourished, falling over terraces and walls, giving the tan stone life and color. It was all so lush and yet, technological.

"Welcome, friends, to Kah'Boom Village," said Luk Luk Ci Ci as he dismounted once more. "Let us find you food and lodging. Tomorrow, we shall talk of our great shame: The Plight of Unga Jungle."

Still utterly dumbstruck I just bobbed my head in acceptance.

Now, the first thing to understand about Kah'Boom Village is, it is just a village. There were house and shops, but to my estimation, there couldn't be more than two or three hundred Unga living here in the city proper. There was only one inn, and it was not Banana Hut Treehouses. It was a cozy inn with warm, if not a little spicy, food, and soft beds, upon which my body yearned to lay down on. There was also a bath, a bronze bowl and running water, which was blessedly warm. After a meal, a bath, and reprieve—thankfully the Unga had discovered relatively modern plumbing—I found myself stumbling to the bed and drifting off into sleep.

A verdant field of green spread out before me. I saw five children dancing in a circle. I wanted to join them, though I could not tell why. Perhaps it was the joy in their faces, maybe it was the camaraderie I yearned for. Either way, they just seemed so happy, so full of joy. As they danced, where their bare feet fell, waves of light emanated throughout the grass, sprouting flowers and budding life.

They sang as they danced, a song that seemed so familiar to me.

Around and around they danced until the sky began to darken. Their song slackened and their faces fell. The sun... he sun began to set, and in its place, two moons rose, one dastardly red.

Fear filled my heart as the children ran, ran crying and screaming.

I wanted to do something, but could not move. My body felt as if I were wrapped in chains. I made to scream, but no sound escaped my mouth. I thrashed and roared, neither to any avail.

Then, a demon rose from the darkness, a figure of fire and smoke, and in his hand he held a bident of flaming gold, set with a ruby of burning red. Laughter rolled from his blazing maw as he stretched forth his bident, scorching the earth before him.

The five children ran and ran. But as they ran, they were separated, just as the sun utterly vanished from the sky, leaving only the two moons and the towering figure of smoke.

"Wake up!"

I jolted upright, panting and soaked sweat, heart hammering in my chest.

"Archy, are you alright?" Treoilae asked, her voice devoid of its normal mirth and childish glee.

I took a moment to gather myself, running shaking hands over my face and body. It had seemed so real. So very real. There was a pitcher of water on the nightstand. I had set it there last night before taking off my clothes and watch to go to sleep. I quickly took a drink and strapped my dad's watch about my wrist, feeling a calming sensation come over me as the familiar chill of the metal plate touched my skin.

I was okay. It was just a dream. I was okay.

"Just a bad dream," I finally said, feeling foolish for having caused such a commotion.

"You were talking, well, more like yelling, in your sleep," Treo said cautiously. *"Dreams can be powerful here in Neverwhere. What happened in your sleep?"*

"I dreamed about kids and then a shadowing figure burning away a field, living flowers and verdant grass, just burned away. I don't know why it seemed so real. It...it just seemed so real."

"Hmmm," Treo said, pondering my words, which admittedly, weren't the most concise or coherent.

"I've always had weird dreams, but here lately, they've become so vivid," I said, feeling a burning need to get it all off my chest. "Before I fell into Neverwhere, I had a dream with the same guy holding the bident. I just don't understand what it means."

"He is the bringer of ash and shadow. That is the Lord of Darkness," Treo said with a shudder, her voice small and scared. *"We of the Fae do not dare speak his name lightly, for we were first to fall to his snare. He promised light, but brought fire. He promised new, but brought destruction. It was he who broken the Golden Sun and cast the curse upon the lands of Neverwhere."*

"And that is who Lord Erle'em means to stop?" I asked.

"Yes," Treo said with a small bit of hope in her voice. *"If he can return the Golden Sun, with your help, he can cast off the curse of this land and return light to the realm."*

"What if he has my dad," I asked, more to myself than to Treo. An unexpected wave of despair struck. " If that...that thing has my dad. What I am I to do against something like that?"

"Lord Erle'em is mighty," Treo said, her voice growing in confidence and full of zeal. "It is foretold that the Promised Elven Lord will reunite the Golden Sun and save us all. If can but help him return to his strength, then he can complete his great task and bring peace and light back to Neverwhere, cleansing the realm and saving all our people."

I wanted to feel motivated by Treo's words, by the zeal and excitement that emanated from them. But I couldn't. It was too much. Too heavy. How was I supposed to help do anything? I barely managed to beat a few mobs, and that had been more out of luck than anything. I was terrible with a sword and even worse with words. Heck, I couldn't even have a three-sentence conversation with Georgia without fumbling around.

"Come," Treo said, bobbing up and down, her coloring a soft pink with shades of lavender flowing throughout. *"Georgia is awake!"*

I hurried got dressed, pulling on my new boots and strapping my bandolier around my chest, slinging my sword and shield on my back. It felt weird, you know, putting a sword and shield on. Despite everything, that was perhaps the oddest part. I was sixteen, and I was arming up with sword and shield to go fight monsters.

The inn's dining area was quaint and smelled of spices and honey, warm breads, and aromatic cheeses. Georgia was at the table already, laughing and talking to Elder Luk Luk Ci Ci. I loved the sound of her laughter, the way she sometimes snorted. I would be mortified if it were me, but she just leaned into it with a confidence I couldn't comprehend. I couldn't tell if I was jealous of her abilities to make friends so fast and carry such casual conversations or if I was down-right grateful. It seemed so exhausting to always be talking and laughing with others.

"Hey, look who finally decided to wake up this morning," Georgia said, finally noticing me, her eyes bright and filled with excitement. "Luk Luk was just telling me how, when he was a kid, that he and his friends would hunt Tripple V's for fun, wearing their mouths as hats. Could you imagine it? It's the darnedest thing I've heard."

"What's a Tripple V?" I asked, pulling out a chair and sliding into my seat at the round table.

"Tripple V is many fewer words than Viscous Venus Viscera," Luk Luk Ci Ci said as he rubbed at his chin stubble with one of his four arms. "Very nasty, but very fun to hunt, Unga say."

"He was also quite the looker," said Georgia. "Or at least that's what the matron and her staff say."

Luk Luk grew red in his cheeks. "Now, now, human child. Luk Luk very old. No need for flattery here. But, Luk Luk Ci Ci happy sleepy one is awake. We have many words to speak. Much need. Much sadness for my people."

Luk Luk proceeded to tell his people's origin story, going into painstaking details about how the first Unga became one with the "Great Heart of Power". It was their fusion with said Heart that melded bronze with flesh, and mechanism with blood, and thus the first Unga became as they are now, part living organisms and part machine. He went on to tell of the Five Forces and how their village was trusted with one such Totem, and for generations it kept the Unga safe and prosperous. That was until the Day of Darkness.

"Since that day, our great chief, Ta'Boom, has not been seen," Luk Luk Ci Ci said, his elderly eyes turning watery.

"Long has our Totem been lost to the Darkness. Long have we Unga suffered. Vines and rot, Wyrd monsters and creeping things, Unga Jungle has turned sour and bitter to us."

"Why doesn't anyone just go and find the Totem and bring it to Lord Erle'em? We were able to take a train to Kandarian Forest. I am sure Briggaforth could bring it from the station to Lord Erle'em," I said, thinking through everything Luk Luk had said.

"Many Unga go into the jungle, they go deep to the great Ziggurat, temple of our peoples," Luk Luk said with a heavy shake of his head. "No come out again. Hearts of Power turn black. Eyes go red with evil fire. They do not act as Unga should."

My own heart fell at the elderly Unga's words as fear crept up my spine. Their hearts were corrupted and their eyes turned red with evil fire?

What was I doing? I asked myself for the umpteenth time.

"But because we're not all mechanical and whatnot, y'all think we can go in without being turned?" Georgia asked before I could formulate a coherent response.

"Yes," said Luk Luk, eyes filling with excitement as his posture straightened. "You two can do what the Mighty Unga cannot. You can go, reclaim our Lost Totem. You can take it to Lord Erle'em. He can make it bright once more."

I knew it was dangerous. I knew I was in over my head. But I could see my mom's face, how heartbroken she was when Dad disappeared. I felt my own loss, my own hurt, and I knew I would give it my all. "We'll go and reclaim your Totem. We'll find a way."

"Ha!" exclaimed Luk Luk as he clapped his four hands

together. "This makes Luk Luk Ci Ci very happy indeed! To help with this, let us give you a sacred treasure."

Luk Luk reached into a satchel at his side and produced a glowing Dewdrop.

Blessed Dewdrop - rare item; upgrade item

Blessed Dewdrops are an uncommon item found throughout Neverwhere that are used to upgrade sacred items, potions, and flasks. Once used, they cannot be reused. If consumed, untold concerns and/or changes may arise.
Do Not Ingest Directly!
2 of 3 recovered for upgrading.
2 of 12 known Blessed Dewdrops found.

I took the Dewdrop with a word of thanks, the magical item seeping into me as I took it. I could see it in my special inventory slot, under the upgrading and crafting materials section.

"Unga Ziggarat stores many powerful items," said Luk Luk as he gathered his composure once more. "Look for those things that will grant you strength. Much rests on your shoulders, little humans. Be strong, like Unga, and you shall prevail."

With those words, Luk Luk led us out of the inn and into the village center. Dozens of Unga were making their way here and there, going about life. But there was a heaviness over them all, a downcast demeanor that permeated through their very essences.

"Help us, friends, and we shall grant many more rewards," Luk Luk said as he directed us to a gate at the back of the village. "Be swift and strong. Beware the Blatherpanter! Her cry is very, very strong!"

"Wait! What's a—" I tried to call out. But it was too late.

The gates closed in Georgia's and my face with a finality that resonated to my core. I turned about slowly, and as I looked deep into the jungle of Unga, I felt a strange sense of dissociation wash over me. If I were not so terrified, I would have taken the time to pounder upon the rich, lush beauty of the leafy jungle. But all I could see was the subtle signs of wrongness. The way the vines twisted menacingly, droplets of inky black tipping unnaturally sharp thorns. There is a darkness upon this jungle, both metaphorically and actually. And I was resolved to cleanse it now, more so than ever.

"Well, we ain't gettin' nowhere fast just standin' around," Georgia said, elbowing me in the side. "Let's get truckin'."

Giant Mechsquito!
Level 1

This bloodsucking, mechanical, flying freak of nature is more likely to beat you to death with its four sets of bronze wings before driving its proboscis into you and draining you of your insides.

"What the heck?" I cried out as I dove into the dirt, narrowly avoiding the onslaught of linebacker sized mechanical bugs that were honing in on Georgia and I. We had only been walking for about two hours before we first heard them flying about, loud as war helicopters, their wings beating out a rhythmic *thump thump thump* of terror.

"I only have one blasted offensive spell, Archy! Do some-thing!" Georgia cried out as she dodged again.

"Running Strike!" I cried out as I used my sword more like a baseball bat than an elegant weapon, crashing into the Giant Mechsquito with everything I had. The leafblade cut through insectoid flesh and mechanical parts with ease, cleaving the thing in two. I did not have time to loot the disintegrating body though, for three more Mechsquitos were already upon us.

"Ouch!" I screamed as one drove its proboscis into my left shoulder, slamming me into the ground. I saw one of my five heart containers immediately go dull and the one next two it started to tick down in quarters until it too went dim.

Thwack!

The enormous mechanical bug spattered into a tree, its whole body a crumpled mess of bent cogs and leaking oil. Standing over me was the most wild-eyed version of Georgia I had ever seen. She was holding a branch, whose end was slightly bulbous and now dripped with Mechsquito sludge.

"I. Need. A. WEAPON!" She breathed out with exaggerated frustration. "What's a girl got to do to get an offensive spell?"

I stared up at her from my prone position at Georgia, her green eyes aflame and her hair tussled. She had a smear of dirt on her cheek, and maybe some oil, marring the freckles. Despite this, I couldn't help but be captivated by her, her strength and her courage.

"You...you saved me," I said, utterly unable to come up with anything more profound to say to her.

"Well, yeah," she scoffed, offering me her hand to help me up. "What else was I supposed to do? Watch out!"

Thud!

Georgia cracked another Mechsquito from the sky, sending it plummeting into thick, leafy vegetation. A little Soulfire lit up in the distance and she smirked at where it had landed. "I'll take that," she said with a triumphant humph as she trotted off into a swath of alocasia and calatheas where the Mechsquito had turned to nothing more than pixilated ash.

I walked over to the Mechsquito I had cleaved in two and picked up the little Soulfire, pressing the warm blaze into my chest. My XP rose slightly, but not enough for me to level up again. Georgia, on the other hand, let out a yip of glee as she managed to increase her level once more.

This glee turned into a tirade of frustration as we continued onward, as none of the Mechsquitos' Soulfires had given her the ability to level up, or dropped any useful loot. That's not to say nothing was dropped, as I was able to collect three monster cores and four Mechsquito wings; The others were too damaged to reclaim.

This was a phenomenon I had come to understand. I could only loot the items for monsters or foes that were not damaged or not useful. Treo tried to explain the difference between useful and not, but eventually I gave up trying to draw a distinguishable line between the two. I had a boot that was classified as a hat thanks to one of the Gibblins I had fought, but I couldn't loot the Mechsquitos of their proboscis and use them as a lance or sword, because... reasons?

Anyway, Georgia and I started making far better time than before, not wanting to be overtaken by any more jungle foes. And we were doing really good until we heard the cry of what sounded like a great cat. Simultaneously, Georgia and I stopped, turned and looked each other in the eyes, and cried out, "Blatherpanther!"

We did not take the time to look about. We ran. We ran and ran and ran. We ran so hard even my stamina bar began to dip down into the danger zone. Since arriving in Neverwhere and leveling up a few times, I hadn't experienced weariness like I had back home. Now. Now I was utterly exhausted. My lungs felt like they were about to burst like an over-inflated balloon.

"We. Have. To. Stop." Georgia cried out through gasping breaths, her voice as shaky as my knees felt.

As if all of my strength had been waiting to abandon me in one fell swoop, my legs gave out and I tumbled to the jungle floor. My hands shook and my eyes watered. Despite this, I strained my ears, searching the plethora of sounds for that horrid cry of the Blatherpanther.

"I think," Georgia said, laying sprawled out on her back, eyes facing the canopy. "I think we're okay. For now."

"For now," I echoed, unable to think of anything else to say.

We lay there, unmoving while our bodies struggled to regain their strength and stamina, for what seemed like an eternity. Slowly, the light began to dim, day slowly transitioning to twilight. It was an eerie feature of Neverwhere, just how short the days were and how long the nights lasted. I just chalked it up to the curse. What else could it be?

"Hey, Archy," Georgia's voice had regained it steadiness and when I looked over, she was staring not at the sky, but at the ground on which we laid.

"Yeah?" I asked in return.

"Does this look like a path to you?"

Sure as daylight was turning to dark, the ground upon

which we had settled was in fact a path. A bit of renewed energy came over me as I drew myself up from the ground. Georgia, who was smiling triumphantly at her discovery, had also gotten to her feet.

"I bet this leads right to that ziggurat," Georgia said as she scratched her chin in an over exaggerated manner. Her eyes were wide and I could tell she was getting nervous.

We followed the path, which was marked by stone heads of ancient beasts, overgrown the lichen and vine. The whole of it gave off an uncanny sense of dread that I could not push away. Georgia seemed to be taking it in stride, now that we weren't being harassed by Mechsquitos or the cry of the Blatherpanther. That was until the foliage began to fall away and we stared into a clearing larger than three Citi Fields combined.

I stared up in awe at the ancient ruins of what I could only assume was the first of the three citadels which I had been instructed it find. Towering above the trees, loomed the vine-strewn ziggurat, capped with a great bronze point. A pathway led to the ancient building, as old and broken as the citadel itself. Alongside the path were dozens of stone statues that did not look too dissimilar to the Totem Poles that First Nation's peoples of Southeast Alaska used. These, however, all bore the same four faces of the same gorilla with large fangs, one laughing, one howling, one looking angry, and the fourth being that of surprise.

"Wow! I ain't never seen anything like this before," Georgia said in awe. "My Pawpaw would have a conundrum if he were here."

"I didn't expect it to be so... big."

"Right? The way the glowing guy talked, I thought it

would be just a tomb or something like they have down in New Orleans. This is... big."

I felt my hand instinctively go to the belt that Erle'em had given me. My hand rested atop the pommel of the sword. I was surprised that the metal was cool to the touch, despite the sweltering heat of the dense jungle.

"I still can't believe he gave you a sword. All I got was a wand that casts healing spells and a stupid spell on my bag," Georgia said with a harrumph as she looked over at me, eyeing the weapon at my side.

"Hey now," I countered. "You've already created a new spell all on your own. Besides, have you ever even used a sword?"

"No!" she answered stubbornly as she pointed the tip of her wand at my chest with a menacing glare that I wasn't sure was playful or not. "Have you?"

"My dad was a two-time champion fencer at Dartmouth. He made me go to practice for years." I answered without even thinking. Sometimes my brain did that, just allowed myself to talk without thinking. Stupid, stupid brain. "But that was with an epee, this looks more like a 13th Century British arming sword."

Georgia rolled her eyes.

"What?" I said, lifting my hand from the acorn-shaped pommel to the back of my neck, which was getting hotter by the second.

"Do you know everything about everything?" Georgia answered after a long, awkward silence, throwing her hands up in the air. "I mean, how much stuff can you fit in that brain of yours?"

"Sorry, when I hyper fixate on something, I kinda go over the deep end on it," I answered honestly. "It has always been that way. Mom said I knew the alphabetical names of over one hundred different dinosaurs at four years old."

This, thankfully, got a smile out of Georgia. "Bless your mother's heart."

"She is an awesome mom. I feel bad for how hard it must have been on her to raise me. I am just...different."

"Bah, we're all a little weird. At least your smart weird, not...weird weird. Like, keeping pictures of people in your locker weird and stalking them on the internet."

This was not the right time to say that he had, more than once, used yearbook pictures and Facebook to learn everyone's names in order to start conversations by calling them by their first names and stating a random fact I had found out about them. This rarely ever led to anything other than odd looks and hurried escapes. It had gotten better when I hit fourteen and sprouted like a weed, though I could not understand why.

"Hey there, Boy Scout, what's got your hitch in a get-up?" Georgia asked, showing a bit of concern.

"Nothing," I answered, pushing away the tidalwave of thoughts that were beginning to cascade onto my mind. I needed to move forward. Move. Forward. "We need to get inside before dark. Who knows what is lurking around in this jungle."

"Well, if this Erle'em guy is to be trusted, not good things," Georgia said with a halfhearted laugh. "But didn't he say he couldn't go in these because of a curse?"

"Yeah," I answered, feeling less sure of myself than I was trying to project. "But that is because he was cursed with this place. That's why we have to get those stones statues. If we can recover them, he can save my dad."

And there was nothing I wouldn't do to save him.

Chapter Seventeen:
I Deal With Monkey Business

Archy Lawerence Jr.
Level 6
Health Points - 6
Focus Points - 3
Endurance - 6
Strength - 5
Dexterity - 6
Esoteric - 1
Speed - 4
Charisma - 3

THE DOOR of the ziggurat was made of wood so old it looked as if a touch would cause it to turn to ash. This, however, was not the case. The wood had somehow turned nearly to stone, and the massive hinges were so caked in rust that there would be no moving them.

"I don't know how we'll ever get into this place," Georgia said as she rapped a knuckle against the wooden doors, which thudded solidly. "These are sealed tight."

Frustrated, and a little nervous at the setting sun, I looked about for any other means of entry. And then, it struck him. The vines!

Casting my eyes skyward, I searched for any other means of entry. And there was one, above us. A window which had a heavy vine protruding from its dark opening in the second tier of the ziggurat.

"I have a plan," I said, nudging Georgia's shoulder. "But I don't think you're gonna like it much."

"What do you—" Georgia's face went pale. "Nope! No, no, no, tall boy! No way, no how!"

"Come on, Georgia," I said placatingly. "Do you see another way in?"

"Ugh," she groaned as she glanced about one more time, seeking any other point of entry.

An animal call, like that of a big cat, rang out through the trees as the sun began to vanish behind the leafy canopy. That was enough for Georgia, who let out a little squeak at the roar. I too felt my hair raise on my neck and sweat gather at my already soaked back. But I feigned composure and grabbed hold of a vine.

To my surprise, as I gripped the thick, green vine, it shimmered, like fish scales in the sunlight. I stared open-mouthed for a brief moment before a shook my head and began climbing. Shimmering vines were the least of my worries right now, but I would come back to that later.

There was a Blatherpanther on the hunt, and I wanted nothing to do with that creature.

Up and up we climbed, probably twenty or so feet before we reached the next level of the ziggurat where, to my aching muscles' and burning hands' relief, I finally was able to catch my breath. My brief respite was short-lived as I remembered that Georgia was still making her way up the sheer face of stone. Quickly, I leaned over the side, propping my feet against something solid inside the dark window, and reached for her hand.

Her skin was soft and warm, if not a little sweaty. I could not help but notice my hands were so much bigger than hers, enveloping her right hand and much of her wrist and forearm as I heaved her upward and into the ziggurat. She landed on me it tangle of limbs and awkward rolling. When the dust settled, I was on my back, her on my chest, and our faces were...really close.

"You're not very soft, Archy," Georgia said with a half-laugh as she pushed herself quickly off of me. She then proceeded to rapidly dust herself off before tucking a lock of arrant hair behind her ear.

Not very soft? What was that about?

I felt heart burn the tips of my ears. Was I supposed to be? My whole life I had viewed guys with lots of muscles as conceited and strange. I hadn't really ever wanted to be big like that before. Suddenly...well, being a muscular guy didn't seem like such a bad idea anymore.

Ding!

"We need to find the way deeper into the Ziggurat," Treo said from seemingly nowhere. And when I looked about, all I could see was a little dancing flame, for Treo had all but lost

her form. "My power is waning fast here due to the darkness. I can't hold my form.

"What was that about me not being soft?" I asked without meaning to, trying to hide my concern of Treo diminishing. She would be alright. Everything was going to be okay. As soon as I said it though, I felt a pit form in my stomach.

"It was a joke, Archy," Georgia said, placing her hands on her hips and rolling her eyes. "Thank you, by the way, for helping me."

"It's no big deal," I mumbled, feeling oddly self-conscious.

"Ooo!" Georgia shouted, rushing past me in excitement.

Confused, I whirled around to see what all the fuss was about. What I saw drove the air from my lungs nearly as hard as our recent tumble into the ziggurat. Two or three dozen pots of antique design and rimmed in gold were littered across the wide room we had stumbled into, and inside each pot was a large gemstone.

"Wow!" said Georgia. "These must be worth a fortune!"

"These look like Mayan pottery, but much, much larger and with a funny kind of seal across the top," I said as I kneeled down in front of one of them, studying the symbols so carefully painted into each one of—

CRASH!

"What?" I shouted, nearly jumping out of my skin as I turned about to see, in horror, Georgia hefting another pot over her head and then throwing it.

She rushed over to where the pot shattered onto the ground. With a gleeful smile she lifted the emerald and dropped it into her enchanted backpack saying, "Maybe this will be of more use than I thought."

"What are you doing?" I gasped, hardly able to form words.

"Listen, Archy," Georgia said with a look I couldn't quite understand. "Your family is rich. My Pawpaw is got a heart problem and my folks ain't got much. Do you know what a gem like this could be worth?"

Flabbergasted, I reached over to one of the ancient vessels and twisted the top, allowing the two parts to separate with ease. I then took out a purple gemstone and held it out to her, voice trembling, "You don't have to break them, they come apart like this."

Georgia didn't take the amethyst from my hand but bent over and took up another pot and dropped it at her feet, making my body twitch. With a smile focused hard on me she reached down and picked it up, placed it in her bag, and said, "I didn't ask to be sent on this mission, but here I am. I don't even know if any of this is real. For all I know, I am going to wake up soon, late for first hour, and not have time to eat breakfast. Or, I am going to make it through these three trials and go back home with something other than an expanding backpack to show for it."

"But the pots," I babbled, trying to gather words.

"They're just pots. Besides, whoever left them here isn't coming back. They are like, really old."

"That...that's the point," I said, pressing my fingers to my forehead. "Old things are valuable."

"Gems are valuable," Georgia said with a shrug of her shoulders. After that, she zipped up her backpack and slung it over her shoulder, muttering, "I should've got the sword."

Trying my best to calm my nerves and steady myself, I searched about myself, trying to find any clues as to how we could delve deeper into this massive ziggurat. The room we were in seemed to be some kind of storage room. Which was odd.

Who stored pots of gems next to a window?

Across from the window from which we had entered, I spotted a doorway whose door had long since rotted away. The hall beyond it was dark; however, next to the frame, an iron torch lay abandoned.

"Look around, see if you can't find anything to start a fire," I said to Georgia absentmindedly as I began to scan the room.

I looked high and low in the cramped room, which was lined with shelves, each covered with jars, some holding gems, others filled with liquids that smelled like soap or moss, while others were filled with sand. Georgia was chattering on about something I couldn't focus on, not with all of my attention on finding something to start a fire with.

"Hey! Listen!" Georgia shouted, nearly causing me to jump out of my skin.

"What?" I said, heart racing.

"I have a lighter," she answered, cocking an eyebrow at me. "You really need to take a step outside of your own head every once in a while."

Well, she was right there. But how could I? What with all the artifacts, gemstones, and, oh ya, the fact that we were in an ancient ziggurat in a parallel universe...or something like that. I still wasn't exactly sure on the specifics of that.

"Hey!"

"What?"

"What do you need the lighter for?" Georgia officially rolled her eyes at me this time, and I couldn't help but smile as she did it.

"By the door there is a torch," I said, walking past her and grabbing the lighter from her hand while doing so.

I wrenched the dusty metal from its bracket, which gave off a horrid noise. I clicked the light and the torch, thankfully, ignited perfectly well. "That's surprising."

"Surprising? Wouldn't you expect a torch to light?"

"We're in the jungle. It is humid. Plus, this room doesn't look like anyone has been here in ages. I guess, well, it might be like the movies in this place sometimes…"

"Yeah, well, let's hope there aren't spike traps and giant rolling stones," Georgia said as she walked up next to me, looking down the hall, which danced with torch light.

Those words made something in my guts twist.

How much like the movies would this place be? Because, if one thing was certain, my gangly body was not one of action star proportions. And my personality, it was anything but brave and domineering. I liked math and science, debate even, or a good game a chess. But running for my life while a spherical bolder rolled climactically behind me. Nope! Nope, nope, nope, nope.

"You alright there, buddy?" Georgia asked, bumping me with her hip. "Let's get going. Ain't gonna get nothing done standing around here."

I swallowed my fear and anxiety and, beyond my better judgement, stepped forward into the ziggurat.

"Oh. My. Gosh." said Georgia in a long, exaggerated sigh. "We've been walking for like, ten years!"

"It's been twenty-three minutes," I answered flippantly, as I looked over to the floating ball of fire that was our friend and guide, Treo, before adding, "Give or take."

"Twenty-three minutes?" Georgia blurted, stopping dead in her tracks. "Twenty-three minutes? How would you know? It is dark. We don't have cellphones. And our watches all went haywire when we fell through the portal. How on god's green earth can you possibly know it has been twenty-three minutes?"

"Bohemian Rhapsody," I answered, eyes still forward, looking for any means to go either up or down. We had been walking in a giant square and were no closer to finding our way deeper into the ziggurat.

"What is that supposed to mean?" Georgia asked, rushing to catch back up to my longer strides.

"5 minutes and 55 seconds, I think," I answered. I did not think, I knew. "And I am almost done with my 4th pass through. Helps me think, to focus on something."

"You're kind of weird, Archy," said Georgia.

And though I expected something like that from anyone. I hadn't expected it to be said the way that it was. This caused me to stop. I turned around and looked at her smiling up at me.

"Every time I think I am beginning to understand you, you go and do something like that. Of course you would know the length of a song to the second. And of course you would be using it to keep time. I bet, I bet it is how you keep track of where we're at somehow."

I blinked.

It was how I kept track.

My stride was roughly sixty-two inches, give or take. And at an average walking pace, I was able to deduce that this hallway's perimeter was about a mile about, each side of the ziggurat being a quarter mile in length. Well, a little shorter. We had passed this point already, and I hadn't started singing in my head right as we started walking.

"I could give a good guess," I answered sheepishly.

"You're just like in my books! That is so cool! I wish I could do that. It's like a super power."

Was that adoration? Was Georgia...did she like the fact that I was able to keep track of time and distance? No...

"Though, had you spent a little less time humming to yourself, bet you would've seen the pattern in the wall," Georgia said, this time as if she were gloating. And her face. She was absolutely beaming. "Ha! You didn't spot it, did you?"

"Spot what?" I asked, unable to keep my emotions or concentration in one place.

"Triangle, triangle, square, lama!" Georgia said proudly.

"And..."

"And where is the lama?" she asked, pointing to a portion of the wall that had replaced a simple drawing of a lama in red —which had repeated dozens upon dozens of times—with a red circle. "While you were measuring time and space, my mind was going pattern, pattern, pattern...but then. I remembered when we started seeing the circle and trying to spot another one. We went around this whole thing again before I realized there was only one. And it is just after the next turn ahead."

Without uttering a word, I turned about and began to run down the hall.

Triangle, triangle, square, lama. Triangle, triangle, square, lama. Triangle, triangle, square, lama. Turn. Triangle, triangle, square, lama. Triangle, triangle, square, lama. Triangle, triangle, square, Circle! Circle! There was a circle!

"How..."

"Smarter than I look, eh?" Georgia said through huffing breaths, knocking into me again playfully.

"Don't say that, you look very smart."

I felt a pit form in my stomach.

Did. Did I just say that?

"Aw, thanks man."

Georgia said those words with a playful nudge, her elbow digging into my side, but for some reason, I could not find a way to smile. Not only had I said something dumb, but I suddenly realized I had misread perhaps everything up until that moment. That pit that had formed in my stomach dropped into an endless chasm and I felt the sudden need to sit down. Only, as Georgia stepped forward and pressed on a stone that slightly protruded from the center of the painted circle, the growl of stone sliding against stone washed away my petty internal turmoil. A gust of stale air rushed up from the darkening void before us.

We were going into the heart of the ziggurat.

Perhaps my proclamation that we were going into the heart was incorrect. At least, partially so. We were going deeper into the ziggurat, but we sure as heck were climbing higher too. Every step was a stair step it seemed as we wound back and forth, ever climbing, ever delving deeper into the dark.

Ding!

Treo shot out in front of us, her azure light turning an angry red-orange. I drew my sword and shield and prepared myself for what was surely about to come careening toward us.

"Halt!" roared a voice that sounded more mechanical than vocal chord. "No one come closer or Trounce smash!"

An enormous Orangutan with two natural arms and a third arm of bronze and whirling gears coming up out of his back like a scorpion's stinger came bounding into the room. On his natural hands, he had on a pair of stone-like gloves that were ridiculously oversized. Unlike the other Ungas I had seen before, this one looked...wrong. Its eyes were filled with a ghastly flame of burning red and where others' shone with Powerstone's green light, Trounce leaked an oily black essence. The health bar that extended nearly wall to wall had a strange border that was that same oily black coloring.

Pervaded Trounce
Level 12
Floor Boss

Trounce was once the favored captain of Ta'Boom, the Great Chief of the Unga Tribes.

Trounce was gifted a pair of gauntlets that were said to be blessed by the Force of Nature.

He went with Ta'Boom to find out why the jungle had turned sick.

He was never heard from again.

"Trounce SMASH!" The enormous Orangutan's already oversized gauntlet grew as tendrils of black power flooded into them. He brought them crashing down, nearly squishing me to a pulp.

Luckily, I used my shield's deflect ability, which notably was not a pain-free method of stopping a strike, just in the knick of time. The force of the blow, however, sent me straight into the wall with a bone crunching thud. My heart containers flickered and dimmed until only one remained.

"Take from darkness, form to light, heal my friend so he can fight," I heard Georgia chant as she moved her wand about hurriedly.

A beam of purple light poured out of the end of her wand and cascaded onto me. I half expected it to feel like I was being drenched in some kind of viscous liquid. I found the actual sensation to be rather pleasant, like stepping out of a dark, cold room in which you had been sitting too long into the warmth of the summer's sun.

Blip, blip, blip!

My heart containers refilled in an instant, and even a 6th, esoterica colored container formed over my head.

"That's pretty much all I got. I don't have any Soulfires to form a needle in here," Georgia cried out.

"No needle! Only smash!" roared Trounce once more as his two stone fists and third prehensile tail-fist came down again in a flurry of jabs and punches.

I dodged and rolled, catching a few errant strikes here and there, but mostly staying out of his reach. I did, however, manage to get a single strike in, nicking him on the arm. Where the sword touched flesh, the blackness receded, leaving only red, hairy, orangutan flesh.

Of course. The sword was imbued with light. These things were corrupted with darkness. An idea flashed into my head, looking at the creature again, now that my eyes had adjusted. In its chest, there was a plantlike growth, with wriggling vines that seemed be seeking out new flesh. The heart of the plant was black and vile. If I could sever the growth from Trounce's heart, perhaps I could spare him.

"Georgia, I need a distraction!" I cried out, dodging another onslaught of strikes.

"Curse me for a dang fool!" Georgia said as she picked

up the torch she had dropped in the fighting and began charging at Trounce, waving the flames in his face.

"Burn Trounce! Bad! Bad fire!" the great orangutan cried out, waving his hands at Georgia, trying to knock the torch aside.

I used the distraction to sneak up around the back side of him, hoping beyond hope to cut the vines that seemed to run straight through his chest and wriggled round the base of that third arm. I would start that. I would—

That third arm jutted out, catching me off guard and striking me across the chin. I saw sparks and light flash before my eyes as my head seemed to burst with pain. Once more my heart containers dipped.

Trounce turned his full attention on me, lurking over me with a predator's grace. He raised his two fists high over his head and brought them down, directly on top of me. I clenched my eyes shut, knowing this would be the end. I had failed, and now I would never see my dad or mom again.

Lucky Glance!

Whomph!

I wrenched my eyes opened and stared in dumbstruck amazement. Trounce was whirling about like a top, crashing into wall after wall. Georgia was standing over me, hands over her head and knees knocking together. She had the aurora of a green clover over her body.

Before I could say anything, the emerald light dissipated, being reabsorbed into her body. When she opened her eyes, one of the bright green petals that had been in her iris vanished. And when it did, Georgia sagged to the ground, one one quarter of health remaining in her final heart container.

"Quick, drink this." I shoved a healing flask into her mouth and tipped it up.

One by one, her hearts began to refill. That had been too close. Too close indeed.

"Ughhhhh," groaned Trounce as he tried to lift himself up from the ground. His eyes were rolling in his head, which was firmly grasped between his two natural hands.

I had to act now. There would not be another chance.

I leapt to my feet, mustering all the fear and anger inside of me I could. I held my sword in both hands as I charged headlong into the mechanical orangutang. Trounce noticed me a second too late. He tried to lower his hands, to extend his third arm. But it was all in vain. I rammed the tip of my sword directly into the center of the bulbous growth in Trounce's chest. A burst of light erupted as my blade sank into the viny plant.

"Ouch!" cried out Trounce as he stumbled backward, black liquid pouring from the plant as my blade slid free.

Trounce began to howl and flail about. I thought, for a moment, he was about to start attacking me. But the red fire dissipated from his eyes. He was attacking something though, just not me. He was ripping and tearing at the growth on his chest. With a final cry of agony, Trounce tore the thorny obtrusion from his chest and cast it onto the ground before my feet, before collapsing to the floor in sobs of pain.

Pervading Pustulous Plant!

Level 19

Beware! These plants are wildly invasive.
Do not touch!

"Archy! Stay away from that!" Treo cried out.

I brushed Treo's warning off as I walked past her floating body. She tried pushing on me, but it felt like nothing more than a gentle breeze. Anger. There was so much anger inside of me. This thing had almost lost me my chance to save my dad, to see Mom again. It had almost crushed Georgia. It had almost crushed me.

"Impaling Thrust!" I roared as I leapt into the air and brought the tip of my sword down once more into the wriggling mass of black tar and plant matter.

Hisss! Pop!

"I think I'm going to be sick." Treo said as she darted away.

Sludge splattered across my face and body. But as I yanked my sword free, I felt a swell of pride at my victory.

Foe Defeated!

A bright Blue Soulfire burned where the writhing plant had just been, now nothing more than pixilated ash. I knelt down and picked up the blue flame, and for a second, I thought about giving it to Georgia. But I needed to be stronger. I had almost lost...everything. I crushed the Soulfire into my chest and watched in amazement as my XP skyrocketed.

Threat Annihilated!
You have annihilated a threat well above your level!
You have leveled up!

Congratulations!
You use a finishing blow on an opponent.
Wicked cool.
You have gained an additional 30% XP.

You have leveled up!

You saved a foe, making them an Non-Pugnacious Citizen
once more.
+2 to Charisma

You slew a mini boss that was more than twice your current
level
+2 to any stat of your choice

I blinked as my heart containers increased by two, one for each of my two new levels. I felt a surge of confidence as well, as if I suddenly gained some perspective I had never held before, a subtle control I had always been missing. I did not have time to revel in these newfound feelings, before I heard Georgia exclaim, "Wow!"

I jerked my head in her direct and saw her eyes wide with excitement. When she noticed me looking at her she waived her hand, beckoning me to come and join her. "Hey, check this out. I leveled up, and I got a +2 to Charisma for saving your life and +3 to Esoteric for using Lucky Glance."

"Wow," I echoed, looking at her. She was absolutely radiant with excitement.

"Ughhhh..."

Georgia and I both whipped our heads about to where Trounce was laying on the ground. Treo didn't wait for us, but shot across the open space to where the great orangutan was struggling to stand.

"Help. Trounce." Trounce said in apparent pain, seemingly unable to lift his fists from the ground.

I gave a questioning glace to Georgia, who simply shrugged her shoulders before heading over toward Trounce, shouting, "You alright, big fella?"

"Trounce weak. Trounce lost magic juice. Trounce sorry." The great Unga sounded absolutely miserable.

"It's all right. We know you didn't mean nothing by all that," Georgia said as she placed a careful hand on one of his massively muscular arms. "Y'all were all possessed and whatnot."

"Chief Ta'Boom, big trouble. Trounce tried save him, got Mighty Fists to open the door. Ta'Boom chucked vine at Trounce. Trounce felt very sick." Trounce spoke faster and faster, the fractured sentences pouring out of him like a burst dam. "Trounce failed friend. Trounce failed Unga. Trounce hunt little people. Trounce is bad warrior."

I wanted to say, yeah you are. I wanted to yell at him. I just felt so...angry, despite that momentary clarity that had struck only moments before. But before I could make a fool of myself, Georgia continued talking to him as she patted his arm reassuringly.

"It ain't your fault, not one bit. We're just glad we got that nasty plant off your chest."

"That was good," Trounce said, a little bit of confidence returning to his voice. "Little woman, you very strong. You took a blow from Mighty Fist and still stand. Trounce no longer has magic in his veins, nasty plant consumed it. I give you, Mighty Fists."

With those words, Trounce rotated his wrists. There was

a loud *Crack!* Like the very earth was being split open. This was followed by a low hiss, as if pressurized air was being released. "Take the Fist! I sense much magic in you, human!"

"I couldn't," Georgia started, but Trounce cut her off.

"No! Must! Door to ziggurat is can only be opened by Fist. These are key, not just weapon. Take them. Not question. Must!"

Georgia blinked at the rebuking tone with which Trounce lectured her. She looked over at me. I thought for a brief second about the varying benefits and implications, but ultimately gave her a little smile and shrugged my shoulders, just like she always did to me.

"Not helpful," she said under her breath, but I could hear the excitement in her voice.

Georgia stepped forward toward the two fists of stone. They were nearly as large as she was. Without a word, she lowered her hands into their gaping openings. The announcement that rang out was audible even for me to hear.

Legendary Item!

Mighty Fists!
These Esoteric finger flexors are 100% goated!
+ 50% increase to strength at base level

Unga's Boon!
When incantation, Unga's Boon, is in use, +5,000% to strength for 10 seconds
This does require a minimum cool down of 100 hours divided by Esoteric level.

Fists of Fury!
Special Move. This strike is worth 1FP per attack. This is a two-fisted whomping of epic proportions.

The stoney gauntlets formed around Georgia's hands until they were the size of boxing gloves. Georgia looked at them and gave a grunt of distaste.

"Does warrior not like Mighty Fists?" Trounce asked in confusion.

"Hold your horses." Georgia said, eyes bearing down on the gauntlets as if she were trying to—

The gauntlets shifted again, this time morphing into what looked like fingerless bikers gloves with stony knuckle-dusters on the back. "Much better!" Georgia exclaimed, her face beaming with triumphant glee.

I had begun to feel many different things about Georgia, but never until then had I ever felt slightly afraid. She was wearing a pair of gauntlets that could increase her strength exponentially and she was grinning like she had just been given a pony.

"You good?" I asked, testing the waters.

"Never better!" she said. "I *finally* have a weapon."

"That you do, warrior!" Trounce laughed, a deep, belly laugh. "Trounce is happy you have a means to defend yourself other than your head. Though Trounce is certain he has never seen a head take a blow like that and not crack. You two make Trounce think many wonderings. Trounce must go now. Must tell the village of the deeds that have transpired. I am no more help to you here."

"Wait, before you-" Before I could finish my sentence, Trounce pulled at an amulet about his neck and vanished into a pixilated light burst. "Tell us what we're up against?"

My words fell flat on the floor.

"Don't look so grim, Boy Scout," Georgia said, still eyeing her new gloves. "We're okay, we know where Ta'Boom is, and now we have a means to open the dang door!"

I blinked. Did she not realize how close we had come to losing? To dying? This was crazy. But, what else was I supposed to do? I was already in the ziggurat, wasn't I? So, I swallowed my fear and, as nonchalantly as I could, said, "Lead away."

The rest of the way through the ziggurat was more of the same. Lots of stairs and right angled turns. Lots of small doors with little puzzles that took no more thought than two seconds to figure out. Once or twice we came across a few low-level Unga, but like Trounce, once the plant protrusions were destroyed, they were freed. Frustratingly, they too had those necklaces that allowed them to teleport away. Every time, I tried to get them to explain more details, but they all just vanished away without giving me the time of day. Which, admittedly, they would have no idea about. It was pitch black and who knows how long they were being possessed for.

"That's gotta be it!" Georgia shouted, breaking a long stint of silence, causing me to jerk in surprise and let out a very unmanly yelp. "Look at the size of that thing! Would you just look at it?"

"I am, I am," I said, trying to calm my nerves and play off my pathetic squeak as me clearing my throat.

"I bet you there is about four million dollars of gold in that door," Georgia said, hands on her hips.

"What makes you say that?" I asked, looking at the intricately carved door of normal stone depicting what I assumed was the gifting of the Totem of Earth to the Unga.

"My eyes, duh," Georgia said with a scoff. "Can't you see it all? It's all throughout the door. So much gold, it's like rivers."

"It must be something to do with your Esoteric scaling. I can't see anything," I said, saying the thoughts aloud as the formed, more to myself than Georgia.

"Oh! Good point," Georgia said excitedly. "I bet that's what Trounce meant by the gauntlets. Oh! And look here," Georgia exclaimed as she found two handprints in the stone on either side of the depiction of the Totem of Earth, carved to look like the receiving hands of an ancient Unga chieftain.

"Hey, before you go—" Before I could finish my sentence, Georgia enlarged the stone gauntlets and placed them in the opening.

The whole ziggurat seemed to shake and tremble. Georgia let out a cry of alarm and I stumbled about like a toddler, bouncing off of the wall behind me as the massive stone door began to slowly slide upward.

"Let go!" I cried out as Georgia's feet began to rise higher and higher, her hands still firmly affixed to the door.

"Don't you think I'm trying?" Georgia screamed, her hands stuck fast to the now fully lifted door, leaving her feet dangling about eleven or twelve feet from the ground. I rushed forward, leaping with legs far stronger than I remembered them being, soaring up into the air. I caught hold of her ankles, her new boots providing a solid grip.

"How is this supposed to help?" Georgia cried out, her voice a mixture of frustration and fear.

"I don't know?!" I answered, feeling a sudden head rush

as I realized just how high up I was. "I was just trying to help."

I said the last part a little sheepishly, realizing to what I was clinging. I had the sudden urge to let go. But my stomach did a backflip as the idea of dropping filled me with dread.

Fortunately, or rather unfortunately, the decision of whether to let go or not was taken from me. Something sinuous and barbed wrapped around my midsection, squeezing tightly and drawing blood where dozens of thorns sank into my abdomen. Georgia let out a scream that was knocked from my chest as two more vines lashed themselves about her legs. We were unceremoniously yanked from our lofty position and pulled into the chamber before us.

Several things happened simultaneously, my adrenaline-drenched mind trying its darndest to comprehend as many of them as possible. We were in a large, square room with cut stone floors and a central altar raised upon a dais. Atop the alter rested a jade Totem, though it appeared to be utterly consumed with an inky black ooze that ran from its eyes, ears, and mouth. The room was lined with pews of carved stone and in those seats, dozens of corrupted Unga sat, eyes blazing with red flame. And before the altar, prostrated upon the ground with a gigantic, bulbous, Pervading Pustulous Plant sprouting from his back, wriggling and writhing, was Chieftain Ta'Boom.

How did I know this?

No sooner did my body strike the ground than the silver scrollwork text fill my vision, reading:

BOSS BATTLE!

Pervaded Chieftain!
Level 23 Temple Boss

All of the corrupted Unga began to beat their various appendages against their chests and chant in unison. The sound sent a shiver through my aching spine. It was perfectly timed, deeply resonating, and utterly devoid of emotion. Like an ancient prayer mantra that had lost all meaning and emotion, a husk of what should have been a great tune.

I forced myself to rise to my feet, quickly scanning about once more to find Georgia. To my immense relief, the vines had loosened their grip on her as they had with me. She was on her feet, her nose bloodied, fists raised like a boxer who had been knocked down, but clearly wasn't out of the fight.

"Come to take my cherished," Chieftain Ta'Boom intoned as he lifted a massive hand to caress the leaking Totem. "Come as others. Die as others."

"What? No. It's not like that," I tried to from words, but my ears were ringing and my head throbbing from how hard I had cracked the stone. Honestly, had I not been leveling endurance, I'm pretty sure I wouldn't be much more than a splat on the ziggurat floor.

The ground cracked with a thunderous explosion as Chieftain Ta'Boom slammed his raised hand down onto the ground. "I felt you take my Trounce from me. Severed him from the Source." Ta'Boom raised himself, the viny protrusion sprouting from his back shooting tendrils into the walls, as if they were there to support his lumbering mass.

Slowly, he turned himself about, revealing a ghastly sight. More machine than ape, Ta'Boom must have once been akin to a Silverback gorilla. He had also had four arms, though one was missing entirely, a thorny vine protruding from the bronze socket. His other arms were covered in angry scars or mechanical parts. But the most harrowing sight was the bronze burial mask that was placed over his face, concealing anything that could have shone emotion or life.

"I will have back my prize," Ta'Boom said with his deep, rumbling voice. However, this phrase was not directed at me, but Georgia, to whom he was pointing a meaty finger. "Those are Unga blessings. Give them back."

"How's about a trade," Georgia said cooly. "I'll give you these, if y'all had over that there Totem and let us be on our way. Everyone wins. And who doesn't like a win-win scenario?"

"How about I break you?" Ta'Boom roared from behind the mask, though it did not dampen the sound of his in the slightest.

Georgia took a step back, and I rushed over to her side, readying my sword and shield.

"No more talk! Crush!" Ta'Boom thundered as he beat two of his fists against his clockwork chest, sending sparks flying.

The room erupted into taunting jeers and leers from the Unga that surrounded us, though none of them seemed to be willing, or able, to move from their seats. Bolstered by their cheering, Ta'Boom thrust his third hand into the ground and ripped a stone from the floor and flung it at us.

Georgia shouted a spell, and I used Parry!

The slab crashed into my shield, which had been forti-fied by Georgia's enchantment, ricocheting into the wall. An Alert! popped up over the shield, notifying me that it was severely damaged. Thankfully, neither Georgia or I had taken any damage though.

"We need a plan!" said Georgia, who was holding a wand in one of her oversized, stone-hands.

"Working on it!" I said back as Ta'Boom sent his hand careening back into the ziggurat floor.

The ground shook as he ripped up another stone, but I did not let it daunt me. I began running toward him, sword ready. I had been able to sever the plant from Trounce's body with a slash. I set my footing and prepared to leap.

Thwap!

An errant vine struck me from out of nowhere, knocking me sideways and sending another heart container into to the dim. I rolled, shield and sword sliding before me.

"Ouch…" I groaned as my head spun.

Boom!

My head jerked around to see Georgia standing in a dust cloud, chips of stone still falling about her feet. Had she just punched that stone out of mid air? I thought I had been the one upgrading strength? Maybe I was doing this all wrong.

Ta'Boom, to my surprise, gave an approving grunt at her strike, following up with, "Lady girl strong. But Ta'Boom stronger!" As he roared out the final word, the vines seemed to pulsate as the eyes of the chanting Unga flared brighter, though their bodies seemed to shrivel somewhat.

"Archy, did you see that?" Georgia called out from across the temple.

"Ya, he is draining their lifeforce from them!" I called back. I had a sickening feeling that whoever the true Ta'Boom was, he would be utterly mortified at what the plant was forcing him to do. I felt a chill run through my spine followed by a resounding thrum of anger. These things, they had my dad.

"I will stop you," I grunted through my teeth as I rose up once more from the ground. I wasn't sure where this extra sense of confidence was coming from and quite frankly I didn't care. I picked up my sword and shield, shrugging off the dusty rubble that clung to me. I would defeat this monkey and I would save my dad.

I ran at him once more at the exact same time Georgia hurled a chunk of stonework at his head. To my dismay, he caught the stone with two of his hands and use his third had to send a punch directly into me. I got my shield up in time, but it was of little use. The power of the punch sent me tumbling backwards, flipping head over heels until I stopped at Georgia's feet.

"Ta'Boom is strongest!" the masked monkey roared.

"I can't get close to him," I said through labored breaths. "He's too fast.

"The vines seemed to be holding him up," Georgia said through panting breaths. "What if you cut those?"

"That would have me leaving you exposed," I said.

"I know, you've been trying to put yourself between me and him instead of just taking him out," countered Georgia, a bit of frustration showing through her tired demeanor.

"But what if he hits you?" I argued, feeling an over-whelming rush of dread filling my body at the thought of her getting hurt.

"I have these," Georgia said with a feigned confidence as she pointed to the magic clover in her eye. But that wasn't all I saw in her emerald eyes. There was something else there, something deeper. Defiance?

"Okay," I said, trusting my gut more than my brain,

which had all but unplugged and shut down for the night. "I'll try and cut the vines. You keep him distracted. But, if you find yourself getting overwhelmed, let me—"

My words word cut off as the second stone flew through the air, separating the two of us as we jumped in either direction.

"Just go!" Georgia shouted at me. To my utter astonishment, she was not fleeing or fumbling but grabbing hold of a broken chunk of stone and flinging it back at Ta'Boom. It struck his chest with a resounding boom!

"Ouch!" roared the pervaded primate as only the vines connecting him to the wall kept him upright.

A renewed sense of confidence and determination filled my own heart as I watched the unexpected exchange take place. If she could do that, I could cut some measly vines. Couldn't I?

Well, the vines, much to my dismay, were a little more active than I would have liked. As I rushed toward my first target, half a dozen little vines shot off from buds along the main growth, moving toward me like hurled javelins. I dodged and ducked, which led me to my second issue. Where Ta'Boom hand plucked the stones, gapping holes formed, which plunged into a deep darkness below.

Great.

Just great.

"Archy, watch out!"

Georgia cried out just in time, warning me of a vine that was sneaking up around the back of me, seeking out my ankle. I swung my sword, slicing through the vine with ease. Hot fluid spewed out from the weed, soaking my leg in a burning liquid.

One of my heart containers immediately dimmed as pain

shot through my body, making my eyes heavy and head dizzy. But I wasn't down. I could still fight.

I pushed my legs forward, rushing to the far wall, farther away from Georgia and Ta'Boom, to where the vines had sunk their tendrils deep into the stone. I could see now how they sprouted across the stone pews and intermingled with the droning Ungas. With a roar of my own, I hacked down on an exposed vine, severing it with relative ease.

Ta'Boom howled.

The vines shook.

The Unga screamed. But the section of which I cut, all of their eyes returned to normal as they collapsed like marionettes whose strings had been cut.

"Three more," I said as wicked sneer carved itself across my face. "You're going down monkey-man!"

"Ta'Boom not be stopped!" He beat his chest back and forth as he spoke, but I saw it. I saw a little deflation, a rotting to the vine at his core. This was it. This was the trick. Sever the vines, then cut free the growth.

"Catch this!" Georgia cried out, taking the momentary distraction as a chance to pick up another chunk of flooring. She hurled it at Ta'Boom, who had to return his attention to her or suffer being struck by a half ton of stone.

"Thanks!" I cried out as I ran to the next section of vine.

Like the first, tendrils tried to stop me, inflicting poison. But just as with the first, I hacked them away. I did, however, have to drain a healing flask, as my hearts were getting dangerously low, as was my stamina. But I was saving that green juice for something extra special. I would need a full bar for what I was planning. I could carve through these basic vines on my own. I just needed to pace myself.

The ground shook once more. This time several of the

stones fell down, down, down into the darkness, leaving the floor looking more like a stretched chessboard, where the white squares were solid ground and the black squares, a pitfall. I needed to cross the whole room, but the two remaining vines were now moving into overdrive, sending shoots and thorny tendrils at me time and time again.

"I can't cross!" I called out to Georgia, looking at the gaping distance between the far wall and me.

"Ta'Boom win! Ta'Boom win!" Ta'Boom laughed aloud, his deep voice like that of a mountain slide, as he raised his arms in triumph. However, as he did so, I noticed that his fourth, vine-like arm was all but withered away, as if every slicing of the main four vines was causing the pervasive plant to deteriorate.

"Hey, Monkey man," I called out in a daring fit of unearned confidence. "Why do you only throw rocks at the girl? Scared of me?"

"Ta'Boom not scared of no one!" howled the masked, multi-armed gorilla. "Ta'Boom crush little man!"

"What are you doing?" shouted Georgia, clearly not thrilled with me taking the boss's attention away from her. And why wouldn't she be? We had a plan, and I was already messing it up.

"Trust me! I got this," I called back as Ta'Boom slammed his fists into another block of stone, wrenching it from the ground.

I ran toward him, the holes in the ground too large for me to span with a jump. I raised my shield, pouring all of my years of video game knowledge into the hope that the mechanics would work the same here and that we weren't bound by actual physics.

Ta'Boom hurled the stone at me just as I leapt from the

ground. Instead of crashing into me, splatting me like a bug, I ran across the surface of the stone, using the edge of it as a springboard to catapult me over the gap. I land with triumphant glee. Glee that was literally smacked off of my face as Ta'Boom backhanded me, sending my body flying through open space and into the far wall.

My heart containers dropped to one blinking heart, half filled with light. My vision was tunneled and flecked with red. I tried to get up, but my body was depleted of strength. That move alone had drained my stamina bar down to nothing.

It had been a risk, and it had not paid off.

"Ta'Boom crush!" the Unga Chieftain cackled, though it sounded like he was underwater to my busted ears.

Something warm and yellow permeated my body, drenching me in the most soothing sensation I believe I had ever experienced. My heart containers began to blink, one by one, as they filled and my vision focused. I whipped my head around to see Georgia dropped to one knee, her wand extended in my direction. She was out of FP and stamina now, though her hearts were still mostly filled. But if her FP was empty, that meant she couldn't use the gauntlets. She was a sitting duck, and without stamina, there was no way for her to use her Fleet Foot ability granted her by her magic boots.

"Ta'Boom win!"

"Enough!" I roared back. "Ta'Boom, you are sick. And I am about to carve the decay from your body!"

To my surprise, and relief, my outburst caused Ta'Boom a momentary pause. He stared at me through that mask, and though I could not see his actual eyes, I could feel them boring into me, measuring me.

Well, I hope he didn't like what he saw.

I ran at the vine in front of me, the vine Ta'Boom had inadvertently knocked me toward. I hacked it down with a swing of my sword. I did not stop, not as the poison splattered across my skin, not as tendrils and thorns shot my way, sticking into my arm and back, though I raised my shield against the majority of the onslaught. Ta'Boom roared and began hurling stones, but he was moving far slower now, and the stones did not fly as far nor as fast as before. I did give one cursory backwards glance at Georgia, just to make sure she was still okay. To my relief, she was drinking something, though I could not tell what it was. I couldn't recall which potions she had picked up from Crossroads Station. But whatever it was, a small glow started emanating from her body, soft and purple.

She would be fine, I told myself, turning my head back to the final vine. She would be okay.

With a final stride, I reached the putrid, thorny vine. I hacked into it with all my strength, cleaving the stinking thing in two. Ta'Boom let out a wail of agony. The last of pervaded Unga chanters fell silent. And then mayhem erupted.

Ta'Boom, no longer supported by the four vines, toppled over. As he collided with the ground, the remaining chunks of floor surrounding him gave way, falling into the abyss, leaving the now diminished boss atop a singular pillar that rose up from the depths, lying atop the altar.

Pressed against the wall, toes at the edge of the gaping hole, I looked between Georgia and the boss, the three of us making a perfect right angle, none able to reach the other.

"What do we do?" I called out, trying my best to keep the concern from my voice.

"Archy, I have an idea, but you're not going to like it," Georgia answered, rising to her feet, body now glowing like one of the lightning bugs we had captured.

I looked down into the nothingness before me, my stomach doing somersaults.

"I don't think it could be worse than this," I said back with a laugh that was a little more shaky than I wanted it to be.

"Ta'Boom's body is saturated with Esoterica. If you could get me any piece of his armor or something, I could use it to form another needle. Then, I could send that over to you and you could ride it back. I can keep it up for enough time for that. I think."

"You think?" I answered, voice rising an octave in pitch.

"Well, I am more concerned with the first part of the plan than the second?"

"Oh?" I said.

"I have one more stone. I can chuck it between you two, but you're going to have to jump," Georgia said with chagrin.

I knew it. I knew that was going to be part of it. And in truth, I had known it from before. I had been holding my stamina for something just like that, and a combo move I had been mulling over in my head.

"Okay," I said.

"Okay?" Georgia's voice held a little more surprise than I would have liked, not really boosting my confidence in the moment.

"Ya, let's do it," I called back as I pulled a flask filled with green juice from my bandolier and downing it in a single, long gulp. "Hurry, before I change my mind."

"Ta. Boom. Get. Up."

"You're right," Georgia said with haste as she hefted a massive sandstone block. "Here it comes."

The next seconds happened in slow motion. The stone sailed from Georgia's hand, hurtling through open space. Ta'Boom, true to his word, began to rise up, his hulking body turning in my direction.

I drove my heel into the wall behind me and pushed off with a bound filled with strength I had never known before. Wind whipped at my face as I soared over the chasm, bringing tears to my eyes. But I did not doubt myself. Not when my boots collided with the stone, not when I took two leaping bounds, and not when I leapt directly into the opening arms of Ta'Boom.

Running Strike!
Slicing Edge!

COMBO MOVE!

I saw the text fill my vision just as I felt my sword cleave the growth Ta'Boom's body in blinding flash of light. I felt both my stamina and my FP drain in a sickening whoosh of exertion and power. But the blow landed.

Ta'Boom collapsed once more. This time, however, the plant that had been attached to him turned into pixilated ash, falling away into dust.

Victory Achieved!
Boss Defeated!

Sanctuary of the Earth Totem has been cleansed.

At the announcement of those words the door behind Georgia fell away and Treo came shooting inward, chiming and dinging as she fluttered around Georgia. At the same time, four large stone windows ground open above me, allowing light to flood the ziggurat. Along with the light came a burst of fresh air, so sweet and clean, I almost choked on it.

"Ta'Boom. Free."

I looked down at the Unga who lay upon the altar before me. He no longer looked hulking, but emaciated, his body a husk of what it had once been. He raised a hand to the bronze mask that covered him and tenderly removed it. The face it revealed was proud and handsome, for an Unga.

"Ta'Boom is freed from darkness," he said, looking at me with the biggest, brightest eyes that were brimming with tears. "So long the night in Ta'Boom's mind has been. Thank you for letting me see day one last time."

"Hey buddy, you're going to be okay," I said, getting choked up in the moment.

"Ta'Boom is okay, little warrior," Ta'Boom said as he let his head fall back against the altar. He let out a low chuckle. "Free."

"Listen, we got Trounce out. He is going to Unga Villiage. We can get you out too," I said, panic and fear beginning to swell in my chest, making it hard to talk. I didn't know this guy, other than the fact he was trying to crush my two seconds ago.

Ding!

"Archy?" Treo said quietly as she rested upon my shoulder.

"Faerie?" Ta'Boom asked, his eyes losing their focus.

"One travels beyond the vale? Is light coming back to Neverwhere?"

"*Mighty Chieftain, the light is coming back,*" Treo said softly. "*But we need to your sacred Totem to help it return.*"

"Take Totem," Ta'Book said as he slid his hand down the altar and took hold of the now clean and shining jade figurine. "Take and do good. Bring back light. Save Unga."

With those words, Chieftain Ta'Boom handed me the jade figurine.

Earth Totem!

When the Five Forces left Neverwhere, they swore to leave the means for the various nations to defend themselves. Mightiest of those were the Unga, proud and strong. To them was given the Earth Totem, representing the balance between life and living things, the strength of the earth and the bounty found therein.

Quest Completed.
Find the Earth Totem!

Quest Update.
Collect the Three Lost Totems!
1 of 3 collected.

Ta'Boom let out a sigh, gentle and serene, before smiling at me one last time. His body turned to pixilated ash. A small *thud* resonated through the silent sanctuary as the bronze mask fell to the altar, clattering a few times before falling still. The mask, and the large, purple flame of a boss level Soulfire were all that remained of the once-mighty

Chieftain. Yet, as his remains floated away, a ray of light shone down upon the mask and I heard his voice calling from above me, saying.

"Brave hero, you have freed me from the curse of darkness, but more importantly, you have saved Unga Jungle. Even now, the curse that laid waste to our home is falling away. Thank you."

"Did you hear that?" Treo asked, zooming up into the lights above me.

"Yeah, I did," I answered, fighting back the well of emotion that rose inside me.

The ziggurat seemed to groan with the passing of its defender. The walls shook and what remained of floor began to slowly crumble, but that was not the worst of it. The pillar upon which the dais was raised, and the altar sat, the one on which I stood, began to sway.

"Archy!" Georgia called out.

Right! I needed something with a strong pulse of Esoteric—the mask! I took up Ta'Boom's mask, which seemed to shimmer with a deep, resonating power. Turning about, I hurled the mask over the open space. It flew with a speed I had not expected, nearly knocking Georgia square in the mouth. Luckily, as my strength had increased, so had her reflexes. She also had those stone gauntlets, which protected her hands from physical damage.

"Sorry," I called back sheepishly.

"Don't you worry yourself about me, Boy Scout." Georgia called back with a smirk. She then did something that utterly blew my mind. She absorbed the mask. It was the strangest thing. It turned a deep red, became fuzzy, and then went into her. "This is gonna come hard and fast! I am going to shoot it past you, it'll bounce of that wall back there, and headin' back to me. You just catch hold of it and it should get you back to me. You hear?"

My mind raced to keep up with her words and my heart flipped at the thought of snatching a gigantic, rocketing needle out of the sky and riding it over the gaping hole before me. But, another shake of the ground and sway of the pillar reminded me my options were limited.

"Yeah, I got you," I said, my voice lacking the confidence I was trying to force into it.

"Get ready!" Georgia said as she pulled out her wand and began to move it about in a perplexing pattern. "One! Two!"

I turned around, quickly grabbing hold of massive, purple Soulfire. Immediately it absorbed into my chest, though a few errant flames darted through open sky over into Georgia.

"Three!"

My HUD flashed up a proverbial wall of text, starting with:

Purple Soulfire!
Wow! You have uncovered your first Purple Soulfire. This is one of the rarest forms of Soulfire and is typically only found after encountering an immensely difficult foe!
400% to XP
30% to the stat of your choosing
4 points to award to stat of your choosing

RARE ITEM DROP!
Blessed Dewdrop!
Unique Item Drop!
Shield Upgrade!

Unique Skill Drop!
Shield Bash!

Uncommon, Wearable Item Drop!
Necklace of the Chieftain
+20% to Strength
+1 to Charisma
This item as a uniqu-

"Agh!" I cried out as the needle shot past me, causing the silvery text to blur momentarily.

Ting!

I mentally wiped the eyes free of the HUD as I turned on my heels and began running toward the edge of the dais. I could sense the needle rushing up behind me. I leapt, just as the pillar shook a final time before collapsing into the darkness below. With a hope and a prayer, I thrust my hand outward, pleading that it would find the haft of the needle.

My fingers grasped cool metal, and I clung on for dear life, my feet being whipped behind my body as both the needle and I began to dip at an alarming rate downward.

"Oh no!" I heard Georgia shout as I saw that my trajectory was rapidly turning to a miss.

With a bone-rattling thud, I struck the side of chasm that was forming, the needle driving its pointed head deep into the stone. It took all the strength and fortitude I had to maintain my grip on the needle, but I could see my stamina bar rapidly depleting.

Fear filled my heart and clouded my brain.

This was it. This was how I was going to go.

I had just fought, and defeated, a four-armed, colossal gorilla that had elemental magic. But this, this was how I was going to go out. Falling into a hole because I couldn't hold onto a needle or pull myself out. If only I had the time to allocated some of those levels to my strength or even equipped that necklace.

Something hard and rough latched on to the back of my neck, wrapping around my bandolier. When I turned my eyes upward, I could not believe my eyes. Georgia was floating above me. Well, not really floating per se. Her left hand was gripping the lip of the chasm, enlarged to humorous proportions, and her right hand was grappling with my shirt and bandolier. Suddenly, the needle vanished. But, instead of falling to my demise, Georgia hurled me up over the lip of the sanctuary floor and onto solid ground, before she pulled her own self back up over the edge.

"Well that was close," she said as she slapped her hands together a few times, as if she were knocking the dust away from her already shrunken gauntlets.

I just stared at her, legs sprawled out, with eyes that must have been filled with as much terror as humanly possible. I tried to mutter a thank you, but I couldn't get a single word out, just a few incoherent mumbles.

"I'm sure whatever it is you're trying to say is lovely, but we need to get up out of here before this whole thing comes tumblin' down," Georgia said with a smile, and if I wasn't mistaken, a slight reddening to her cheeks and neck.

"Right," I said, my senses finally coming back to me in a wave.

The ziggurat chose that moment to shake violently. All of the Unga that had been under the spell suddenly awoke with a myriad of yips and yelps of dismay. They, unlike us, however had those things that allowed them to vanish. One by one they popped away from this place.

"Wait!" I cried out, grabbing Georgia by the arm as I mentally opened my Item Menu.

"What? What's wrong?" Georgia asked, raising her fists up again as if she were about to fight.

"I have an idea!" I said. "Ah, here it is!"

Necklace of the Chieftain
+20% to Strength
+1 to Charisma
This item as a unique ability.
The Unga, renowned for their abilities to work Powerstones into the natural and supernatural, long ago found a way to travel via Way Points. This necklace allows the wearer to traverse between three different Unga Points: Unga Village, Ziggurat of the Earth, and Unga Station.
Where would you like to equip this item?
Yes! Or, no...

I mentally pressed the *Yes!* button as the floor began to tremble violently.

This item requires 1 FP to utilize.
Do you wish to travel to a Way Point?
Yes! Or, no...

My frustration grew alongside my fear, as now the whole of the ziggurat was shaking and crumbling. Georgia looked at me with terror, her eyes filled with questioning. Surely she was wondering why we were just standing around instead of trying to find a way out.

Yes!

Where would you li—

I mentally slammed onto the button that said Unga Village as I pulled Georgia tight against me. It said wearer. I only hoped if I was holding her tight enough this was going to work.

A low *pop* filled my ears as pressure like diving to the deep end of a pool flooded over me. Light bent around me and before I could do anything else, Georgia and I vanished from existence.

Pop!

I tumbled to the earth as something collided into my back in the process. I rolled, and it rolled on top of me. Tangled and flopping, I finally could make out light and trees, ferns and birds. And on top of me was Georgia.

Before I could do or say anything, Georgia took me by either side of my face and planted a kiss right on my lips. I was so utterly shocked I did not know what to do. I had never even held a girl's hand before, much less kissed one.

Abruptly, Georgia pulled hers lips from mine, her face flushed and her eyes wide. "Oh my gosh, I am so—I don't. I didn't. I—"

I could not act. I could not think. My brain seemed to be short circuiting and all I could do was just stare back at her with wide eyes.

"*Wow! You to smashed into each other hard!*" Treo chimed. "*Your faces were really crushed together. Are you okay?*"

At Treo's innocent inquiry, Georgia's face was set ablaze with red.

I felt awful for her, but my mind was still so focused on the fact that I had just been kissed I could not form a single word. Instead, I did, perhaps, the worst possible thing I could have done. I laughed.

"What? Why are you laughing? I thought you would be hurt?"

Sure. We were hurt. Both Georgia and I were muddled with scrapes, bruises, and dirt. But, I had just been kissed a girl. In that moment, to my teenage brain, I am pretty sure I would have fought Chieftain Ta'Boom by myself for another chance like that.

"We're fine," I said trying my best to both reassure the worrying wisp and show that I was not upset with Georgia, who looked to be on the border of tears. I needed to save this. I needed to act now. "Hey, I, uh—"

I was cut off before I could formulate my reassurance by the beating of familiar wings and a descending shadow.

"Squawk! It is I, Briggaforth, of the Court of Lord Erle'em Ud'din Nidlahm, Lord of the Wood Elves and Once-Sovereign King of Neverwhere. Glory be to his name! I have come at the turning of the shadow to help aid your return to where you need to go. Where would you have me take you?"

Pulling up the tribal necklace that hung about my neck, I looked between the giant pelican and Georgia, "This didn't have the strength to get us all the way to Unga Village. Could you take us there?"

To her credit, Georgia collected herself, casting me one last apologetic glance. I, unsure what else to do, rubbed at the back of my neck. I needed to get back to Elder Luk Luk Ci Ci, to tell him of the fall of their Chieftain and the cleansing of Unga Jungle, though I was almost certain that all would aware of that second part by now.

"Well, best be on our way," Georgia said as she elbowed me playfully, though not as hard as she had before. "You know how Brigg is."

"Yeah," I said once more, clearing my head with a shake. "Yeah, let's go."

Chapter Eighteen:
I Get Linked

UNGA VILLAGE BLARED with drums and clamoring life as we climbed off of Brigg's back. Cymbals clattered and clanged as the mechanical primates danced and gyrated to the primal beats of the musician's jubilant strains. I nearly laughed out loud as I saw Elder Luk Luk Ci Ci dancing about, face painted and flowers strung into his hair, holding hands with several of the younger Unga children. I was swept up into the ruckus almost immediately, the Unga lifting Georgia and I over their heads like we were crowd surfing at a rock concert. We were moved effortlessly, drifting across the tops of Ungas until we were finally lowered before the feet of Trounce.

Unlike the rest of the Unga, Trounce did not seem to be taking part in the revelry. His face was unpainted and heavy. His eyes were filled with sadness that bespoke the truth we had not yet told. I felt the glee and joy that had built in my own heart grow dim.

"Mighty warriors," Trounce said with a loud but solemn proclamation that ceased the revelry around us. "You have done a mighty deed for our people. We owe you a life-debt."

The Unga all began slamming their fists against their chest at this statement. Trounce raised a hand, calming the masses.

"But we have suffered a great shame and a great loss," Trounce continued. "We have lost our Chieftain, and we have lost our sacred totem, entrusted to us."

"Do not speak so, Mighty Trounce," said Elder Luk Luk Ci Ci as he ambled forward, not deigning to pluck the flowers from his hair. "We have won a great victory, and that we must be proud of. Our warriors returned to us, telling of the great victory. It is because of these two so many of ours return home at last. Be happy in your heart."

"How can I be happy, Elder? We are without our Chieftain and we are without our Totem," Trounce asked with a trembling voice.

"If I may," I said awkwardly as I held out my hand and I mentally opened my inventory.

Rare Item
Earth Totem

The jade figurine appeared out of thin air into the palm of my hand. No sooner had I revealed the totem to Trounce then the Massive Unga let out a howling screech that nearly shattered my eardrums.

"Home!" his screeched morphed into a singular word. "Home! Our Totem is home!"

"How you did this thing?" asked Elder Luk Luk Ci Ci with wide eyes.

Apparently, the Ungas that escaped the ziggurat had not seen me take the Earth Totem into my inventory and so would have had no way of knowing I had rescued it. All they would have seen was their fallen chieftain and the collapsing of their sacred sanctuary.

"It was on the altar, I just put it in my inventory," I answered unabashedly, not enjoying the heaps of attention that were being levied upon me at the moment.

Luk Luk's eyes widened further. "When we met in Lord Erle'em's Court, we Unga could not have known that he had gifted you the ability to hold such Sacred things."

"What do you mean?" I asked, extending the Totem to the Elder.

"No! No!" Luk Luk said with haste. "We do not touch! The power is too much for Unga. The very Force of Earth is in that Totem. We bow to your strength, Mighty Archy!"

In a moment that surely must have been meant as a great honor, but to me was of such pure embarrassment I wished a mountain could have hid me, all of the Unga around me fell to their knees and prostrated themselves before Georgia and I.

"Well, you don't see that every day," whispered Georgia under her breath as she leaned in close.

"Yeah," I answered, my face burning with heat.

Luk Luk rose back up once more and clasped me on the arm, the force of his massive hand nearly taking me off my feet. "You are more than meets the eye, Archy of Earth. You have the Unga's gratitude. Take this Totem and bring back the Light with Lord Erle'em. A new dawn shall rise upon Neverwhere once more, says Luk Luk. A new dawn at long last."

"But what of the Unga?" asked Trounce as he too rose to his feet. "What shall we do without our sacred totem and without a chieftain to guide us?"

"Our Jungle is cleansed and the Light must return, we can share our totem today," said Luk Luk Ci Ci with a small smile. A smile that grew wider and wider with excitement. "But for chieftain, I declare Mighty Trounce to be our new Chieftain. Second to our great Ta'Boom, Light take him home. Who amongst the Unga stands opposed to this?"

Silence fell across Unga Village.

"Then it is declared," Luk Luk said as he turned his eyes on Archy and extended a long finger to the necklace that hung about his neck. "May I have that?"

"Uh, of course," I said, unsure what else to say.

With a courteous nod, Luk Luk Ci Ci removed the necklace from around my neck. I felt the loss of the necklace acutely, the immediate drop in stats impacting me in ways I did not expect. My hands felt heavy and my eyes watered slightly. To keep from dropping the Earth Totem, I returned it to its place in my inventory system.

"I proclaim you, Chieftain Trounce," Elder Luk Luk Ci Ci said as he slid the necklace over Trounce's head. "Unga!"

"Unga!" Roared the crowd in approval.

"So it is!" cried out Elder Luk Luk to a thunderous bout of applause that lead into further beating of drums and dancing.

The rest of the day passed with so much partying and music that my head began to ache from the constant barrage of noise. Just as dusk was settling, I slipped out of the ruckus, sneaking back to my room in the inn. The silent stillness of the small room was perhaps the most welcoming sensation I had ever experienced; thanks to the wildness of the day I had just endured.

I unfastened my bandolier, allowing the leather strap that contained now mostly empty glass flasks, as well as my sword and shield, to fall to the ground. I wasn't worried about it breaking. I literally just had a temple floor thrown at me. It would be fine.

Speaking of flasks, I realized I was going to need to brew a few potions before I left. Thankfully, this little room had a small workbench with a cutting board, mixing pot, and what looked like a mad scientist's glass chemistry set, along with a Powerstone fueled burner. I opened my inventory, turning to my craftable items, selecting the necessary items to begin working.

Knock knock!

I turned my head, facing the door that I had left open. Georgia stood in the hallway, one of her knees turned in, her body still covered in dirt and muck. I must look equally disheveled, I mused to myself. I nodded my head, beckoning her to come in wordlessly.

Blessedly, neither of us spoke for a long few moments, the continued silence not one of awkwardness, but understanding. We had just survived something neither of us ever could have imagined just hours ago. Were we in shock? Maybe. But we were alive, and stronger for it. That realization bolstered my confidence enough to speak.

"You were pretty incredible in there," I said as I began to chop up some red berries I had collected from my scavenging, something I always found myself doing when I had the opportunity.

Georgia shook her head and let out a subtle scoff before adding, "This is crazy, you know that, right?"

"Yeah," I answered, allowing myself to softly laugh along with her.

Another long bout of silence.

"Have you leveled up yet?" Georgia asked, still not looking directly at me as she scooped a bunch of dust from a little pouch into the black-iron cauldron.

I blinked. I hadn't. I hadn't even thought of it. But now that Georgia had said something, I could feel the burning heat of not one, but two very powerful Soulfires blazing within me.

"I didn't figure," She said, elbowing me softly. "I wanted to wait, talk to you before I did again. I got some from both of the fights, and some other weird technicalities as well. I figured, we worked pretty dang good together and if we are going to continue together, we need to make sure our stats and abilities continue to line up."

"That is a really good point," I said, feeling dumb that I hadn't thought about that.

"But, I don't know if I'll even need you anymore now that I got these," Georgia said with a playful laugh, holding up her hands, the rocky, fingerless gloves, giving her a fierceness that I hadn't seen before today.

"You really were handy with those," I said, nudging her back.

"Ugh! Not a pun," Georgia rolled her eyes dramatically. "I thought you were above those."

"Nope," I said with a confidence I did not recognize. "As a matter of fact, I am quite skilled with both puns and limericks."

"Oh, Archy," said Georgia with a chuckle. "What am I going to do with you?"

There was something about the way she said my name that made my stomach drop and butterflies fill my chest. I was at once acutely aware of our proximity and filled with the memories of that kiss. I looked over at her, her attention turned back to her endless bag, searching for something.

Was this the right time? Should I kiss her back? Tell her I hadn't meant not to? I wished I was like my dad, he was so brave and bold. I wasn't either of those things.

Before I could drum up the courage to act, Georgia pulled out what looked like strawberries, excepted they were clustered like grapes. She handed them to me as she reached her hand back into her backpack, arm sinking impossibly deep, past the elbow, until she retrieved that spellbook with two chains of gold instead of iron wrapped about it.

"Says I need to be at an Esoteric Level of Fifteen or higher to open this," Georgia said as the book thudded down, abruptly concluding my moment to act. "I am currently at natural Nine plus the +3 from using Lucky Glace. I was hoping to put more into FP, but I guess I'll need to burn three more levels to get to opening this grimoire."

"How...how did you learn all this so fast?" I asked, totally bamboozled once again at Georgia's seemingly innate knowledge of how the magic system of this world worked.

"Lord Erle'em, when I was on the other side with him, he told me to get as many spellbooks and grimoires as I could. It isn't like it is on earth, once you open one, you just know it," Georgia said with a shrug. "I just haven't been able to open this guy here and I've been wanting to for days now."

"Why?" I asked, curiosity getting the better of me. "What is so important about that one?"

"I don't know," said Georgia. "It just seemed cool."

"Works for me," I said, standing up. "You want to go first or me?"

"What do you mean?" she asked.

"Leveling up," I said as I stretched. Georgia's eyes widened a little bit as I did so and I felt an immediate rush of embarrassment wash over me unexpectedly. Had I done something wrong?

"You've, uh, gotten a little stronger," she said with a wink.

"What do you mean?"

"You've got a vein in your arm now, that wasn't there before," she said, pointing to my extended arm.

Mortified, I dropped my arms to my side, wishing I had been wearing a hoodie or anything.

"Don't be like that," she said, elbowing me a little harder, like she did before she had kissed me. "I don't mind it."

"Well," I said, fumbling for anything at all. "Your eyes are more sparkly."

That did it. I felt something akin to fire burn up the back of my neck, so sudden and overbearing was the rush of tingling mortification.

To my surprise, Georgia didn't laugh at me. She didn't run away or poke fun. She just shook her head and said, "I just don't understand you sometimes, Boy Scout."

"Well, I, uh," I stammered, trying my best to salvage the conversation, though I was pretty certain there was virtually no hope for that now.

"Why don't you go first, we don't even know how many levels you have," Georgia said, saving me from further humiliation.

"Right," I said, trying to act confident once more, though this time it was quite obviously feigned.

I threw open my HUD, allowing it to encompass most of the room. Lines, bars, and stats flooded my vision.

Archy Lawrence

Level 12

Health Points - 8

Focus Points - 3

Endurance - 6

Strength - 5

Dexterity - 6

Esoteric - 1

Speed - 4

Charisma - 3

I was surprised to see 8 Heart Containers instead of 12, even though my Health Points were at 12. As I hovered over it, as smaller tab. I mentally selected it. The following words filtered before my eyes:

Hearts containers progressively become more challenging to build as levels increase. At your current level it takes 2 Health Points to increase 1 Heart Container. At Level 14 it will require 4 Health Points to increase 1 Heart Container.

I filed that information away and turned to my attention to a tab titled: *Available Status Points and Upgrades.* From there, I saw that I had leveled up five times since I had last checked. I also had those unique points already directly added to Charisma from the necklace removed, dropping me from 5 to 3.

An errant thought popped into my head. Before I could squash it, I could not help but wonder: what if the only reason Georgia had kissed me was because of that? And now, I no longer had the necklace.

A sudden urge to drop all five available stat points into Charisma struck out of nowhere. What was I thinking? I needed to be practical. How was Charisma going to help us in a fight for our lives?. Besides, looking at Georgia now, her stats lined up beside her, she had enough Charisma for the two of us.

"I have some stat bonuses to Strength, Endurance, and Dexterity, especially when coupled with my Skill Attacks," I said as I perused my own stats, not wanting to make eye contact with Georgia during this moment. "What if I put one into Speed, two into Focus, my FP is too low for my liking. I could then increase at 1:1 ratio my Dex and Strength or pour it all into either?"

"Well," said Georgia as she stared at her own HUD, her face screwed up in deep concentration, making little wrinkles form at her nose. "Maybe Strength isn't as important with my gauntlets. I'd say Dex or Speed actually."

"Good point," I conceded, feeling strangely emasculated at her casual dismissal of my Strength stat. Hadn't she just commented on me getting a little bigger? Wait? What was I doing? I wasn't becoming one of 'those guys' was I?

Hurriedly, I moved my stat points around:

+2 to Speed

+2 to Focus

+1 to Dexterity

The rush of energy that flowed through me nearly took my breath away. All of the colors in the room seemed to suddenly become more vibrant, I could sense the dust motes that floated lazily in the twilight rays that soaked the room through the open window. The air became sweet and heady, the aroma of honey and fresh fruit wafting in from the celebration outside. There was something else too, something like fresh cut grass after a rainstorm or the refreshing scent of Spring after the chill of winter dissipates.

I turned about trying to take it all in, literally feeling my body adjust to the newfound increases of my physiological makeup. The floor felt more solid, though I could feel a pulse of nature under the soles of my shoes. There was a thrum of living things, a motion to the world around me I had been blind to up to this moment. And now that I could feel it, I felt as if I needed to gasp for air.

"You alright?" Georgia caught me as I stumbled about. I hadn't noticed how the green in her eyes turned slightly brown near the irises, nor had I realized that she had more freckles on the right cheek than the left, twelve to be exact.

I blinked.

"You look like you're about to be sick," Georgia said, her voice filled with concern. I could see her throat bob and a bit of sweat mixing with dust on her brow, like a little stream collecting particles as it flowed downward.

"Maybe level a single stat at a time," I gasped, my lungs struggling to keep up with the amount of air that was flowing in and out of me.

"Noted," Georgia laughed as she helped me onto the edge of the bed. I could feel the fibers in the sheets, coarse now to my touch, every minor fray a mountain of texture. "Well, I plan on mainly leveling FP and Arcane. I'm not sure what that will look like, so just be ready. I have seven stat points to divvy out."

"Seven? How did you get seven stat points?" I blurted out.

"Bonus points for using my head for more than a battering ram I'd guess." she said with a wink as she stood up and aligned herself on the floor. She took out the three grimoires she had bought from Crossroads Station and another one I had not seen her acquire, laying them out on the floor around her. Next, she pulled out the wand Lord Erle'em had given her, as well as various items she had looted from the ziggurat and arranged them in between the books, forming a triangle. Lastly, Georgia retrieved a bit of chalk from her bag, drawing straight lines of white, followed by curved lines connecting the circle with the triangle, herself stationed in the center.

"This might get weird," Georgia said as she looked over her shoulder with a sheepish grin.

I wanted to protest, saying this seemed a little weird or a bit much. But I couldn't find the strength to do so. I did, however, make a mental note to never upgrade in the field. It was too dangerous. The only benefit I could see out of that was, when you did level up your Stat Points, it auto-refilled your HP, FP, and Stamina bars. Speaking of those, my FP was starting to look nice now, five hashed lines now appearing alongside a slider that had not been there before. I assumed that had to do the percentage increases from special abilities, as my Stamina bar had the same.

Whoosh!

My eyes shot up, unable to comprehend this sight in front of me.

A pillar of light had shot up from the floor. The books that had been laid open were now hovering in the air, rotating slowly around the place where Georgia had been standing. Fear ripped at my heart, but when I tried to get up, a secondary, concussive burst blasted reverberated through the small room, sending me flying into the wall. I flopped back onto the bed, eyes blurred from the light.

Georgia let out a scream of panic.

There was no way I was going to let whatever was happening to her continue. Something was obviously wrong. Drawing on what strength I could, I pushed against the torrent of wind and crackling light that was cascading outward from the pillar of light. Every step felt as if my legs were made of lead and my feet had been set in concrete. Despite this, I pushed out, extending a hand into the light to pull Georgia free.

Heat seared my skin as my hand disappeared into the column of winding lights. Pain like that of a razor blade slicing up my fingers, palms, and forearms burst across my flesh. I almost pulled back, but just before I did my hand met Georgia's. With an effort of will and strength beyond anything I had known before, I latched onto her hand and pulled her free.

That moment, the exact millisecond, her body left the pillar of light, it vanished with a horrifyingly subtle *pop*. the books fell to the floor in a clatter. However, all of the items, wand included, were gone. And in Georgia's hand, a scepter of gold with an emerald gemstone set in its head remained.

"You were right about the leveling," Georgia muttered under her labored breaths. "That was rougher than two porcupines sliding down a sandpaper waterslide."

I burst out laughing. Georgia joined in after me, both of us just laying on the floor in each others arms, letting go of all of the weirdness that had been and would be in this place called Neverwhere. Our laughter was cut short when Georgia took up my hand.

"Oh my gosh, Archy, your hand," she said with a voice seeped in remorse.

I looked down at my right hand. It was covered in what looked almost like cybernetic scarring, a faint greenish-blue glow to them. The shock of seeing it only caused me momentary alarm, because when I looked at Georgia, actually looked at her, fear for myself vanished in an instant. She had the same markings, not just on her hand that I had taken, but all up her arms. I could even see some of them on her neck, peeking up from that tattered collar of her shirt. And her eyes, they were even brighter green, positively radiant with light. It was as I was staring into them, that I noticed the missing clover leaf in her right eye.

"You're missing a clover petal," I said dumbly.

"Yeah, don't you remember? I took a nasty hit," she said, her voice somewhere between fear and feigned confidence she used every time things got hard or scary. "But hey, it worked, didn't it?"

"Yeah, I guess so. Oh, and you got them same markings as me, except, kind of everywhere," I said, moving my hand in an awkward gesture to encompass everything.

Georgia shot up, running across the room and staring into the mirror. "This. is. So freaking cool! My Pawpaw is gonna flip! I always wanted a tattoo!" Georgia's voice was brimming with excitement and pride as she looked over her arms, hands, and even pulled up the front of her shirt to look at her stomach. And though I couldn't see, I was almost certain I knew she bore the markings there too, judging by the wicked smile that flashed across her face.

"You know, it's not even legal for us to get tattoos yet," I said matter-of-factly.

"Don't be a killjoy! We just fought a four armed mechanical monkey. I don't really care about the rules anymore." Georgia turned about as she lowered her shirt. She walked back over to where we had been sitting together and picked up the scepter she had forged in that pillar of light. "Now this. This is going to be fun. I have three new spells and plenty of FP."

She did in fact have plenty of FP. That wasn't all. My mouth almost fell open as I looked at her stats:

Georgia Stoddard

Level 14

~Human Sorceress~

Health Points - 9

Focus Points - 7

Endurance - 3

Strength - 3

Dexterity - 5

Esoteric - 15

Speed - 4

Charisma - 8

"I literally do not understand how you are leveling so fast," I gawked. Despite my humorous tone, I really did feel like I was being cheated. What did it take to get a class? Was I really that useless that I could not gain my first with Georgia moving now to her second? "It is not fair!"

"Hush," Georgia said as she shoulder checked me. Despite her playful action, I could see the color rising in her cheeks once more, barely perceivable, even with my added stats.

"Ooooh!" Treo chimed as she zipped into the room, showering us with sparkles of azure and white. *"A Linking Charm! How did you manage that?"*

"A what?" Georgia and I asked in unison.

Treo dove onto the back of my hand. As her light mixed with the strange markings, I felt a jolt of power. My expression was mirrored in Georgia's face as her eyes widened, then began darting back and forth as if she were reading something-

You have initiated the Charm, Linking!

You will need a faerie and 3 FP

You have:

A Wisp

3 FP

Do you wish to finalize, Linking with, GEORGIA STODDARD?

Yes! Or, no.

Mentally, I tapped the yes icon. Upon doing this, Treo darted back and forth, bouncing off of our marked hands. When I realized what she was doing, I felt my jaw slacken once more. Treo was carrying tiny strands of light, weaving them between Georgia and I, and with each tether I felt a strange sense of connection to Georgia that went beyond anything I had ever experienced before.

"Get ready!" Treo chimed as pulled the last two strands tight, exuding a tremendous level of strain, that caused her tiny body to tremble.

You have completed the Charm, Linking!
You can now communicated with with, GEORGIA STODDARD, over distances via scrollwork. You can now speak with, GEORGIA STODDARD, over greater distances as if they were present. You can now pass +1 Heart Container to, GEORGIA STODDARD, for a limited time. To increase time allotted and number of Heart Containers, Linking must be upgraded.

This is a Complex Charm.

This is your first, Complex Charm.

You have completed your first, Complex Charm.
+1 to Esoteric

"This is weird." Georgia's voice rang in my head.
"Wow! How did you—" I thought back.
"Agh!"

"Oh no..."

"Does this mean?"

Ding

"You can activate and deactivate the charm by pressing on the center marking and willing 1 FP into the mark. Only the initiator is required to produce the FP. The receiver will feel a vibration, alerting them of an incoming message or request to speak. They can choose to accept or decline. If declined, the initiator will receive their FP back," Treo said matter-of-factly. *"This is how most faeries and Elves communicate. I did not realize humans could do so. This is so exciting, I'm about to burst! Perhaps we could form a bond next time, when we level up the Charm?"*

Georgia and I looked at each other, both our thoughts running together into one pool. And at the bottom of that pool was the shared notion that neither of us were ready to have a faerie bounding around in and out thoughts and conversations at any given time. Thankfully, Georgia spoke up before it became awkward.

"You know, if we do find the means to level it up, that is a good thought."

"I am glad you agree! This will only help me in my aid of you on your journey!"

"I'm going to shut off the link," I sent mentally to Georgia.

"Okay," she sent back, a relief to her thoughts that was palpable. "I didn't want to be rude. But this is kind of weird and invasive."

"Yeah, my thoughts exactly," I said dismissively, before I could allow any more feelings to bubble up to the surface.

Do you wish to sever the Link?

Ye-

I pressed yes before it even had time to finish scrolling out the silvery, looping text. There was a subtle *pop* and my thoughts became my own once more. I wish it wouldn't have hurt so bad to see the relief on Georgia's face, but at the same time, I was equally grateful not to have her in my own head. What if she knew about how much I was thinking of her and her eyes and...

"Hey, Boy Scout, you ready to go?"

I snapped my head up, "What?"

"I've leveled up, have three new spells - well, technically four if you count the linking charm - and a desire to test them out," Georgia said with a smile. "What do you say we try and catch the midnight train out of the jungle?. I am about tired of sweating."

"Could we at least get cleaned up first?" I asked, the exhaustion of the past few days returning as the thoughts of going once more struck me. "Maybe sleep a little?"

"Ugh, fine," Georgia said impatiently as she slung her backpack over her shoulder. "But hey, I want to go at first light. I am itching to try out this one called Thunderstrike!"

"First thing," I said reassuringly. "I just need some rest."

"Alright, Boy Scout," Georgia said with a roll of her eyes as she shut the door behind her.

Ding!

"I noticed you have yet to select a class," Treo chimed, nearly causing me to jump out of my skin. *"You have several available to you now."*

I turned about to face the wisp. This. This was what I was waiting for. Admittedly, I was a little perturbed at how long it had taken, and ashamedly, I was also jealous of Georgia's aptitude with this new world. From what I had seen today, she hadn't only been able to gain her first class, but increase from Mage to Sorceress. Though I did not understand the finer details, that had not gone unnoticed by me. Excitement began to swell within me, pushing away the impending tide of weariness that was pressing against my will to stay upright. I was exhausted, but I wasn't about to pass up the opportunity to gain my first class.

"Ah! So I take it you are ready?" Treo mused.

"Yes!" I nearly shouted the word in my eagerness to begin.

"One's Class is very important, and the chose of such should not be taken lightly. I will take you on a journey, to a place where you can make your first transition. Be aware, you are only allowed three transitions, each one impacting the next in ways that can be unforeseen. Are you sure you are ready?

"Come on, Treo." My words were fraught with impatience.

"Just making sure," Treo said with a bob that sent a cascade of azure sparkles all over my body. *"What is done next cannot be undone."*

"Hey, why do I feel so—"

My words were cut short as I fell through the floor at an alarming rate. I fell through the floor, the canopy in which Unga Village was set, through the leaf-strewn jungle floor, colors and shapes whipping past my eyes, melding into a blur. I fell until I landed on a thin lake, not unlike where Lord Erle'em had trained me.

Chapter Nineteen:
I Get Classy

"You have to warn me next time," I began complaining, but stopped short as my eyes focused and Treo came into view. And she was unlike anything I had ever seen before.

The towering faerie smiled a knowing smile as she dusted off her rather distracting dress. Like Lord Erle'em, Treo did not take the same form in this place. Unlike Lord Erle'em, she was far more glamorous. Her golden skin seemed to glisten, covered in trails of azure sparkles. She was about twelve feet tall. And, well, she looked like a goddess with enormous dragonfly wings sprouting from her back.

"How did you...why?"

"*Cat got your tongue, Archy?*" Treo laughed, her voice less chiming and more lustrous in this mirror realm. "*This is my inner form. As you make your first choice in class, you will release your inner form as well, building upon it as you level.*"

"I won't look like—" I started, but then bit off my words in embarrassment.

"*Like me? Ha! No, as you are not any of the subrace of Faerie. Some classes are only linked to races, while others are not. Like Georgia, any of the sentient beings of Neverwhere can level Esoteric and journey the path of the magic,*" Treo explained. "*But you, you have not elected that path, and it would require a tremendous amount of time and levels for you to journey that way. I would suggest one of the following three classes to begin with.*"

Three pillars of light burst forth from the water in front of me, one gold, one orange, and one green. In the first pillar, a set of knightly armor floated, just above the ground with an enormous towershield next to it. In the second, a strange looking hat and backpack, along with three floating bombs. And in the third, a green tunic and leather gauntlets was suspended, as well as heart container with an emerald casing. As I stared at them, bars of text appeared before them.

Guardian: Guardians are the protectors of the realm. They specialize in strength and have indomitable will. Guardians receive a proficiency in defensive tactics, healing potions, and a percentage increase in Charisma as they level, regardless of where their stats are placed. Guardians are able to equip heavy armor and still move at medium speed, gaining a +3 to Endurance. Guardians can wield colossal weapons and are strong against golems, trolls, and drakes.

Sapper: Sappers make things go Boom! Not only that, but they can build at 3x speed. Sappers are proficient in creating bombs, explosives, and have a percentage increase in crafting a plethora of items. Sappers utilize wit, knowledge, and concussive force to overcome their problems. Sappers get a time bonus in puzzles, crafting, and bridge building, as well as a percentage damage increase when using placed and thrown explosives. Bomb bag automatically upgrades to Level 2. Bombs automatically upgrade to Level 2.

Champion: Champions fight for the greater good, willing to sacrifice to save. They specialize melee combat, have a proficiency in light and medium armaments, and a +2 to Dexterity and Speed. Champions gain a special ability, Heart of Courage, allowing them to double either Speed or Dexterity for 10 seconds once per combat encounter. Champions get a bonus against Corrupted mobs and have a debuffing affect on dark or shadow types.

"It is up to you to choose," Treo said as she proffered her hand, gesturing to the three pillars of light. *"But remember, every choice made cannot be undone. You start yourself down a path you cannot reverse. Choose wisely."*

An image from Indiana Jones filled my mind, when the Templar Knight had said the same. I only hoped that none of these decisions would leave me a crumbling pile of ash. They were just Class choices, right?

I looked at them again. As much as the Charisma and Endurance seemed nice, as well as the advantages against larger foes, I almost instantly moved past Guardian. I just wasn't that guy. I wasn't big and strong. But I was smart. Sapper immediately drew me in, tantalizing me with the ideas using brain over brawn. Yet, there was something about the Champion class that held my attention. I had already poured a lot into Dex and Speed, and the idea of having a permanent debuffing effect on dark or shadow type enemies seemed to be the most useful of all the options. Not to mention the special ability, Heart of Courage. I could think of a dozen practical implications of that.

I walked closer to the Sapper's pillar of light, studying the bag. It looked much nicer than my troll-skin sack. The hat looked pretty cool, too. But, in the end, I moved toward the Champion set.

Unsure as to exactly what I should do, I placed my hand on the glowing pillar.

Champion Class!
Do you wish to proceed with this choice?
Yes! Or, no.

I swallowed my nervousness and mentally selected, *Yes!*

Energy flooded into me, wave upon debilitating wave, first taking me to my knees and then to my back. Water soaked my shirt and pants, seeping into places I wished it wouldn't. But I did not have time to think about that discomfort, as more and more light fell upon me. I stared up, eyes unfocused, as the world warped around me.

When the light faded and my senses returned to me, I could not help but let out a cry of exhalation. Power seemed to course through me, as if I had lightning in my veins. I felt stronger, more alert, more...everything. And deep within, I found that the spark of confidence that had been growing as I had overcome trial after trial, passing the insurmountable, and burst into flame.

"Archy, don't you look dashing," Treo said, covering her mouth with hand as she let out an oddly girlish laugh.

I looked down at my hands, which were covered in the gauntlets from the green pillar of light, my grandfather's watch that Dad had given me strapped over my wrist. Staring past my hands, I saw my reflection rippling in the water upon which I stood.

I was garbed in the green tunic, and could feel chainmail underneath. I did not look that different, save for an spectral green glow that permeated from my skin, rising around me like ghostly flames.

"Champion indeed! You are seeing the power of the Champion, a extra planer power that can only be seen physically here, but will remain with you for as long as you retain you current class. This is know as the Champion's Power and is built up through battles. This power is what is used to access the ability, Heart of Courage. Do you wish to do a trial run with new ability, Heart of Courage?" Treo spoke the words with excitement, leaning in closer to me,

staring at me with wide eyes that seemed to bore through me.

"Uh, sure," I said, a little hesitantly, thrown off by this version of Treo and feeling more than a little uncomfortable in her towering, goddess-like presence.

"Initiating Trial of the Champion, Champion Class tutelage."

The world spun once more as water shot up like geysers around me. And when it came crashing back down, two dozen Gibblins stood before me in a semi-circle. Shock and fear filled me as I stared out at them, confused as to how they had come to this place. Large, scrolling text appeared over the sounder of Gibblins:

Trial of the Champion
Heart of Courage

Stage One:
Defeat Gibblin Sounder using Heart of Courage
Fill up Champion's Power so you can initiate Champion Class's unique ability, Heart of Courage.

Instinctually, I threw open my HUD, quickly looking over my stats:

Health Points - 8
Focus Points - 3
Endurance - 6
Strength - 5
Dexterity - 8
Esoteric - 1
Speed - 6

Charisma - 3

Next, I attempted to pull my sword and shield, but was met with a strange error had not encountered as of yet:

Shield damaged.
Do you still wish to use?
Yes! Or, no.

Looking at the rapidly approaching sounder of Gibblins, and seeing no other real option, I selected, *Yes!* No sooner had I done so, then I could retrieve my sword and shield.

Sword of the Promised Elven Lord
Level 2 - Legendary Item

Wooden Shield of the Adventurer
Warning: Damaged!

The grip of the sword felt satisfyingly different in my now gauntleted hand, as if the one was meant to hold the other. And like I had already noticed, I did feel stronger, the leafblade feeling almost featherlight in my grip. The shield, on the other hand, felt oddly off balance, as if it were resisting me as I moved it up in front of me. This must have been due to the damage inflicted upon it.

I did not have time to think on any of this further, for no sooner had I brought my shield in front of me, than did the first trio of mallet-wielding Gibblins spring onto me. Moving with practiced speed, I dodged to the side of the first, checking the second with my shield and slicing through the third. As on the surface world, the defeated foe turned to pixilated ash. The only difference here was that no Soulfires burned.

Training grounds. I was in a simulation.

I wondered for half a second if how real this was and what differences could be felt here. This was answered swiftly as the Gibblin I had sidestepped slammed its maul into the small of my back, sending me toppling forward.

Beep!

One of my heart containers dimmed to a dull grey.

So I can take damage. Great.

I rose quickly, shaking off the pain and refocused myself on the fight. The two Gibblins had recouped as well and were rushing at once toward me. We clashed quickly and viciously, and I allowed some of the frustrations and angst that had been building up inside of me to bleed out, quickly dispatching the two with rapid cuts and a well-timed thrust.

My sense of accomplishment was, to my dismay, short-lived. For no sooner had I defeated the trio, than did five Gibblins break aware from their line, rushing toward me. This proceeded time and time again, until all were defeated.

Stage One:

Defeat Gibblin Sounder using Heart of Courage
Fill up Champion's Power so you can initiate Champion
Class's unique ability, Heart of Courage, has been completed.

To see your Champion's Power, access your HUD and select,
Unique Abilities

I followed the text's direction, throwing open my head and locating, Unique Abilities. Sure enough, next to

Running Strike and *Slicing Edge*, a third ability was located. This one, however, was in emerald text: *Champion's Power*.

Add Champion's Power Meter to HUD?
Yes! Or, no.

I mentally selected yes and watched as my Inventory closed and the new, emerald meter populated on the bottom left portion of my HUD, just above my bombs and coin purse. It was filled to the brim, emitting a bright light.

Stage Two:
Defeat Gibblin Warlord
Use your Champion's Power to initiate Champion Class's unique ability, Heart of Courage, to defeat a Strong Foe well above your level.

Water shot up once more, washing away the piles of pixilated ash that had been two dozen Gibblins. As if teleported in from thin air, a hulking, pimply Gibblin in scaly armor and holding a warhammer that could have been pulled straight from a video game appeared no more than ten feet away from me.

Gibblin Warlord
Level 27

Gibblin Warlord has unique ability, Battle's Fury. The longer the fight, the stronger the foe! Better act fast, or it will batter you even faster.

Resistant to Slash

> *Resistant to Pierce*
> *Weak to Mental Assault*
> *Weak to Spells*

I looked at the beast, feeling an impeding sense of dread wash over me. I had a sword and shield. It was resistant to Slash and Pierce. The irony was not lost on me that this place would put a foe before me that was resistant to the only damage types I did. But it was a training simulation, I told myself. There had to be a weakness I could exploit.

"Warlord crush little green man!" the Gibblin Warlord roared as it raised its massive warhammer over its head, shaking it violently over its oversized head.

Well, I had played enough video games to know that if there was ever an indication that something was supposed to be hit, make it big and round. So, I mentally slammed on the Champion's Power. Two of my attributes populated, jumping back and forth:

> *Dexterity - 16*
> *Speed - 6*

> *Dexterity - 8*
> *Speed - 12*

> *Dexterity - 16*
> *Speed - 6*

> *Dexterity - 8*
> *Speed – 12*

I tried to focus, my mind rapidly playing through which

would be more effective in this fight, and honestly, neither of them seemed like they would be that beneficial, as neither would increase blunt force trauma like a 2x to Strength would. The whole time this was going on, the Warlord was rushing toward me, warhammer poised to smash me like a bug.

Ding!
Dexterity - 8
Speed - 12

The whole world seemed to lurch into slow motion, and my mind began to race.

This is unexpected, I thought to myself with a smirk. The Gibblin Warlord looked as if he were wading through syrup. Was this how I had been able to think on the spot so much better in fights and stressful situations? Had my mind itself sped up as I had leveled speed? Cool.

Speaking of ideas, I had one come to me.

Bombs. I still had them. Just because I hadn't chosen that class did not mean they were not still at my disposal. And nowhere in the Trial rules had anyone or anything been said about limiting me to just my sword and shield.

Bomb Bag: Base Level
Formed from the mangled, flabby skin of the fallen Hill Troll, and held together by the string of his loin-cloth, you have received a small-explosives Bomb Bag!

This sack allows you to carry explosives like TNT sticks, Bombblossoms, and other small munitions you may acquire. The space is limited and so is the stability of this sack. You will need to upgrade this item if you wish to carry larger, more volatile explosives.

Contents:
Gibblin Boomboom Oil - 4 Pots
TNT Stick - 0
Bombblossoms - 0
Brightshrooms - 1

Inventory:

Volatile Lightning Bug

I grabbed a Gibblin Boomboom Oil pot and three Volatile Lightning Bugs from my Inventory as I easily dodged the Warlord's hammer strike. Fury crept slowly across the behemoth's face, as if it could not comprehend how I had moved from where I had been. But I was already moving once more, shoving the three bugs into the pot and tying the string back around the leather cover.

My stomach lurched as suddenly, everything around me began to rapidly speed up. I felt a wave of dizziness strike as the Gibblin Warlord turned about, raising his hammer once more. I only had a second to react, flinging myself sideways just in the nick of time.

Heart of Courage
Ability: Consumed.
Must gather more Champion's Power to initiate Unique Ability

"Oh no!" I muttered as the big, green Gibblin lurked

forward, a wicked smile spreading across his gap-toothed face.

"Me crush."

My hand felt hot all of the sudden.

"Oh no!" This time I cried out in exclamation as the Gibblin Boomboom oil pot began to heat at an alarming rate.

Not know what else to do, I hurled the pot directly into the Warlord's face. The blast that followed sent me tumbling backwards, head over heels, soaking me to the bone in the standing water of the mirror realm.

Victory!

Stage Two:
Defeat Gibblin Warlord
Use your Champion's Power to initiate Champion Class's unique ability, Heart of Courage, to defeat a Strong Foe well above your level.

Trial of the Champion
Heart of Courage

Completed.

Power surged through me, replenishing all of my heart containers and filling every meter. I felt stronger, focused, ready. Treo winked before blowing me a kiss, a kiss that flew on azure flows of light, taking me from this place of mysticism.

. . .

I woke up on the floor of my room in Unga village, sunlight shining in through the window. It was not the warm rays of twilight, but the golden beams of morning's dawn. I went to place a hand on my hand, but stopped short as I saw the leather gauntlets about my hands.

I leapt to my feet, all the weariness from the day before, gone. No wonder Georgia was in a hurry to go. I felt so alive and energized. Looking down, my baggy t-shirt had been replaced by the green tunic with an emblem of a golden sun breaching the horizon, five rays stretching out across the fabric.

You have been granted, Blessing's Boon. You have received Upgrades to several of your stats thanks to your gaining of, Champion Class.

I threw open my HUD.

Archy Lawrence

~Champion~
Level 12
Health Points - 8
Focus Points - 4
Endurance - 7
Strength - 6
Dexterity - 9
Esoteric - 1
Speed - 7
Charisma - 5

Ding!

The single note sent my eyes darting around the room, searching for Treo. She wasn't there. Confused, I looked about again, seeking out the source of the noise.

Ding!

I turned my attention back to my HUD, where I saw a flashing icon reading, Notifications. I clicked it.

Craftable item.
Blessed Dewdrops
3 of 3 available for crafting
3 of 12 discovered
Do you wish to use 3 of 3 Blessed Dewdrops to upgrade?
Yes! Or, no.

Yes.

Bandit's Bandolier of Recovery Flasks - Rare Item
Upgraded: Level 2
Inventory Slots - 8
Available Slots - 4
Level 3 Required to access Slots 5 & 6
Available Flasks
Health Flasks - 2
Stamina Flask - 1
Focus Flask - 1

Flasks now Recover 12% more
Flasks can now be quick-swapped!
Move between HP, FP, or Stam in an instant.

. . .

Well, that would be useful. I thought as I strapped my bandolier about my chest and fastened it to my belt. I slung my shield over my back, receiving a second Ding!

Shield damaged.
Do you wish to repair?
Yes! Or, no.

Yes.

Error!
You do not have the appropriate items to repair this item.
You do not have the appropriate skills to repair this item.
You do not have the appropriate station to repair this item.

"Well, why did you ask me if I wanted to repair it then?" I shouted into thin air at the wall of text. I chagrined at my action, feeling utterly foolish for crying out at nothing, but thankful Georgia wasn't there to witness it. Unwilling to let my outburst ruin my excitement for gaining a class, I strapped my sword to my side, laced up my boots, and made to leave my room and Unga Village behind.

I wasn't just a lost and scared boy anymore. I was a Champion now. I was going to save my dad, I knew that. Confidence swelled with in my chest. And as I thought, I allowed myself a secondary inclination to form. Maybe, just maybe, I could win Georgia over in the process.

The End of Book 1

ABOUT THE AUTHOR

 DAVID ANDREW TROTTER was born in a small town in rural Arkansas. His mother provided much of his childhood education, and in doing so, instilled in him a love of reading and of learning. As a young man, David courted, and then married, the love of his life, Heather Scott. They now have four beautiful children, Oliver, Lily, Theodore, and Rowena. David graduated from the University of Arkansas – Fort Smith with a degree in Business Administration. David currently spends most of his time juggling a job, an active gym life, and his true passion, writing.

instagram.com/datzme16

facebook.com/david.a.trotter.3

tiktok.com/@davidatrotter92

OTHER WORKS

BIRTHRIGHTS

AZURE TIDES

Chains of a Broken God

The First Oath